GILL

NET

GAMES

ALSO BY M.W. GORDON

THE WESTERN MOUNTAINS TRILOGY
DEADLY DRIFTS
CROSSES TO BEAR
"YOU'RE NEXT!"

GILL NET GAMES

A MACDUFF BROOKS FLY FISHING MYSTERY

by

award winning author

M. W. GORDON

SWIFT CREEKS PRESS EDITION, APRIL 1, 2014
Oyster Bay does not exist. St. Augustine, Gainesville, Cedar Key, Mill Creek, Paradise Valley, Apalachicola, Khartoum, Omdurman, Wadi Halfa, and Aswan all exist but are used fictionally in this novel. This is a work of fiction, and the characters are either the product of the author's imagination or are used fictionally. Any resemblance to actual persons, living or dead, or to actual events or locales is unintentional and coincidental.
Library of Congress Cataloging-in-Publication Data
Gordon, M.W.
Gill Net Games/M.W. Gordon

ISBN-13 978-0-9848723-4-3
Printed in the United States of America

To the authors (and characters) of novels from whom I have drawn inspiration and an awareness of the demands of writing.

C.J. Box (and Joe Pickett and Nate Romanowski)

Victoria Houston (and Chief Lewellyn Ferris, Doc Osborne, and Ray Pradt)

Randy Wayne White (and Doc Ford and S.M. Tomlinson)

ACKNOWLEDGMENTS

This book was written with the encouragement of family, friends, and the many readers of the first three Macduff Brooks novels: *Deadly Drifts, Crosses to Bear,* and *"You're Next!"* Particular thanks go to Jeffrey Harrison, Marilyn Henderson, Roy Hunt, Johnnie Irby, and Shelley Fraser Mickle.

Very special thanks to Iris Rose Hart, my editor, friend, and patient instructor in what the school system I attended was supposed to provide, but either did not or found me an impossible student.

Whatever I have accomplished over the decades would have been impossible without the encouragement and help of my wife Buff.

Several people in Montana have provided quiet places for me to write, especially Joan Watts and Johnnie Hale of Livingston, and Julie and Jason Fleury of Bozeman.

I am indebted to the Department of State, which years ago on the eve of damaging political changes in the Sudan, sent me to Khartoum and Omdurman.

The cover photo of gill nets courtesy of the State Archives of Florida, Florida Memory.
http://floridamemory.com/items/show/122939

PROLOGUE

Elsbeth's Diary

Having my dad, Macduff Brooks, living with me in Captiva is an extraordinary happenstance. Not only his presence, but also the fact that we are living in the very same cottage that once stood on the edge of a salt marsh south of St. Augustine. Dad and Lucinda spent many winters in this cottage. When he said he was no longer able to maintain both his cabin in Montana and the cottage in St. Augustine after Lucinda's death, I had the cottage dismantled and rebuilt here on Captiva as my home. Dad has come full circle—once again he lives in this cottage of memories.

I asked him to continue writing the story about his life, picking up where he left off with the third manuscript of the three that had covered the time many years ago before I arrived at his doorstep in Montana. I knew much about the events occurring after we were reunited, but I wanted him to write them in his words. I also knew I would learn about matters he had never felt comfortable telling me about face to face.

In that tragic accident on the Snake River in Wyoming so many years ago, unknowingly I lost my birth mother. But not my birth father. Finding Dad, with the help of Dan Wilson and Dean Hobart Perry, began a life more animating than I could ever have dreamed of as a young girl growing up in the Maine North Woods.

1

MID-SEPTEMBER OFF SANIBEL ISLAND IN SOUTH-
WEST FLORIDA

A BATTERED AND NEGLECTED FLATS BOAT slapped along the breeze-ruffled surface of San Carlos Bay between the mouth of the Caloosahatchee River and Sanibel Island in Southwest Florida. Sending sheets of stinging, cold spray the boat was not made for racing across a bay on a rough day. Ahead for its two occupants was a day of spin casting live bait for snook along the Gulf beaches of kidney-shaped Sanibel; behind was a disk of orange fringed with heat waves certain to create another intensely heavy early-fall day demanding heavy doses of sunscreen and fluids. There was nowhere to hide from the Florida sun and humidity.

Jimmy Joe Jones was at the helm; his buddy since first grade, Billy Joe Brown, was drinking the first of two dozen Pabsts and Buds that filled the Igloo ice chest beneath his spreading rear. These third generation Florida crackers took remarkable steps to avoid any work that interfered with their fishing.

"Goddamit, Jimmy Joe, slow this freakin' boat down. I'm spillin' good beer every wave you slam into."

3

"Shoot! Billy Joe, you complain 'bout anythin' the minute you step on this boat. You been complainin' 'bout everythin' I do since kinergarten."

"I didn't know you 'til first grade, you dumb ass."

"Gimmie one of them fine American Buds and shut up," responded Jimmy Joe, with all the eloquence he had gained from the ten years he remained in school. Each had departed school for good on the day he reached sixteen, the date the misdirected members of the Florida legislature believe the school system has prepared each new generation of students to enter the world on their own. The system prepares them at best for a life earning the minimum wage—if anybody hires them. But that suited Jimmy Joe and Billy Joe just fine, as long as occasional jobs supported their fishing.

"Billy Joe, how many times I gotta tell you, drink *my* beer—Pabst Blue Ribbon. A real *American* beer. Your Bud ain't an American beer."

" 'Tis too," snarled Billy Joe.

"Ain't! It's a damn Belgie beer. The Belgies bought Bud. You just givin' money to all them Belgies, Frogs, and Krauts that killed millions of Americans fifty years ago, 'cludin' your own grampa."

"You're so dumb, Jimmy Joe. It was the goddamn Krauts that killed Grandpa Bobby Joe. Frogs is French. They didn't kill no one in that war. The Frogs all waved a big white flag when they seen the first Kraut."

"Billy Joe," Jimmy Joe said, as he watched his buddy toss his first empty can over the side, followed by the wrapper for six doughnuts he'd managed to eat in between sentences, "you eat too damn much. Look at you. All I see from back here is your fat ass hangin' off your seat—on both sides."

"Jimmy Joe, if you keep complainin', I'll be back there and beat the crap out of you."

"I'm so scared of you," replied Jimmy Joe, sarcastically.

"Jeeze!" exclaimed Billy Joe, suddenly, easing the mounting tension between the two. "You see that net hangin' off the channel marker we headin' for?"

"Yep. Another gill net. Guess it belonged to some commercial fishin' guy. Po' bastards, the net ban took away all they got."

"But *our* fishin's better since the ban. Screw 'em all," articulated Billy Joe.

"Jesus, Mary, and Joseph! You see what I'm thinkin' I see in that net? Billy Joe, I'm takin' the boat closer."

Slowly they approached the net, which was streaming out from the channel marker with the ebbing tide. On top of the marker a female osprey nestled with two offspring; the marker itself was aerated by a half dozen bullet holes.

"It's a freakin' body! I'm gettin' the hell out of here," Jimmy Joe whined.

"Wait!" insisted Billy Joe. "I seen 'em before."

"Who is he? He look pretty dead."

"I know 'em. He's that stupid sumbitch Sanibel fishing guide. Been talkin' bad 'bout the way commercial fishermen are gettin' round the net ban. And irritatin' good guys like us by his pushin' for prohibitin' treble hooks and only allow usin' barbless single hooks. Them's fightin' words. . . . I remember now. His name's somethin' like Clint Potter . . . or Cotter."

"If the net hadna caught on the marker, then the body'd be floatin' somewhere west of Sanibel headin' for Mexico, and he woulda been shark bait."

The cold wrinkled fingers and toes of fishing guide Clint Carter were caught in the gill net as securely as gills of a fish. Even one of Carter's ears was entangled in the net. His body was completely wrapped from head to foot and jerked and twisted as the tide swept past toward the Gulf. Carter stared out from behind the mesh which, with every wave, tightened its grip on the body.

Carter wouldn't guide any more snook fishing trips along the beaches of Sanibel.

2

Limiting marine net fishing.—

(b)   For the purpose of catching or taking any saltwater finfish, shellfish or other marine animals in Florida waters:

(1)   No gill nets or other entangling nets shall be used in any Florida waters; and

(2)   In addition to the prohibition set forth in (1), no other type of net containing more than 500 square feet of mesh area shall be used in nearshore and inshore Florida waters. Additionally, no more than two such nets, which shall not be connected, shall be used from any vessel, and no person not on a vessel shall use more than one such net in nearshore and inshore Florida waters.

FLORIDA CONSTITUTION, ARTICLE X, SECTION 16.

MILL CREEK, PARADISE VALLEY, MONTANA

"MACDUFF, WHY DO YOU SPOIL WUFF?" asked Lucinda, just as I had begun to read the entry for Florida on yesterday's *USA Today* page that has no more than an inch of "news" about each state. The succinct allotment to Florida for this issue was about a body wrapped in a gill net found hanging from a channel marker on San Carlos Bay between the mouth of the Caloosahatchee River and Sanibel. The gill net news brought to mind the successful state-wide referen-

7

dum in 1994 that banned using most gill nets—or so many Floridians thought.

I looked up from the paper because my usually mesmerizing and spirited Lucinda has been remarkably tranquil for the past week. We were having what I called our breakfast but she called our *petit dejeuner* inside my Mill Creek log cabin in Paradise Valley, Montana, fifty miles south of Livingston. Yesterday was the first day of fall. It wasn't the first time fall arrived in the valley carried in on a blustery dusting of snow. But it will have melted by noon.

My rescued Sheltie, Wuff, was lying by the door watching us, her head moving back and forth as we spoke—as though she were watching a tennis match.

Lucinda Lang, my companion, has persisted in alleging that she is also my fiancée. I'm beginning to believe she's been right. In a few weeks we'll leave for my cottage that sits a nervous three feet above the edge of a salt marsh twenty-five miles south of St. Augustine, Florida. We had already booked an early December stay on Captiva, partnered with Sanibel by an umbilical bridge and not far from where the gill net wrapped body was found. We should barely arrive before the crowds of pale-skinned snowbirds flood in from the North.

"I don't spoil Wuff," I responded to Lucinda. "She's richly rewarded for fulfilling her obligations as a pet. *Without* complaining."

"What obligations?"

"Love, loyalty, protection, honor, obedience . . . I could go on."

"*I* do all that, Macduff, and then some."

"What's 'and then some'?"

"Freshly brewed coffee in the morning delivered to your bedside as you awaken."

"You were a few minutes late this morning. . . . Anyway, when I adopted Wuff, I assured Judge Becker I'd take exceptional care of her. I've done that, and she's responded with undivided attention. . . . I haven't adopted you."

"And I've never taken any vows to love, honor, and obey you. . . . I guess I never will," she added, her head dropping to hide a quivering jaw.

"Neither has Wuff, but she does it anyway," I replied, wondering why she added "I guess I never will." Probably because we've allegedly been engaged for what I thought was at most a year but she thinks has been much longer, and I haven't brought up the matter of discussing a wedding date.

"Furthermore, Macduff, I've never promised to cherish you until 'death do us part,'" she added, "which may not be long considering how many times we've been shot. Not to mention kidnapped three months ago."

"*Never* were you in real danger. I was always there to protect you."

"Have you forgotten? A few weeks ago we were sitting in a drift boat on the Yellowstone River with our hands, ankles, and mouths taped. We were covered with a basket-like wicker man and *explosives*? I remember seeing the timer clock show thirteen seconds were left until we exploded."

"But you had a beautiful wreath of mistletoe in your hair."

"*Mac!* The timer on the explosives was *ticking*, and there were only a few seconds left."

"You survived."

"Thanks to the heroics of Juan Santander," she said.

Juan was new to guiding in Jackson Hole. He was a Navy Seal injured on a mission never made public. He lost his right leg below the knee, his right hand, and his right eye. His recovery was long and arduous. And miraculous—now he's a successful fly fishing guide in Jackson.

I met Juan when I helped Project Healing Waters by taking combat wounded disabled vets on Wyoming's Snake River fly fishing from my wooden drift boat, *Osprey*. I guided Juan, and he has become not only a friend but *maybe* also a life saver. Most recently when Lucinda and I were saved literally as the last few seconds ticked off before an explosive device strapped to us was to detonate. It was dark when an unidentifiable figure dropped off the Mill Creek Bridge over the Yellowstone River and landed in the water next to the drift boat where we sat tied together. We've debated whether it was Juan who pulled the explosives off us, pushed us over the side, and dragged us far enough away to avoid the full impact of the explosion.

"You don't know it was Juan," I muttered, aware I was about to lose another debate with Lucinda. "Juan has denied being in Montana when it happened. Your evidence is all circumstantial."

"Don't play lawyer with me, Macduff. Was I right about Juan saving us a couple of years ago near the tennis courts at the University of Florida after Richard Potter was shot and killed?" she asked.

"Well . . . For the sake of this discussion, I'll concede that."

"And was I right about Juan killing Allan Whitman in D.C. when he was about to tell Juan Pablo Herzog—your Guatemalan nemesis—your new name and location?"

"Let's talk about something else, something that doesn't involve us. Like a man's body found yesterday wrapped in a gill net that caught on a channel marker in San Carlos Bay near Sanibel. The body was bobbing against an outgoing tide. We'll be a few miles from there in December when we go to Captiva."

"A body? Who?" she asked.

"No name released yet . . . but apparently he was a fly fishing guide from Sanibel who was leading the fight in Florida for adoption of stricter net ban legislation and removal of judicial discretion in determining what constitutes an illegal gill net."

The murders of the past year are over. Attempts on our lives on June 21st—the summer solstice—were thwarted. Lucinda is convinced we were saved by Juan Santander. Yesterday, September 21st—the autumnal equinox—passed without incident. But it passed without any sign that the suspects of the five earlier equinox and solstice murders—Hannah Markel and Robert Ellsworth-Kent—had been found or were planning further wicker man and mistletoe murders.

Hannah is the twin sister of late PARA member Helga Markel, one of the killers in the Shuttle Gals murders on the Yellowstone River in Montana two years ago. People Against Recreational Angling—PARA—is a radical Montana-based organization. Hannah blamed me for Helga's death in L.A.

Robert Ellsworth-Kent, at the time of the murders only recently released from a prison on the Isle of Wight off the southern coast of England, had been Lucinda's husband . . . for all of two months. Despite a purported nationwide search, there hasn't been a clue about where either has been hiding.

I'm Macduff Brooks, a sixtyish guy who wants nothing more than to be a respected fly fishing guide and keep my three gals close by and happy.

First, Wuff is my eight-year-old rescued Shetland sheepdog, aka Sheltie or "little Lassie." She's easy to please as long as she's fed precisely at 6 a.m. and 5 p.m. on her own tiny oriental rug in my very small kitchen, taken out to pee on demand, and kept from being shot on my drift boat—again!

The second gal who entered my life after I became Macduff Brooks is Lucinda Lang—an enchanting, lovely 5' 6" lady with captivating and communicating hazel green eyes, a sculptured classic straight nose, and a broad Cheshire cat grin. Her light brown hair is cut to barely touch her shoulders. Often when she tilts her head slightly to the right, it's obvious that she's listening to you.

I first met her nearly seven years ago when I accepted an unexpected invitation to Thanksgiving dinner at her imposing lodge at Arrogate Ranch, about two miles upstream from my modest log cabin on Mill Creek. I slipped on ice on her front stoop just as she was opening the door. Lessened pride and sore butt aside, I soon learned I was the only dinner guest. She was single, and six colleagues of hers at the Manhattan investment firm she worked for canceled at the last minute. That dinner led to more dinners and somehow to where we are now, living together on Mill Creek in Paradise Valley, Montana, a stone's throw north of Yellowstone Park, during the summer, and on Pellicer Creek, a longer stone's throw south of St. Augustine, Florida, during the winter, while Montana is frozen over and—for most intelligent species of flora and fauna—is uninhabitable.

Lucinda claims we're engaged; I don't remember the night I apparently said "probably" when she asked if we *were* engaged. I haven't raised the matter of the next step—marriage. The arrival on the scene of my third gal may affect that step.

The third of my ladies is Elsbeth. She showed up on my doorstep three months ago and *announced* that she was my seventeen-year-old daughter. There's no doubt: she's a mirror image of my late wife, El, who drowned nearly eighteen years ago in an avoidable accident on the technically demanding Deadman's Bar to Moose section of Wyoming's Snake River. We were expecting our first child. Nearly two decades would pass before I learned that by some miracle our daughter to be, Elsbeth, survived the accident.

Foster parents raised her in Maine and raised her very well. We've spent the nine weeks between her arrival and recent flight to Maine to begin college with hardly a moment apart. She told Lucinda and me everything she could remember about growing up in Maine, how she learned that she was not the Carsons' natural daughter, and about her help from Dan Wilson at the CIA and Dean Perry at the UF law college—without which she would never have found me. Lucinda talked freely about her life, how we met, and our nearly seven years together. When it came to my life before moving to Montana, I didn't know how much to tell her. I downplayed my time spent with the State Department and pursuit by my Guatemalan and Sudanese adversaries. Elsbeth seemed to sense there were some parts of my life that she would learn about only over time.

Elsbeth's in Maine this very moment, three weeks into her first year at the flagship state university in Orono. I talk to her almost every evening, a practice I hope to carry to the end of my days. We find much to discuss and laugh about: whether she'll remain at Orono for four years, what she would like to do with her life, and other decisions of adulthood that will challenge her but that she needn't make soon.

If I have one nagging concern that confronts me every day it's whether I can keep my three gals from harm. I came to Montana to live quietly as a fly fishing guide. My life hasn't been very quiet.

Seven years ago, in my first year of guiding, I embarrassed a client—Park Salisbury from Newport Beach, California—in front of his attractive wife, Kath, by leaving him on the bank of the Snake River north of Jackson, Wyoming, to walk out four miles. He had disregarded my explicit instructions not to kill any trout and instead to release them carefully into the river. After helping Kath learn to cast, I returned around a bend to see how her testy spouse was doing. What he was doing was using a three-inch-thick piece of driftwood to club to death a beautiful native cutthroat trout. He did not take my response to heart. Weeks later he tried to shoot me from the shore but missed and killed my client, retired ambassador Ander Eckstrum, who was Juan Santander's uncle.

A year later, disguised as an overweight, heavily bearded Oregonian fly fishing with me on the same Snake River in my wooden drift boat, *Osprey*. Salisbury shot Lucinda, Wuff, and me before we killed him, admittedly with help from the Teton County Sheriff's Office swat team and a sharp tree branch that impaled him when I steered *Osprey* into a strainer—a pile of trees jammed up in the middle of the river during the previous spring snowmelt runoff.

Wuff survived the incident with a slight limp. I was patched up and released from the Salt Lake City hospital in a few days, but Lucinda was in a coma for two weeks and came out of it with amnesia that lasted much of the following year.

Three years ago three women were murdered on the Yellowstone River. Each one was mutilated and nailed to a large wooden cross that was tied to my boat trailer—to greet me at the end of a day's float. Not surprisingly, my clients were not thrilled at finishing one of those floats with me only to find a dead body on my trailer. The victims were members of the

Shuttle Gals, a group that moves my SUV and trailer from where I put the boat in upriver to where I will take it out after a day's float downriver.

Those murders were solved. They were committed by four different people. One fled home to Mexico and couldn't be extradited to the U.S. for trial, and two died in an auto accident in L.A. But the fourth was apprehended and remains in the midst of the interminable journey from arrest to gas chamber.

Last year Lucinda and I spent twelve months wondering whether we would be kidnapped and sacrificed in a "wicker man and mistletoe" ceremony that ended the lives—one by one—of five people I knew. The murderers were fanatics about Druids and the symbolism of the solstices and equinoxes. Who did the murders became increasingly certain over the year, but the perpetrators escaped after their last attempted sacrifices—of Lucinda and me—were thwarted. They remain at large, which is not a comforting thought.

These actions are enough for me to occasionally consider if Wuff needs to be rescued again by a more normal household, if Lucinda should move back to Manhattan and resume her safe occupation as a highly compensated financial advisor, and if Elsbeth needs to consider spending her life in Greenville, Maine, as Elsbeth Carson—as she was known for her first seventeen years.

"Macduff," Lucinda stated, touching my hand across the table, "you're a thousand miles away. You haven't heard a word I've said for the past ten minutes."

At least I have her talking. "I was thinking about the body wrapped in the gill net. But it doesn't affect us."

"Doesn't *affect* us?" she exclaimed. "Didn't you give a lecture to a fishing club at Captiva last winter where you analyzed a proposal for a new public referendum to tighten the gill net ban? Plus, you supported the adoption of new provisions that would limit judges' discretion in interpreting the gill net law."

Lucinda and I have rented a house on Captiva in early December, and I'm bound to run into someone who was present at the discussion, which had been held at the South Seas Plantation. It was the annual meeting of the Fly Fishers of America South Florida Council.

"Yes," I answered, "but this involved a man *caught* in a gill net. It could have happened a hundred different ways. There's no mention of the net ban or foul play."

"I'm on my cell phone searching for local news from Southwest Florida," she said. "It's been a day or more since the article you're reading was written. Right now it's mid-morning in Florida, two hours earlier than here. There must be more news. . . . Here! In today's *Ft. Myers Globe*. . . . There *is* news! The body has been identified as Clint Carter, a fly fishing guide who works out of Sanibel. What's the name of the guide you lectured with last winter?"

"His name was Clint Carter. He was president of the group that organized the meeting," I whispered, as though the killer might overhear me.

Is the madness starting all over again?

3

THE FLORIDA NET BAN

THE VIOLENCE SURROUNDING THE NET BAN may have resurfaced, and unintentionally I may have thrust myself into the middle of a new gill net ban debate. Last winter I reluctantly agreed to provide a Western state guide's personal opinion on the proposed new constitutional amendment to further restrict net fishing and limit judicial discretion. Those weren't my ideas—I was only offering an educated guess on whether they would pass muster: Would they be accepted by the Florida Supreme Court as valid citizens' initiatives and be allowed a public vote? But I *was* at the program. In the view of some that makes me guilty by association.

At the Captiva panel discussion, I described myself as merely an outside third-party—a resident and voter in Montana. Meaning I had no axe to grind in Florida. I *am* law trained—in another life before I became a fly fishing guide—but for the discussion I had assumed only the role of a fishing guide and not a lawyer.

The second part of the current proposal, limiting judicial discretion, arose out of an incredulous decision—even to a layman—by a Florida Panhandle county court judge. It was nothing new for Florida's impetuous county and circuit courts. Prior to the net ban, Wakulla County Court Judge Roderick McLeod seemed intent on overruling a state law that made January and February the open season months for mullet, rather than November and December as favored by commercial fishermen. Judge McLeod ruled that mullet, which uniquely have a gizzard—a digestive organ—in common with birds, should not be called fish and therefore were not subject to the gill net ban. Newspapers throughout Florida had articles about the judicial observation that proclaimed a mullet to be a bird.

The new net ban proposal has created a clash between the Florida Marine Fisheries Commission, at the time more accurately identified as the Florida Commercial Fishing Protective Association, and both the Florida Coastal Conservation Association and the more pro-active Fly Fishers of America South Florida Council. The CCA is more accurately identified as the Florida Recreational Fishing Protective Association.

Florida voters outside the Panhandle were generally in favor of the original 1994 gill net ban, but for the most part those along the Panhandle coast opposed it. Some of the Panhandle judiciary proved to be an embarrassment to the state. A few judges withheld adjudication improperly, ignored the clear intent of the net ban, and became an informal activist opposition to the enacted ban by substituting personal notions of how political, economic, and social pressures might affect their re-elections. When their decisions were appealed, the challenged reasoning of their decisions invariably was overturned.

4

ON MACDUFF'S PORCH AT MILL CREEK

BY THE NEXT DAY the news of Clint Carter's death was in every large-city Florida newspaper, as well as some local papers in sparsely populated commercial-fishing towns in the Panhandle. Overnight the earlier descriptions referring to Carter's death by assumed drowning were changed to suspected homicide. Nothing yet had appeared in the local Montana papers.

Wearing sweaters, we took our morning coffee and sat on the cabin porch. It was cool, as was our conservation, which was remarkable for its long silences. No chatter about "love, honor, and obey" or when and if Juan Santander had saved us. Lucinda was nervous; I was uncertain. New to the mix—in contrast with our past adventures and concerns—was Elsbeth's joining our lives.

"Macduff, Elsbeth has been with us for less than three months and this happens!"

"She seems to be adjusting to life as a freshman at Maine," I responded. "Do we tell her? . . . Or warn her?" I added, seeking help more than providing answers.

"Put yourself in Elsbeth's place. We've told her every detail of our time together, and the events that transformed you from Professor Maxwell Hunt to fly fishing guide Macduff Brooks. We should tell her about Carter. But what do we tell her *to do?* . . . 'Buy a gun and carry it with you.' . . . 'Stay in your dorm when you're not going to class.' . . . 'Don't date.' . . . We can't do any of those."

"Is she at risk at all?" I wondered out loud. "Probably more so if Juan Pablo Herzog or Abdul Khaliq Isfahani learn who and where I am. Or if Hannah Markel or Robert Ellsworth-Kent, *knowing* who and where *we* are, renew their attempt to kill us. Likely none of them even knows Elsbeth exists."

Juan Pablo Herzog is one of the wealthiest men in Guatemala, but most of that wealth came from organized crime rather than from his coffee plantations. He has ambitions to become the country's president. Because I did some work in Guatemala for the CIA, he detests me. My work was insignificant, mainly filling in some information about when he was a student in one of my classes at the University of Florida. He's learned I survived the near fatal beating he gave me in Guatemala City seven years ago that led to my being placed in the CIA's protection program with a new name and location.

Abdul Khaliq Isfahani was in that same class at the university, was present but didn't intervene when I was beaten, and joined Herzog in trying to find me to impose more permanent discomforts. Five years ago I tried to kill Isfahani for the CIA, but failed.

Hannah Markel, Helga's sister, and Ellsworth-Kent, Lucinda's husband of two months, are wanted for the solstice and equinox murders. Thus far they've evaded efforts to locate and arrest them. Lucinda and I should be more worried than we are.

"There's no reason any of those four would go after *Elsbeth*," I continued, "unless they try to get to us through her."

"Or kill her to cause us grief."

"Don't even think of that," I said, shaking my head.

"We have to think of that," she ventured.

"Should I fly to Orono and talk with Elsbeth?"

"If you think that's what she would expect."

"Lucinda, you know her as well as—really better than—I do. Remember that she came into my . . . *our* lives only three months ago. . . . We'll be with her in Florida for the Christmas holiday."

"A lot can happen between now and Christmas."

"You've convinced me," I said, suddenly determined. "I'm going to Maine. I don't have a float for a few days. I'll stay in Orono a couple of nights and be back in time for two weeks of daily fall floats."

"Can I trust you to eat sensibly?"

"Of course."

"You need more *greens*. They provide vitamin A. That's good for helping your irregular heart beat."

"I've had that since the day I met you. Maybe the *moment* I met you. And I ate greens this morning."

"What greens did you have . . . before breakfast?"

"Green mint M&Ms."

"M&Ms aren't leafy, Macduff! . . . You need *leafy* greens, like lettuce and spinach."

"The mere mention of spinach turns my stomach. I doubt they even allow the sale of spinach in Maine. . . . I'll trade you, Lucinda. I get one glass of Gentleman Jack for each spinach leaf—to wash it down. Or even better would be to soak the leaf in Gentleman Jack. . . . I could write a book on how to prepare meals using Jack Daniel's whiskey."

Ignoring me, she said, "I'm preparing pasta for tonight, made with New Orleans Andouille sausage, tomatoes, rosemary, and slivered green-pitted olives. Cooked in *Ribera del Due-ro* Spanish wine."

"Anything cooked in wine is good. Do the olives count as leafy greens if you sliver them very thin?"

"Why did I ever insist on being your nutritionist?"

"To keep me alive so I can eat more of your meals disguised as healthy food."

"To think of all the chances I've had to let someone shoot you or blow you up! . . . Or leave you wrapped in a gill net on the Yellowstone."

"Macduff," she continued after a moment of stirring something I couldn't identify, "you told me a little about the Florida net ban. What's a gill net?"

"I'll tell you after lunch."

5

Limiting marine net fishing.—
(c)   For purposes of this section: (1) 'gill net' means one or more walls of netting which captures saltwater finfish by ensnaring or entangling them in the meshes of the net by the gills, and 'entangling net' means a drift net, trammel net, stab net, or any other net which captures saltwater finfish, shellfish, or other marine animals by causing all or part of heads, fins, legs, or other body parts to become entangled or ensnared in the meshes … but a hand thrown cast net is not a gill net or an entangling net [.]

FLORIDA CONSTITUTION, ARTICLE X, SECTION 16.

AFTER LUNCH

// LUCINDA, A GILL NET IS SOMETHING LIKE a tennis net, long but not very high. And the gill net mesh is much less visible because it's made of fine monofilament. Imagine ten tennis nets that form a three foot high net that's about 360 feet long. Add weights along the bottom and floats along the top. Then stretch it across a channel's tidal flow. Or make a half-circle with the net off a beach and then pull in each end of the net at the same time.

"These nets catch a lot, and not solely the one or two species the fisherman is primarily after. It's called a gill net because fish swim into the net and get caught in the mesh by their gills.

It's also called an entanglement net—the meaning of which is obvious. Unfortunately, not only targeted fish are caught, but also innocent creatures such as sea turtles and dolphins."

"Turtles?"

"You've probably heard of shrimp boats and other trawlers using turtle excluders—or TEDs—in their nets. They're required by federal law and designed to let turtles escape from the net. But the law isn't always enforced, and trawlers sometimes simply tie the opening and close the excluder device, increasing the number of fish caught at the expense of the turtles.

"Anything caught in a gill net that isn't the main target is called the by-catch, which can mount up significantly when a fishing boat, for example a shrimper, drags nets across the bottom."

"That's what we see off the beach at St. Augustine—shrimp boats moving slowly with their nets out to each side. They're like wings," Lucinda exclaimed.

"That's right. They're scraping the bottom for shrimp, and often cod and flounder, but catch a lot of other creatures. They alter the bottom habitat, destroying complex structures and smoothing or homogenizing the seabed."

"People have been fishing commercially for centuries," Lucinda noted. "Aren't a lot of people out of work because of the net ban?"

"Yes, including hard working people from families who have fished commercially for generations. Too many people are after mullet. They use 'modern' techniques, meaning more fish are caught per hour of fishing."

"Should there be licenses and limits on the number issued."

"There are licenses, but not very capable regulation or enforcement. But that would require a responsible legislature and state fisheries commission and effective policing. We don't have any of that when it comes to regulating commercial—and in some cases recreational—fishing. Plus, there's the judge issue; the best and brightest law graduates usually are too successful in practice to accept an appointment to, or run for, a lower court judgeship. These are all reasons that the citizens' initiative for a referendum on banning gill nets was promoted. It would have been entirely unnecessary had more of our state 'officials' acted responsibly. . . . I don't expect that will change."

"Macduff, isn't it hard to get a constitutional amendment passed?"

"Almost impossible. But the net ban proposal passed by the widest margin of votes for any proposed amendment in Florida—ever! Seventy-two percent! Twenty years later that record still stands. Not many proposed amendments had been successful at the time of the gill net ban vote. Previously, there had been 132 filed petitions for referendums. Fifteen made it to the ballot, and only ten were approved. The public doesn't want to amend the Constitution unless it's clear the legislature has refused to act. Too many lobbyists handing out too much money."

"Is there really a need for a ban?" she asked. "That's pretty severe. And why was it needed in 1994 any more than forty to fifty years ago?"

"Imagine a small coastal town that a century ago had ten families fishing commercially full-time. Then each family had three children and two decided to carry on the family tradition. A century later—maybe five generations—there may be 300 families in the town commercially fishing, not ten. It's simply too many people chasing after a decreasing number of fish and using more efficient means to catch them."

"But once the fish stocks have diminished, a lot of those fishermen will be forced to find other work."

"True," I agreed, "there's a certain balance over time. But what may happen, especially when the fishermen have sizeable boats with monthly payments to make, is that they move to other locations where the fishing hasn't declined or hasn't been regulated. For example, what if the commercial fishermen in St. Augustine are forced to move further north or south along the coast? They may meet boats based in Jacksonville coming south and others from Daytona coming north. Result? No more fish unless they head offshore and probably fish for a different species."

"Like the sword fishermen who long-line and have had to go further and further out in the Atlantic to find fish. Into some pretty bad weather. Remember the book, *The Perfect Storm?*" she asked.

"I do. A frightening and tragic story. But it's a way of life for a lot of people. I admire them. It's hard work in exchange for a certain freedom. There's a mystique to fishing, whether it's for swordfish or lobsters off New England or mullet or red snapper off Florida."

"I'm exhausted thinking about it. . . . What does it have to do with a *body* found wrapped in a gill net? That's a strange kind of by-catch."

"Carter wasn't a by-catch. The latest news online suggests foul play. Once an autopsy has been done, we should know more."

"At least it didn't happen around us, Macduff, although I feel sad for Carter's family."

"Me, too. But he's not the first person who may have died because of the clash between commercial and recreational fishermen. And he won't be the last."

26

"I don't want *you* to be among the next!"

"I won't repeat my speaking appearance; I'm out of the dispute as of now. I want to protect my three gals."

"Walk with me to my ranch," she said. "I want to check on the status of a few chores I need to complete before we head to Florida next month. Its work I want to do while you're in Maine."

We walked, but when I reached to hold her hand as I do often, she withdrew it and crossed her arms for the rest of the walk.

Something is troubling her.

6

Passage of the amendment would finally halt the runaway netting by commercial fishermen that has plundered our nearshore waters and caused a fisheries crisis. The exploitation by the nets has caused unprecedented depletions of fish and other marine animals.

Special to the Orlando Sentinel, October 30, 1994.

A WALK UP MILL CREEK ROAD THAT AFTERNOON

L UCINDA'S RANCH IS AN IMPOSING SPREAD with a half-mile of Mill Creek winding through the middle and fed by spring creeks. It's a working cattle-turned-bison ranch, in addition to being a beautiful place of rest and contemplation. Between my modest acreage and Lucinda's ranch is federal land that's part of the Gallatin National Forest.

As we walked toward her ranch, we noticed new signs randomly tacked to trees, but we couldn't read them because of the distance. When we reached the ranch, the signs reappeared, stapled to Lucinda's ranch fencing every hundred feet. We walked over and pulled one off its staples to read it:

RECREATIONAL TROUT FISHING IS NO LONGER
PERMITTED ANYWHERE ON MILL CREEK,

WHETHER THE LAND ADJACENT TO THE CREEK IS
PRIVATELY OR PUBLICLY OWNED.
ANYONE FOUND FISHING IN THIS CREEK, OR ANY
OF ITS TRIBUTARIES, WILL BE SUBJECT TO THE
SEVEREST OF PENALTIES TO BE APPLIED BY PARA.

At the bottom in large bold letters, these words appeared:

PEOPLE AGAINST RECREATIONAL ANGLING

"Mac!" Lucinda exclaimed, "PARA is the group Helga
Markel helped form. I thought it would dissolve when she and
Professor Plaxler died."

"I'd hoped that was the case," I responded. "Who do you
suppose is behind the group now? And how big is PARA?
These signs were printed to deal specifically with Mill Creek.
Could the same have been done for other creeks in the area?
And what about the Yellowstone River?"

Helga Markel and Professor Henry Plaxler, as members of
PARA, were among a small group cast out of People for Equi-
table Treatment of Animals. At a PETA meeting at Chico Hot
Springs Resort three years ago, the ouster occurred because the
group that had formed PARA approved the use of violence to
achieve its goal.

PETA's focus has been less on challenging the nature of
angling and more on promoting the well-being of fish, such as
removing dams or building adequate ladders for salmon to access rivers where they have historically spawned.

Markel and Plaxler responded to their dismissal from
PETA by killing the second of the Shuttle Gals—Olga Smits.
They left her body nailed to a wooden cross attached to my

drift boat trailer. I discovered her after a float on the Yellowstone. Markel and Plaxler were never apprehended; they were later killed in an auto accident in Los Angeles.

"As I think more about it, I suspect this is a local matter, Lucinda. PARA was never a large group; they acted almost exclusively in Western Montana. Maybe they've targeted other places between here and Missoula, but I doubt that it goes further."

"Macduff, I worry because Helga's sister Hannah was half of the duo that killed five people you knew over the last year and a half—the wicker man and mistletoe murders. Hannah and her partner, Ellsworth-Kent, have never been found. Could she be after you again?"

"You have a knack for scaring me half to death. But you're usually right. Let's walk back to my cabin, go online, and see if we can find out how extensive this warning notice distribution has been."

On the return walk Lucinda seemed preoccupied; she hardly spoke, until she stopped, grabbed my arm and asked, "Do you think it's possible that the body found in Florida is related to these signs? You said the person, Carter, was a recreational angler—a fly fisherman."

"He was a fly fisherman, but he was also a guide," I answered. "Because of the small size of PARA and its focus here in Montana, I think it's a local issue. Plus, if the man in Florida was *murdered,* the gill net he was wrapped in points more at commercial fishermen than at PARA."

"But PARA means people against *recreational* fishing," Lucinda countered, "which excludes the commercial fishermen. The commercial group isn't very kind to recreational folk either, but they do respect the sea and its bounty, however much *they've* unreasonably been reducing that bounty. PARA members have little quarrel with using violence to stop *recreational* fishing; I suspect they don't much care what goes on with commercial fishing."

"I think it's time to do some online research," I suggested. "Let's walk a little faster."

7

THE "MUSIC ROOM" IN THE CABIN

W E RETURNED TO MY CABIN, grabbed a bottle of Gentleman Jack and two glasses, pulled on a bookcase that swung out and revealed a door, and went down stairs to a basement that I call my "music room." The room is filled with weapons and sophisticated communication equipment and computers. Plus, giving the room its name, it's where I play my oboe and English horn.

The music room reflects my passion for classical music, especially compositions for the oboe and English horn. The music room is soundproof; without fear of complaint, I deface the carefully written notes and instructions on some of the greatest oboe classics, especially my favorite Venetian Baroque concertos by Albinoni, Cimarosa, Marcello, and Vivaldi. I play only when Lucinda is away—my version of playing supports the old phrase that "The oboe is an ill wind that no one blows good." My English horn blowing sounds a little better, not quite so ill.

At the far end of the music room are racks holding various weapons. The most intimidating is a CheyTac Intervention M-200 sniper rifle, with a laser rangefinder, a telescopic sight, and a muzzle brake and suppressor. It's the rifle I used several years ago in my unsuccessful attempt to assassinate Abdul Khaliq Isfahani in the lush Guatemalan highlands. He's the Sudanese friend and former classmate of Juan Pablo Herzog at UF. Both are trying desperately to find me. My poor shot left Isfahani alive but with a disfigured face that has been subjected to a half dozen plastic surgeries in Zurich. They haven't restored his former dark, swarthy, handsome features. He's determined to reciprocate for the attempt on his life, but with more accuracy than I exhibited.

As soon as Isfahani recuperates from his most recent surgery, undoubtedly he'll join with Herzog to continue their persistent pursuit of me. I'm certain they know I'm alive and have been placed in a protection program. That means they'll be more determined than ever to discover my current name and whereabouts.

I also store several quickly accessible pistols in the music room—three Glocks and a Sig Sauer. But I've proven not very accurate with them at any target more than three feet away.

Upstairs are more guns, including a loaded Coach 12 gauge double-barreled shotgun and a .44 magnum Ruger revolver; both are loaded and kept out of sight in my bedroom. Several Winchester and Henry lever action rifles are hung in various places, mostly for display and reflecting my fondness for the "guns that won the West."

Another part of the music room has desks with computers and the miscellany needed to communicate by satellite directly and secretly with Dan Wilson at the CIA headquarters at Langley in Virginia near the edge of D.C.

It was to these desks that Lucinda and I disappeared for our search about the origin of the PARA signs on Mill Creek and the gill net wrapped body in Southwest Florida. We agreed that Lucinda would research the sign issue and I'd focus on the Florida killing. I'm reasonably familiar with the estuary of the Caloosahatchee River where the body was discovered.

After a couple of hours, we had collected a few helpful facts to exchange.

"Macduff," Lucinda reported, "PARA is not gone. I guess we've been so focused on the wicker man and mistletoe murders over the past year that we haven't thought to check on what's happened to PARA. There are currently PARA chapters in several Montana counties; their headquarters appears to be in Bozeman."

"It's a relief they're still confined to this area," I added. "I was worried there might be one in Florida."

"You didn't let me finish. A group in Florida has been organizing a chapter. Its address is a P.O. box on Sanibel!"

"Sanibel!" I exclaimed. "Why isn't it in the Panhandle?"

"Sanibel's a big recreational fishing area. As you go north along the coast to Cedar Key and beyond, commercial fishing holds sway. Or it did until the gill net ban."

"Did you find anything about PARA being involved in the death in Florida yesterday?" I asked.

"Too soon to know, I guess," she answered. "You know the snail pace of police work and how muddled the FBI can make a routine investigation. . . . You told me earlier that PARA has no quarrel with commercial fishing. Why? That involves killing fish?"

"PARA doesn't tolerate fishing for fun; commercial fishing is the way some people feed their families. PARA accepts that."

"Then you suspect the Florida death was the work of angry commercial fishermen—continuing the recreational versus commercial fishermen conflict—rather than an act of PARA against recreational fishing?"

"That's my guess. We haven't found anything about the PARA warnings we saw today that's resulted in violence. I think we need to wait a couple of days and keep checking."

"Will this ever be solved?" she asked.

"Not to all groups' satisfaction. Conservation's on the side of the recreational angler, at least for now. Florida might benefit by more appointed rather than elected judges. That would help the disparity between county and circuit court judges and those on the district courts of appeal and the Florida Supreme Court. Something more in common with the federal judicial system might be useful. . . . Enough! I don't think Florida's going to do anything."

"I'll call Ken or Erin at the sheriff's office in Livingston and see what they know about the PARA signs."

When Lucinda called—setting the phone speaker on—Ken Rangley, Acting Chief Detective at the Park County Sheriff's Office, answered. Ken's a long-time friend who took over the head detective role after then Sheriff Jimbo Shaw was indicted for the murder of Pam Snyder, one of the three Shuttle Gals killed a couple of years ago. Shaw sits somewhere in a Montana jail—"waiting for justice." In Montana that means the gas chamber.

"What's up, Lucinda?" Ken asked. "Don't tell me. There's more trouble. It's barely three months since the last attempt to rid the world of Macduff Brooks and Lucinda Lang. Or is it now Lucinda *Brooks*, as it should be?" he asked.

"We didn't call you for domestic advice, Ken," I called out. "Lucinda and I found some signs by PARA on a morning walk along Mill Creek Road. Do you know anything about the signs?"

"No. And nobody else has called about them. They must have been put up not long before your walk. After dealing with Helga Markel and the Shuttle Gals murders, I don't like *anything* about PARA."

"We'll call you if we hear more."

I turned off the phone and looked at Lucinda. "Forget PARA. Let's go fishing. . . . Before I leave for Maine."

8

THE FOLLOWING MORNING FISHING ALONG THE PASSAGE FALLS TRAIL

"SHALL WE DRIVE TO NEARLY THE TOP OF MILL CREEK where we like to picnic? Or hike up to Passage Falls?" Lucinda asked at breakfast. We began on the porch with Guatemalan coffee brewed from freshly ground beans grown on mountain slopes near Antigua, but were abruptly chased in by a fall morning chill. The kind you don't feel until you begin to shiver uncontrollably. Porch coffee will have to wait until Florida.

"Let's stop at the Passage Falls Trail parking area," I replied. "If the creek doesn't look promising, we can drive a few miles further to the last picnic area."

"You get the fishing gear. I'll get the lunch," she said. I knew what "get the fishing gear" meant, but I worried what she would produce for lunch.

With the exception of one small, mud-caked SUV, the parking lot at the Passage Falls trailhead was barren. Not unexpected on a weekday with schools and colleges back in session. The trees were turning colors; the brazen gilt of autumn aspen leaves shivered in the chilled breeze. Leaving her bamboo rod for me to rig, Lucinda quietly moved toward the creek at the southern side of the parking area, working her way through dense challenging brush along the edge of the water.

"Macduff, pass my rod through the brush to me—carefully," she called, in a muted voice. "I didn't think I'd see any fish here, but there's a pool below me where the water's calm. I can dapple a fly and see what happens. . . . I think I saw a flash of silver and crimson but it may be well-wishing."

I handed her the bamboo rod I'd made and given to her for Christmas the year we met. Once it served as a conversation piece over her mantle in her Manhattan apartment, drawing comments from colleagues about her slumming with a guy from the wrong side of the tracks, or in my case the wrong seat in the drift boat. For the past few years Lucinda has used the rod to catch dozens of small trout in the creeks off both the Yellowstone and Snake rivers, as well as in many of the isolated streams and creeks of Yellowstone Park.

"Thanks," she said, taking the rod. "I see shadows from two trout. Native cutthroats, I would guess. Maybe eight, maybe nine inches—good for here. They're feeding on something I can't see. What about using a tiny caddis—darkish green? Do you have anything like that?"

"Yes. I'm going to hand you a #18 brown elk hair caddis. It's an Al Troth creation, imitating an adult caddis fly. Easy to tie, the body is hare's fur wrapped with fine gold wire and cock saddle hackle. Look at the wing made of elk hair. The head isn't built up of thread, rounded, and cemented to leave it glossy black, as on many flies. You can see the hair in front of the wrapping thread is cut off, leaving a short bristly stub. You're about to use a classic fly, one that's on most fly fishers' ten best dry flies list."

She tied on the usually reliable caddis fly with a clinch knot, lowered it to just above the surface, and then flicked it backhand to the upstream edge of the pool. The creek had enough flow to start the caddis drifting across where the two trout rested near the bottom in little more than two feet of water. Neither fish even lifted its head and looked at her fly. She tried again, and then a third time. No movement at all.

"I found another elk hair. This one's olive," I whispered, watching as best I could through the brush. "You said whatever's been floating had a green tinge. . . . I saw you bite off the brown elk hair. . . . Remember what our dentist said about biting off tippets?"

"Something about not doing that," she shrugged, "but this is an emergency." She tied on the olive elk hair, dropped it exactly as before, and the two trout raced for the fly, colliding so neither could take it.

"Why are trout so greedy, Macduff?"

"Vying for your affection. They were surely males. . . . Try it again, but don't drift the fly directly *over* the fish. Keep it a foot away from the side of one."

She did exactly that and this time the closer of the two fish reached the fly, engulfed it, and ran all of twelve feet before it disappeared into some overhanging brush and snapped the thin tippet.

"Macduff! What happened?"

"Early catch and release."

"I'd like to make the catch part last a little longer," she noted, glumly.

"Let's cross Mill Creek at the top of the parking lot where Passage Falls Creek joins, then walk part way upstream and see what's around the next bridge."

"OK. I'll try another olive elk hair caddis. It seems to work."

"Stay with anything that works. That applies to flies as well as to companions!"

"You're so erudite!" she said, with as much doubt as she could insert in her comment. I attributed her momentary surge in spirit to be from her presence on a favorite creek, not from any change to what seems to be troubling her.

The next bridge didn't produce any fish so we continued for a half hour, reached the falls, and rested without conversation, listening to the sounds of the fall forest. Walking back was an easy downhill trek, and we were soon again at the small bridge over Mill Creek at the head of the parking lot.

The bridge provides good cover for trout. I rarely pass by a bridge without fishing in the shadows, especially on the downstream side where there are eddies caused by water rushing past the bridge supports, rejoining a few feet after the bridge and leaving some reasonably still water that fish like to hang in and watch for food to rush past. They dart out, take the food, and dart back, expending as little energy as possible. Somehow they seem to calculate how much effort will be required. If energy to be gained from consuming the food is less than energy needed to reach the food and return, they let it pass by unchallenged and wait for something more favorable to the fish's equation of energy expenditure. I prefer to have the fly float along the seam between the fast water and the eddy, especially when there's a foam line.

"There's more turbulence around the bridge than usual," Lucinda observed as we neared. Two steps onto the bridge she leaned over the railing, looked, and froze, her expression changing from mirth to shock. Dropping her rod and putting her hands to her face, she cried, "It's a body, Mac!"

"I'll see if it's alive," I said, leaning over to look and then hurrying across the bridge and splashing into the water on the downstream side. "It doesn't look promising: The head seems to be stuck underwater. Try your cell phone, but we may not have service here."

I was standing in cold water, wearing my best ankle-high hiking shoes that were no more than ten days old. I hadn't changed into my wading boots, which I usually wear but which lack the comfort of my hiking shoes.

The body's feet and legs were thrusting to the erratic rhythm of the downstream surge of the stream; the torso was caught under the bridge. I left the creek, crossed the trail, and stepped back into the creek on the upstream side of the bridge.

It wasn't certain, but the person *appeared* to be male. The water hadn't yet distorted facial features. Whoever it was must have become wedged under the bridge in the couple of hours since we crossed it on our walk to the falls. The person's hip boots had filled from the flow of the creek. There didn't appear to be enough water in Passage Creek or this part of Mill Creek in September that called for wearing anything more than sandals or shoes. But the water was cold—cold enough to kill.

I tried to look closer, but the head was mostly under the surface. Then the head broke the surface, and I saw a moustache that gave us gender identification. The man wore a fishing vest that had snagged on the corner of a bridge beam. But what caused us to stare was the net wrapped tightly around him.

His shroud was not just any net. It was a gill net!

9

Two shrimpers, one near Jacksonville and the other near Pensacola, were cited for illegal use of trawls. Two men in the Panhandle were cited for gill-net violations.

In Fort Pierce, tacks were placed across a recreational boat ramp and a group of 15 pleasure boats was spray-painted and otherwise vandalized. Three gill nets were also found abandoned near St. Lucie without identifying floats attached.

Orlando Sentinel, July 2, 1995.

AT THE PASSAGE FALLS TRAIL BRIDGE

LUCINDA CALLED THE PARK COUNTY Sheriff's Office immediately after we confirmed that the man was indeed dead. There was little doubt—the gill net had kept the man's head mostly submerged.

"You won't believe this," exclaimed Lucinda to our friend Erin Giffin, a deputy with the county sheriff's department. "Mac and I are looking at a body under the bridge at the parking area on Mill Creek Road where the trail to Passage Creek Falls begins." Erin is a thirty-seven-year-old tiny bundle of energy and competence. Ph.D., author, Japanese martial arts kendo expert, all stuffed into a trim 5'1" body that draws men's attention.

"Are you certain the person's dead?" asked Erin calmly.

"He's partly submerged. We lifted his head as best we could, but he showed no life. No pulse. Should Macduff and I remove his body?"

"If there were any possibility he was alive I'd say 'pull him out and try CPR.' But it sounds as though he's dead. Best to leave him."

"We'll leave him. We don't want to disturb anything."

"Are you sure it's a male?"

"The body has a short haircut any Marine would envy. And a moustache."

"Any idea who he is?"

"Neither of us recognized him. Maybe in his forties or fifties. Immersion is not kind to gender or age determination. He was a fisherman—at least he's wearing a khaki fishing vest. No fly rod nearby, probably stuck in the overhanging brush along the creek."

"Hang on; I'll be there in forty minutes. Any ID on him I can check on the way?"

"We haven't moved him from under the bridge so we haven't checked his pockets. Didn't want to mess up evidence."

"Good. Macduff with you?"

He's here by the body. If it comes loose and starts to float down the river, I assume you want us to stop it."

"Drag him ashore; don't lose him."

Erin arrived in thirty-five minutes, five minutes ahead of an emergency van. No flashing lights, no sirens, no longer a sense of urgency. The crew's sole role would be transporting the body to the Park County morgue in Livingston for an autopsy.

After she took a score of photographs, the emergency crew pulled the body loose from the bridge supports, laid him on a stretcher, and cut away part of the gill net. Erin looked but found no immediate signs of blood, blows to the head, or bullet wounds.

"It looked at first like death by drowning," commented Erin. "Maybe a heart attack or stroke. He may have been fishing upstream of the bridge, fallen in unconscious, floated downstream, and caught under the bridge. He may have been dead before he could have drowned. . . . But that doesn't explain the net. Maybe it was under the bridge, and he became entangled."

"Anything in the pockets?" I asked. "He must have had a fishing license."

"Not a thing. He either didn't carry any identification, including a fishing license, or someone took them. But that sounds like foul play, and I don't want to presuppose anything."

After the emergency van with the body disappeared, scattering swirls of dust down the gravel road, Erin, Lucinda, and I sat on the bridge railings. "Erin," I asked, "have you read about the body found a few days ago in a gill net near Ft. Myers in Florida?"

"Briefly. I scanned the *USA Today* article. But don't start thinking serial killer. As far as I know, the person in Florida was caught in a gill net, maybe his own, and drowned. . . . I haven't seen any recent report, only what you two and I have read in the papers here. . . . But I'll look again. . . . Do you have *any* reason to think the two deaths are connected, Macduff?"

"No. I'm probably overreacting, but the Florida papers we read online this morning hinted there may have been foul play.

I knew the dead guy, Clint Carter, but he wasn't what I'd call a friend. We spoke together at a conference a year ago. . . . I have no knowledge about the guy here—yet."

"Erin, what about the signs?" Lucinda asked. "PARA seems to have returned, and now they're posting warnings. Do you know of any deaths linked to PARA over the past couple of years—since Helga Markel died in California?"

"Not a one," Erin answered. "But I'd like to know what motivated the signs and whether signs alone are the extent of PARA's current plans."

"Has anyone been reported missing around here?" I asked.

"No, but the death presumably occurred only within the past couple of hours; the person may not have been reported as missing for lots of reasons. He could have been single and lived alone. Or married or lived with someone who was away on business or pleasure and assumed the person at home was fine. It's too soon for conclusions. We'll know more when we can. Let's look inside the SUV. Maybe it's his."

The SUV had been broken into, and there was no sign of any registration or ownership. Nothing to help identify the man. The license plate had been removed.

"We're a little jumpy after the past year, Erin." I admitted.

"Can't blame you. . . . By the way, there's been no word about the whereabouts of Ellsworth-Kent or Markel. Maybe no news is good news," Erin said as she started to her vehicle.

"I'll try to think of it that way," I responded as she left. "But it's hard to when a body is found," I mumbled to myself.

10

THE FOLLOWING DAY

B Y MORNING I HAD POSTPONED going to Maine because the discovery of the gill net wrapped body, added to
the threatening PARA signs we discovered posted along Mill
Creek Road, affected what I planned to talk about with Elsbeth
when I arrived in Orono. One thing is certain; she doesn't need
to have me impose a new burden on her.

Elsbeth apparently hadn't heard about the Florida and
Montana gill net deaths—at least she hadn't called and asked
about them. Perhaps if they didn't appear in the Maine newspapers they didn't happen.

After calling Elsbeth late in the afternoon and telling her
nothing that might upset her, I changed my plane reservations
and again called the sheriff's office in Livingston.

Ken Rangley answered. "A lot has happened since we
talked two days ago. . . . It doesn't take you two long to stir
things up. I was hoping Macduff might call and ask me to go
fishing. It's been too long. . . . But at least you two gave us
three months of peace between the wicker man and mistletoe
saga's attempt on your lives—and finding the body yesterday
along Mill Creek. Erin's filled me in on your conversation yesterday."

"Anything new about the guy we found?"

"Yes, an hour ago I talked with our county medical examiner, Dr. Deborah Castle. She's new to the job, but I think she'll be great. Touching the six-foot mark, she played volleyball at UM in Missoula. A *very* professional, disciplined lady. She started on the body early this morning. We hadn't found anything in the man's pockets, around his neck, or even a watch on his wrist. Dr. Castle noted a narrow band of white skin on his right wrist—no tan—suggesting he wore a watch and that it was removed. Whatever flies he used and all the gadgets usually hanging from a fly fisherman's vest were missing. Someone, and I'm not saying a killer, didn't want him identified easily. But we found one item.

"He was wearing gloves with the finger tips cut off, the kind that allow you to change flies in cold weather, add tippet, or do other functions requiring some dexterity denied by full-fingered gloves. When Dr. Castle stripped the body and took off the gloves, she found a ring on his left ring finger."

"Wedding ring?"

"No, a college class ring from the University of Vermont, with a date: 1972."

"Anything inscribed on the back?"

"Nothing. We're trying to do a composite of his face. We'll post some around Paradise Valley and later today send some to the university in Vermont. But he may not have been in Vermont for several decades.

"How about dental records?"

"We're hoping. That could solve the identity matter. A report is due by the end of the day. The man had some expensive gold caps that should help . . . Mac, there's a call from the dental lab. Can I call you back?"

"I'll stay on this line. Take the call."

After a five-minute wait that seemed like thirty, Ken was back on line.

"Macduff, we know who he is. Name's Bill Hendersen. Lives in Georgia, at least in the winter. He's restored a 1920s log cabin on the outskirts of Livingston. It's a modest place high behind a ridge of the Gallatin Mountains about five miles west of here."

I was sitting at the small table by my cabin's rear windows talking to Ken and staring absent mindedly out at the creek, unusually high for this time of year but understandably so considering that heavy rains had persisted the past two weeks. I didn't want to have to shift my focus from what should be good fall fishing to another death.

Ken talked louder, aware that as usual Lucinda was listening. "We'll check local bank accounts, fishing and auto licenses, military records, things like . . . ."

"We didn't see any sign of another vehicle being in the parking area next to the bridge where we found him. Isn't that strange, Ken?" Lucinda interrupted.

"Maybe. There's no parking upstream of the bridge for several miles. I don't think his body could have floated that far without being hung up on brush or wedged between boulders."

"Ken," I asked, "when you know anything significant, please pass it on to me. I'm going to Maine in a few days to see Elsbeth, and I'd like to know if there's anything I need to think about telling her."

"Erin's off the other line. If she has any news, I'll get right back. . . . Hey, Lucinda," Ken said loudly, "hope Macduff likes that sticky rice you told me you were going to make." With that, he hung up.

I sat up and tried as best I could to decipher the meaning of whatever it was that Lucinda was going to put on my plate.

"Lucinda, what did Ken mean by 'sticky rice'?"

"I'm making sticky rice with mango for dinner."

"What does it stick to? The plate? The mango? My throat? . . . You trying to choke me?"

"I would if I thought it would work; you're so unenlightened about nutritious food."

"I've defined good food to you a dozen times," I said.

"Bacon, sausage, eggs, milkshakes, fries, burgers, and hot dogs are not on my list of good food," she responded tartly.

"Sounds like you're going to try to feed me a tofu burger again."

"No, I admit I lost that round last month. My rule is to wait a full year before I try again. . . . But we are having sticky rice with mango tonight. You like Thai food. Sticky rice is a staple in Thailand. . . . It's also called sweet or glutinous rice."

"Thai food was intended for the Thai people. Besides, if I remember my minimal French, *riz gluant* would be French for sticky rice, and it properly means *gluey*. Gluey doesn't sound healthy, much less appetizing."

"Wait 'til you try it."

"That's what you said about tofu. I gagged on tofu."

"You were faking."

"So were you when you said before you served it that you were cooking a delicious, healthy meal."

For dinner that evening I was introduced for the first time to sticky rice with mango. The mango was delicious. I must admit the gluey rice was pretty good.

11

The Florida Marine Patrol on Sunday removed five gill nets totaling about 4,000 feet that were dropped in the waters off Santa Rosa County. . . . The nets weren't meant to trap fish, only boats. . . . The Marine Patrol learned of the nets from a recreational boater who got tangled in them. . . . Roofing nails were strewn across four boat ramps in St. Lucie County; while no one was injured, several cars got flat tires.

Orlando Sentinel, July 3, 1995.

THE NEXT DAY

BEFORE LUCINDA AND I WENT TO BED last night, we double-checked the locks on the doors and windows. I checked my .44 magnum Ruger pistol, put it back in the top drawer of my bedside table, and placed my loaded double short-barreled shotgun under the edge of the bed. I don't think Wuff likes the smell of gunpowder; she sniffed the shotgun, went into the guest bedroom, hopped onto the bed, and was asleep in five minutes. She didn't budge the entire night.

The unruly temperature dropped during the night sufficient to blanket the cabin and ground with another white dusting—reminding us we might soon want to flee across America's wastelands to Florida. But not until I finished my coffee—which we were sipping inside while looking out at the deteriorating weather. More snow is expected tonight.

"Macduff!" exclaimed Lucinda. "No sooner do I hand you a cup of my special Antigua-bean coffee then you spill it all over your mat. You OK?"

We were reading the *New York Times* we found with difficulty late Monday in Bozeman, along with the rural *Bozeman News*. When I opened the first section of the *Times* to international news, I saw an article's headline: "García Carranza Wins Suspect Presidential Election in Guatemala."

"Lucinda, listen to this." I started to read the brief article to her. But I was stopped before I finished the first sentence.

"Macduff, you're always interrupting me. I'm reading 'Peanuts' in the Bozeman paper. It's a cartoon about Snoopy. And Charlie Brown, who can't make up his mind about what Lucy will do next. Sound familiar? When you went through the federal program that changed your name, you should have insisted on *being* Charlie Brown."

I'd spilled my coffee because of the second sentence in the *Times* article: "The losing candidate, businessman and often alleged head of Guatemalan organized crime, Juan Pablo Herzog, condemned the vote as fraudulent and promised to challenge the result in the courts and on the streets. Persons with personal knowledge about Herzog suggested he might challenge it by mounting a coup d'état."

"Lucinda, it's about Juan Pablo Herzog."

"My God! Now you've caused *me* to spill my coffee! . . . I won't enjoy 'Peanuts'—Charlie Brown was just about to throw a pitch to Lucy. . . . Or *at* Lucy. Since I've splashed my coffee onto my lap and lost my place reading, you might as well tell

me about Guatemala. . . . Sorry, Mac. I should be more interested in Herzog than Snoopy, but I like Snoopy better."

"Just listen to me for a moment, and I'll explain 'Peanuts'
to you later. You know Herzog was running for the presidency.
The election was two days ago—Sunday. The winner—José
García Carranza—is about sixty-five. Twenty years ago, as *General* García Carranza, he led a coup that failed to oust then President Manuel Rubioso. García Carranza is a populist and
doesn't generate the fear associated with Herzog. The U.S.
doesn't like García Carranza because during his campaign he
promised to nationalize a score of foreign owned companies,
including several owned or managed by U.S. companies."

"Should we worry? Herzog's been quiet for the past couple
of years."

"He has been quiet for good reasons. He was consumed
by his campaign and his friend Abdul Khaliq Isfahani was un-
dergoing plastic surgery in Zurich to correct the damage I in-
flicted when I tried to assassinate him five years ago. You recall
my shot hit him in the face."

"Will they come after us?"

"I don't know how successfully Isfahani has recovered
from his surgery. Herzog apparently backed off from searching
for us until Isfahani fully recovers. But Herzog's election loss
gives him time to settle old scores, and he may not be willing to
wait for Isfahani any longer. I imagine I'm number one on his
list."

"Why not talk to Dan Wilson about them both?"

"I'll call him today."

12

THAT AFTERNOON

D AN GOT TO ME FIRST. Not on my cell phone but the special line in my music room linked directly to him at Langley. He was calling on a private cell phone, not a protected Agency line.

"Why the secrecy?" I asked him.

"Herzog and Isfahani are both on a general CIA 'watch' list. Herzog, because he's furious about losing the Guatemalan presidential election and may attempt a coup. That's nothing new to Guatemalan politics. Isfahani, because he's returned to planning terrorist activities."

"Is Herzog in Guatemala?"

"Yes, some of his time is at his luxury penthouse condo in Guatemala City, some at his vast coffee *finca* outside Antigua. He's been in closed-door sessions with three army generals. They don't trust García Carranza even though he was one of them. It's the same old anxiety among the generals about the new president initiating social reforms and the military losing its privileges. 'Privileges' means control of the executive, legislative, and judicial branches. That doesn't leave much else."

"Does all this mean the U.S. would prefer to have Herzog in office?"

"Right."

"Meaning the U.S. would like to make him a happy man?"

"Right."

"Without regard to my remaining alive?"

"Right again; you're doing good."

"Maybe by your giving Herzog the information about me he's been after for years?"

"Still right. . . . But that won't happen, Mac. . . . I have something with me. Some files."

"Involving me?"

"*Only* involving you. It's our complete file on your conversion from Professor Maxwell Hunt to Macduff Brooks. There are two hard copy sets. Plus only one in our computer files. That one has been mysteriously erased . . . by me. We don't back-up those files—too many of our people have access to the computer file storage. As to the two hard copies, our person in charge of the protected person has one."

"That would be you?"

"That would be me. The highest ranked person here in overall charge of the program has the other."

"That wouldn't be you?"

"Correct, but I have *both* sets with me. There's a quirk in our system that allows me access to the file storage room, when the head man is on vacation. I'm second in charge. I took your files from his office an hour ago; I have both sets."

"If any of his files are missing, you're in trouble."

"Not likely. I know our head man. He wouldn't acknowledge that he lost a file or left it in charge with the only other person with a set. He could lose his job and, more importantly, his generous government pension."

"But when his boss discovers the backup storage is missing, what then?"

"We don't admit mistakes here. We would deny any knowledge of a Professor Maxwell Hunt. In fact, when the whole process with you commenced, our records showed a John Doe name in place of Hunt. Plus, there's no reference to his being a professor. He was nothing more than an agent of convenience being placed in the protection program."

"What about your agents who were stationed in Guatemala at that time?"

"They know about Professor Maxwell Hunt. They know he was beaten up in Guatemala City by Herzog. They know he disappeared. They were told he was taken to the U.S., where he died of a stroke. But, they don't know anything about the link between Hunt and Brooks."

"But I worked for you trying to kill Isfahani."

"True, but as an outsider who was able and willing to do the job, not as Professor Hunt. Remember, you used assumed names—Ben Roth and Smith—when you shot Isfahani."

"Dan, I'm not so naïve as to believe there isn't some way for someone in your organization to link me with Maxwell Hunt. But I appreciate your actions. . . . Another thing, can you destroy the two hard copy files?"

"I've shredded one copy at a local Office Depot. I don't want to do the same to the other. You might need the file someday. What if Herzog and Isfahani were to die? You'd be free to resume your life as Hunt."

"That's strange, Dan. Last year Lucinda asked me what I would do if I could go back to being Hunt and whether she'd be a part of my life."

"If you have any sense, that wasn't hard to answer. Unless you're still arguing whether you're even engaged."

"Apparently I conceded that debate months ago."

"So what's delaying the wedding?"

"Elsbeth. She's becoming close to Lucinda, but I don't know her true feelings about my remarrying."

"Ask her."

"I may. Soon. I'm going to visit her in Maine once I know more about the deaths here and in Florida."

"Then I'm going to tell you everything I can about all your suitors—Herzog, Isfahani, Markel, and Ellsworth-Kent."

"Before you do, what about the second set of hard copy files?"

"I'm sending it to you by private courier. Not the Agency's. Mine."

"Dan, what if you died a month from now. I'd be a nonentity to the CIA. That would end any protection I have. Am I right?"

"Not really. Jack Ivonsky replaced Paula Pajioli as the Montana agent who, among other things, was assigned to protect Macduff Brooks. No Montana agent assigned to a protected person knows the former identity of that person. . . ."

"I feel more comfortable when you're available, Dan. If you're not, won't I be cut off from protection? How does the Agency know I exist other than what their Montana agent knows?"

"What's been removed from the files is any reference to the original identity of the protected person. That means everything linking Maxwell Hunt to Macduff Brooks. Hunt is referred to as a deceased professor who occasionally acted for us as an agent of convenience. He's history. No reference to Brooks appears anywhere there's a reference to Hunt. Brooks is referred to as a protected person in the program. No cross reference exists to Hunt. Protection for you as Brooks continues. The Agency won't dump you."

"One more concern. . . .When I became Macduff Brooks, there were a dozen people in the room. We know what any one of them could do because of Whitman's attempt to publish his book on his experiences in the CIA."

"Whitman and three others who were involved with your conversion are dead. That leaves eight who also participated. Not all know the full facts; you may recall that people came in and out during the process. Some know your new name but not where you chose to live. Others know about Montana but not your name. Even they don't know where in Montana you went or whether you're still there. I'm the only one who knows everything and has any paper record. And *now* I don't have a paper record."

"Are you in good health, Dan? It sounds like your planning for your own demise."

"Not planning. Prepared. Nothing that seven pills a day can't keep stabilized. Remember, Herzog and Isfahani aren't getting any younger either. You're not *that* much older."

"The two sound pretty healthy to me. Except for Isfahani's face. I was hoping he wouldn't survive the operations, but apparently it was mostly routine plastic surgery. . . . Dan, you mentioned that Isfahani has been active in terrorist activities. Anything specific?"

"Yes. The attack on our embassy in Libya and, more recently, an aborted similar attack on our embassy in his country—the Sudan. Now he's planning an attack in the U.S."

"What do *you* plan for him?"

"We'd like you to visit Khartoum again."

13

THAT SAME DAY AT THE LAW COLLEGE IN GAINESVILLE, FLORIDA

DEAN HOBART PERRY of the University of Florida law college, on his way to work, was stepping out of the sluggish elevator outside his suite when his secretary, Donna, rushing from his office, nearly knocked Perry over. She looked unusually disturbed.

"Dean! Your office was broken into. It's a mess. I haven't touched anything."

"Let's go look. Then we have to call the campus police."

"Most of your desk drawers have been opened and the contents scattered on the floor. I know you don't lock your desk. What's been forced open is the locked filing cabinet in your closet."

"That has special personnel files," Perry noted. "And reports, including the one Gloria Martinez did . . . oh my gosh! If it's missing, could it be Juan Pablo Herzog's doing?"

Perry went directly to the closet and noticed that the second file drawer was on the floor, file folders scattered in the closet. He quickly sifted through the folders and discovered that the report former Associate Dean Gloria Martinez had prepared about deceased Professor Maxwell Hunt was missing. Herzog had demanded that Perry report on the accuracy of the claim that Hunt had died of a stroke while lecturing in D.C.

Nothing else was taken that Perry could identify immediately. Then he sighed in relief and sat down, realizing he had removed that file when he wrote Elsbeth, telling her he was willing to talk to her, and a month later had added some notes about their conversation. Perry was positive that his letter to her had not mentioned the name Macduff Brooks or that he lived in Montana.

Perry also remembered that weeks ago he had placed the Hunt file in a separately zippered compartment of the large briefcase he routinely carried between home and office. He had forgotten to return the file to the locked cabinet. His hands trembled as he quickly opened his briefcase; he was much relieved to find the file with the report.

The report had been made after Herzog promised to fund an endowed chair honoring Professor Maxwell Hunt. Any promise of a $4-million gift was not to be ignored, but after talking with then UF President Killingsworth, who shared the dean's reservations about the motives of Herzog, they decided to reject the gift. Perry kept the report locked in his personal cabinet.

Perry had thought about destroying the file several times, but never finally decided on doing so. He thought he would destroy it when he stepped down from the deanship, which increasingly he thought about.

"What do you want me to do?" asked Donna.

"Nothing. Absolutely nothing. . . . President Killingsworth has retired, partly the result of the shooting here a few years ago at the building dedication in the law school courtyard. The shot must have been meant for me, but the shooter's identity, which we later learned was Herzog's niece, has never been publicly disclosed. Nor has *her* killer been named. Partly because we never tried to help the police in sorting out the facts."

"Dean Perry, there's been a forced break-in, and you're not going to report it?" Donna asked incredulously.

"What's to be gained from doing so? Our new president and I aren't on the best of terms. I don't want to tell him about the report and be asked to start filling in blanks and start naming names and places. Suppose the president wanted to see the report because some federal or state law enforcement official or member of the Board of Trustees or press snoop asked to see a copy?"

"Maybe you *should* have destroyed the report."

"I've thought about that. It *is* a public record, even though access is limited because it deals with a student. . . . But, it doesn't deal at all with Herzog as a student. Only about events long after he graduated and returned to Guatemala. . . . I'm thinking only of former Professor Maxwell Hunt's interests. And Elsbeth's. There's nothing to be gained from keeping the report and having someone demand it. . . ."

"I'll take care of it," Perry said as he walked toward the office shredder, flipping through the folder and removing paper clips. Turning to Donna, he added, "I don't want you implicated by being here when I do."

Donna stepped out. A moment later, from her desk she could hear a grinding noise coming from Perry's office.

The noise of his shredder.

14

EARLY OCTOBER

L UCINDA, WUFF, AND I FINALLY DEPARTED for
Florida after we had dallied to enjoy the year's final display
of floral colors in Paradise Valley. Late one afternoon we wit-
nessed a fifty mph wind denude the seasonal trees of their twi-
light leaves, leaving clear signs of the frigid, challenging months
to come. Long before these trees leaf out soft spring-green
again, Lucinda and I will have lived for several months among
the flowering camellias, azaleas, and dogwoods of a Northeast
Florida "winter."

"We'll make St. Louis in a couple of days in time for you
to catch an afternoon flight to New York," I indicated as we
by-passed Billings and turned southeast to face the placid fea-
tureless landscape of America's inland seascape. "That is, unless
you drive and we reach St. Louis in much less than that."

"You're jealous of my driving skills. I could give Danica
Patrick a lesson."

"But she breaks the sound barrier on a race track; you do it
on everything from interstates to dirt roads."

"Jealousy will get you nowhere with me."

The next day Lucinda was remarkably quiet. She hadn't begun a conversation, asked a question, or made a comment between departure and lunch time. She sat staring out the passenger side window, just as Wuff does when she gets a turn up front.

"You're very quiet," I said. "Problems you might share?"

"Something I need to talk about before we part. . . . Mac, I can't seem to decide where I'm going."

"You're going to New York."

"I know that much. . . . Be serious."

"What is it?"

"We've been engaged for more than a year and we've never talked about marriage. I think I'm glad. I'm so confused. When I met you, I was content with my life. Robert was no longer a part of it. I had succeeded financially beyond my expectations, buying an elegant New York apartment and a magnificent ranch in Montana. Now I rarely use either."

"Do you want to go back to that life?" I asked. "Say the word; you have a right to choose your own way. . . . I've certainly put you at risk. Unfairly. I spend sleepless nights worrying about your safety. The past year has been the worst. I thought it ended years ago after the shooting on the Snake, again a year later after the Shuttle Gals deaths, and finally this year after the solstice murders."

"It's not only that," she noted. "If anything, it's been a thrilling few years. We've helped each other out of some unimaginable circumstances. We're like a couple of cats with nine lives. But, I feel like I've used up eight of them."

"With only one left," I added, quietly, thinking that was negative, like the bottle being half empty rather than half full.

"Far fewer left than lost. . . . I don't know where I belong. Being a stay-at-home isn't what I want. I need a focus. A couple of weeks in Manhattan, the rest of the year split between Montana and Florida—two paradises. . . . I'm confused. Sometimes I feel terribly selfish."

"Do you miss your work? A few weeks a year isn't much time spent on what you do so well."

"I have some clients in Bozeman. A few in Big Sky. More in Paradise Valley. They help. But Bozeman isn't Manhattan when it comes to where the investment energy is centered."

"I don't have to be in Montana as long as from mid-April to mid-October," I offered. "I could limit my Montana time to the best part of the season, mid-August to mid-October."

"That's only two months. You're a guide. You earn your living as a guide."

"Not really. I've never talked to you in detail about my finances. Work isn't a necessity. I inherited and invested wisely while I was teaching. I saved much of my salary over the last ten years as a law professor. Consulting during that time was lucrative. I was pretty reclusive during those ten years. I mostly worked. But you know that.

"Guiding is fascinating, except for the occasional client who wants to shoot us. Or blow us up. I guide because I love the mountains. But no more than the coastal salt marshes of Florida. I'm lucky to divide the year between them. But I don't *have* to do that."

"Mac, I knew you weren't making a living guiding; you do a lot of guide trips for charities."

"Fewer each year. I'm not getting any younger. I'm past the age of most guides. Rowing is a younger man's job."

"Are you OK? Is it health?"

"No. I'm fine. As Dr. Zeuss says, 'You're in pretty good shape for the shape that you're in.'"

"Is Dr. Zeuss your doctor?"

"No, he's my spiritual advisor. As he's philosophically observed, 'You're only old once.'"

"You're not old."

"I'm not young. Six or seven days a week for as much as ten hours a day on the river, with two demanding clients, is pretty exhausting. It gets more so each year."

"I know you've been reducing and spacing your guiding trips every year. That makes sense. . . . But. . . ."

"I'd like to be here for the late-summer and early-fall fishing. I don't need. . . ."

"You *love* Montana and your cabin on Mill Creek," she interrupted. "Two months isn't much time. And Florida begins to be uncomfortably humid by late May. You've always had an urge to leave and be at Mill Creek in time for the spring fishing before the ice melt overwhelms the Yellowstone."

"The Yellowstone is blown out for a month or two, mid-May to as late as the end of July. If I got here by late June, I wouldn't miss much. I'm thinking of you; I sense you miss your work more than you admit."

"Yes. . . . I think I do," she said, diverting the discussion from her main concern. I haven't been fair to my clients the past few years; I'm not giving the quality of advice I once did."

"And want to do."

"Yes."

"Will you stay in Manhattan longer than the three weeks you planned?"

"Yes."

"How long?"

"I don't know."

"Long?"

"Maybe."

The remaining drive to St. Louis said much by its silence. Lucinda rarely looked my way. I thought I saw an occasional tear but didn't ask why. When we reached Lambert-St. Louis for her mid-afternoon flight to LaGuardia, Lucinda finally turned to me and said, "Please drop me at the departures level."

"We can park. I'll walk with you to the security line. Wuff's fine in the car. We have a couple of hours before you leave."

"Drop me where I asked," she said, with stiffness to her voice I rarely heard.

It was not a good parting. Any "sweet sorrow" was all mine. When I pulled the car to the curb in front of the busy terminal, she hopped out while I explained to a security guard that I only wanted to help her get her bag out and would immediately leave. He said OK. But when I got out of the car, I saw the back of Lucinda pulling her bag through the door. Not a word of departure. Nor a hug. Nor a wave. Nor even a glance. She was simply gone.

I sat back and shut my eyes for a moment. Wuff hopped into Lucinda's place and leaned against the seatback, staring at me. It was twenty minutes before I could drive. When I cleared St. Louis, crossed the Mississippi, and aimed us southeast, I stopped at the first rest area along the interstate, walked Wuff, and sat on a concrete picnic table in silence as the hours passed and the day darkened. The sun was setting on a life I never dreamed could be possible after I lost El.

I checked in to a nondescript motel, like those Wuff and I used when crossing the country before I met Lucinda. Wuff had her meal, and I had a Gentleman Jack.

The next day was drudgery; when we passed into Tennessee, the roads were filled with Volunteer fans heading to Knoxville to drink and yell while once again the Alabama Crimson Tide pummeled their football team. Apparently public radio hasn't yet reached Tennessee; all I could get on AM or FM stations were drunks singing "Rocky Top." I scribbled a note to myself: "If I ever plan to drive through these states again, subscribe to Sirius."

At noon the following day, somewhere on a drab and endless interstate, I called Jen Jennings in St. Augustine. She's my cottage caretaker during the summers and my weekly cleaning helper when I'm there in the fall and winter.

"Macduff," she said, "the cottage looks great. I cleaned it today—not sure you three were coming tonight or tomorrow."

"I'll only be there for a couple of days, Jen, before I fly to Maine for three days. Could you take Wuff? Lucinda won't be with me."

"You know I will. I'd like to keep her."

"After another cross-America drive, she'll be happy to stay with you."

"What's in Maine; you'll be too late to see the fall leaves turning."

"I'm going to visit my daughter."

"Daughter! You don't have a daughter."

"I do now. I'll tell you all about it when I get to the cottage."

"I'll be waiting on the front steps to hear this one."

I haven't talked to Jen since Elsbeth arrived on my Montana porch a few months ago. I prefer telling her in person.

"Macduff, I don't want to pry, but is Elsbeth's arrival the reason Lucinda's not with you?"

Without knowing the answer, I stretched the truth. "No, they get along like best friends," I commented, hoping it was true.

Maybe it's why Lucinda said she might stay in New York longer than she first planned. New York is a short flight from Bangor.

15

ARRIVAL AT THE FLORIDA COTTAGE

JEN WAS SITTING on the wooden steps of my cottage when Wuff and I drove in. Beside the stairs the berries on the Nandina had burst into their fall polished-satin red.

With cooler weather having arrived, Jen was wearing jeans and a faded denim shirt. She had let her hair grow; she's an attractive woman, but married. Maybe she seemed different because Lucinda had gone.

"You're not going past me on these steps until you tell me about 'the daughter,'" Jen declared. She didn't ask about Lucinda, and I didn't mention her. For the last few hours of the drive, Elsbeth's arrival in my life had been the only thing I wanted to think about. But Jen made it difficult to keep my problems to myself.

I sat and told her about Elsbeth's young life, starting with how she survived my wife El's death seventeen years ago only because El was found by a couple fishing on the bank of the Snake River downstream from the spot of the drift boat crash. The two were Margaret and Gregory Carson of Greenville, Maine. She was a physician and performed a Caesarian on El.

As the years passed, Elsbeth had no reason to doubt she was the natural daughter of the Carsons. For those same years I wasn't aware she hadn't perished with El. Jen was now added to the few who know about part of my past, but I didn't mention I was law professor Maxwell Hunt when El died.

"You're going to Maine in two days?" Jen asked. At some future time she would inquire more about Elsbeth.

"Yes," I answered, "I should be back in three. . . . There's not much to come back to, except Wuff."

"Don't worry about Wuff. I'll take her home with me. Your cottage will be spic 'n span when you get back."

"It looks good now, Jen; could Jimmy put my boat in the water?"

"Of course. He'll clean it, take it for gas, and leave it at your dock. It should be safe—not many people find their way back here in a boat unless they know exactly where they're going. . . . Anything else? . . . You want to tell me about Lucinda?"

"No. . . . How's Tom?" I asked. Tom is their son who is now at the University of Florida. He's intent on becoming a lawyer.

"Tom's enjoying Gainesville. High honors overall and highest honors in his major—economics. He'd love to see you."

"Maybe I can get over for a soccer game."

If Dan Wilson learned I might go to a soccer game, he'd be livid. He thinks that every time I sneak off to Gainesville, something bad happens. . . . He may be right."

I unloaded my belongings I'd brought from Montana and on a whim called Lucinda. After not getting an answer for a full two minutes of waiting, I closed the cell phone, poured a double Gentleman Jack, and turned off the lights by nine.

16

TWO DAYS LATER IN ORONO, MAINE

THE LAST TIME I WAS IN MAINE is measured more accurately in decades than years. I was in high school. On spring break during our junior year, Jim Brooks, my closest chum, and I drove to Maine from Connecticut in search of summer jobs anywhere on the Maine coast. Jim died a decade ago. I miss him; I took his last name when I was entering the protection program and was told my name Maxwell Hunt was history.

Summer jobs were not easy to find when we were in high school. Jim and I struck out, finally working as construction laborers at home. The week we started, under threat of bodily harm from a couple of thugs driving a brand new Cadillac, we joined the local hodcarriers' union. Good money but not the adventure we had hoped for with jobs on the Down East coast.

At that time, the University of Maine was a small state institution in a small town, Orono. UM catered mostly to in-state residents. The town remains modest in size, possibly 9,000 inhabitants, swelled during academic terms by a student invasion of about the same number. Plus lots of free ranging moose.

Embarrassed from being hung over after two days of staying close to my bottled friend, Gentleman Jack, and after leaving countless unanswered calls at both Lucinda's apartment and office, I dressed for cold weather and flew to Bangor, rented a car, and soon was approaching a sign: "Welcome to UM, home of the Black Bears."

We met in a small coffee shop just off the campus. I arrived first; Elsbeth came flying in wearing a navy blue fleece jacket with a black bear embroidered on the chest. She nearly knocked me down with her enthusiasm and affection. She buried her face in my coat and squeezed; I noticed some stares that suggested that in this conservative, provincial state, people didn't hug in public.

"This is *so* good, Dad! I've missed you every day. I can't wait until the Christmas break. How's Lucinda? And Wuff? Is Florida warm? You know I've only been there to see Dean Perry last year. In December you have to take me to see the UF campus and the town. Can we take Lucinda and Wuff? Are you fishing? What's. . ."

"One at a time," I sputtered, overwhelmed by hearing her so happy. "I thought I might meet your roommate."

"You don't want to. She's an uninspiring, nymphomaniac, alcoholic druggie. So much for my 'college experience.'"

"She sounds . . . *interesting*," I commented, without knowing what I meant by "interesting."

"Dad, there are specific unkind words that better describe her, but I won't use them. She's extraordinarily bright, but misses a lot of classes hung over, spaced out, or still in bed with some guy . . . *any* guy."

"You'll be roommates for four years?"

"Not a chance! I've made some good friends. Especially one. Her name's Sue, and she's from, of all places, Jackson, Wyoming. She wanted a different experience, like when I thought about going to Montana's UM rather than Maine's UM. . . . The dorm rooms here are awful. Sue and I will share an apartment off campus beginning in January. . . . I need to ask you something, Dad. OK?"

"Of course."

"Sue and I are talking about transferring next year. Most of the kids here were born in Maine, grew up in Maine, and are happy with the idea of spending the rest of their lives in Maine."

"You don't agree?"

"Well, for one thing, now I know I wasn't born in Maine, but on the bank of Wyoming's Snake River. I loved growing up in Greenville—not too far from here in Orono. Eleven of my high school classmates are here at UM. I've told you about my long held fondness for reading about the West—Willa Cather, Diana West, and others. Now I know why. I don't want to live in Greenville. Or in Maine. Now that I live with you, I'll go wherever you are. . . . Only as long as Lucinda's still with you!"

"That's disrespectful!" I hoped she wouldn't ask about Lucinda.

"Dad, I love you. You know that."

"Remember, if you go to school in Wyoming or Montana, we won't be at the cabin from sometime in October through April or maybe even as late as June. I hope you're not thinking about transferring to be near us," I said, without knowing any longer what "us" meant. Maybe it meant only Wuff and me.

"*Dad*, I'm busy during the terms. I'm not planning on coming home with my laundry every weekend. But I do want to be with you on holidays."

"Every day you're with me is a holiday."

"If I'm at a college close to you, I might stop by occasionally for a free meal."

"Anytime. . . . Where do you and Sue think you might go?"

"Montana at Missoula. Colorado at Boulder. Maybe Washington. *Maybe* Montana State. . . . We're also thinking about Florida."

"Florida would be great. I'm here for most of the academic school year. At least October through April. But go anywhere you feel good about."

"There's also graduate school. Sue wants medicine. I don't like seeing blood. Possibly law school—like you."

"UF?"

"I think so. Dean Perry was awfully nice to me. And if I'm at UF, I *could* drop in for free lunches. Like maybe three to four times a week. We'd be only sixty or seventy miles apart."

"I can't afford you."

"I hope so. I'll try to live up to that. It'll test your affection. . . . Is Lucinda in Manhattan for long?"

"Another week or so," I answered, with more hope than expectation for her return. I didn't relish dealing with the consequences of Lucinda's departure.

"She should stay in Manhattan until you set a wedding date."

"Not you, too!"

"She's beautiful, intelligent, and wonderful. And she's rich. What more could you want? I know you love her. You're a pain when she's away. You and Wuff mope around the cabin like you're both lost."

I had to get her off the subject of Lucinda.

"Is there any chance you'd consider transferring to Aberdeen? You know you're mostly Scot. I'll pay your way."

"If you send me to Aberdeen, I'll major in cults and become a Druid. Maybe make wicker men for a living. I could go to the Orkneys on holidays. Isn't Ellsworth-Kent there? He could be my mentor."

"Don't mention him. Dan Wilson's told me he's not there. If he were, the Scottish police would pick him up."

"Aren't you worried that he might be in the U.S.?"

"Only when I'm reminded of him. Like now. . . . Do you have anything better to talk about?"

"I'm going to Jackson Hole with Sue for Thanksgiving. My first visit there since the Carsons saved me."

"Excited? Or worried? We didn't go near Jackson after you joined us at Mill Creek. I didn't want to cause you grief. So I never asked."

"I'm excited. I want to throw some wild flowers into the Snake River south of that place called Deadman's Bar, near where your drift boat crashed."

"Next summer we'll go to where the Carsons buried El in the mountains near Encampment in Southern Wyoming. I haven't seen it. There's a marker where she was buried. I learned about it only after you arrived."

"Just you and me, Dad?"

"Just you and me, Daughter."

That was unintendedly prophetic.

17

RETURN TO ST. AUGUSTINE THREE DAYS LATER

I FLEW BACK TO ST. AUGUSTINE, landed at Jacksonville and looked forward to the crisp, cool days of October—when the humidity drops forty points, fall flowers bloom, and highly competitive soccer games are played in Gainesville. And best of all—not a sign anywhere of a single falling snowflake.

When I picked up my bag as it came off the belt—upside down and noticeably more worn than when checked—someone grabbed my arm. I turned as the figure hugged me, but a hug without emotion.

"Why are you *here*, Lucinda?" I asked, realizing I injected a needless cutting edge to my manner. "You said you might be gone for *weeks*. And you never answered or returned even one of my calls."

Ignoring my comment, she said, "Elsbeth called me last night. She said you were distant and you had to keep asking her to repeat something you missed because your mind was elsewhere. I didn't tell her about my comments to you or that I'd been the one who was distant on the drive to St. Louis. . . . Elsbeth said you missed me."

"Are you here because of Elsbeth? She's coming for the three-week Christmas break. If it's Elsbeth you want to see, you might have waited."

"Do you want me to leave? There's a flight to New York in a couple of hours.

"I didn't leave you. You walked away at the St. Louis airport without a word. That was only a few days after we sat on the porch of my cabin on Mill Creek and debated the merits of sticky rice. I looked at you across the porch table and thought how lucky I was. I guess you weren't thinking the same."

"I *was* thinking about us. About what we've been through the past years. Whether it was fair for me to expect you to find a place for me with Elsbeth entering your life. She's a young lady who deserves your full attention."

"She's in college. Not at home any longer. She needs to have some space to work out her own life."

"You don't comprehend what you mean to her."

"She had seventeen years of devoted parents in Maine. The Carsons loved her as though she were their natural daughter. That made her the loving and sensible person she is.

"But she's *yours.* You're her father. *El* was her mother. There's no place for me in what she needs right now."

"I was with her the past three days. She kept turning the conversation to you. Not to me."

"I love you, Macduff. I just don't know if I can live the kind of life we have."

"I haven't exactly been the only target. Your ex, Robert, was the bigger part of the wicker man killings. He's still out there somewhere. Like Herzog and Isfahani."

"But I never tried to harm, much less kill, Robert, unlike your paranoia about Herzog and Isfahani."

"What do you mean?"

"Be honest with me. Are you involved with Dan and planning to kill Isfahani?"

It wasn't easy to answer, but I wouldn't lie. With all my faults in our relationship, lying isn't one of them.

"Yes," I said quietly, knowing we were not heading where I wanted.

"And I'm expected to wait home, not knowing whether you'll come back. Is it worth it, Mac?"

"Dan says our government is convinced that Isfahani is the next bin Laden. And that I'm the best shooter they have to take him out, when we find him."

"I don't buy that, Macduff. The CIA's full of agents who can kill Isfahani. Have you been asked, or have *you* asked, to be involved?"

"I asked Dan," I replied, even more quietly. I had reasons I didn't want to discuss.

"Case closed as far as I'm concerned," she said. "I *will* get that flight back in two hours. Please ask Jen to pack and send my belongings at your cottage to my apartment in New York."

She turned and left.

18

From the environmental standpoint, the ban seems to be working, as many fish targeted by gill netting have rebounded. But that's small comfort for Florida's fishing industry, which has been left adrift. 'It has been a very difficult situation for a lot of old-time fishing companies in the state,' says Cecil Lane, manager of Hudgins Seafood in Fort Pierce, Fla., which was founded in 1911. 'It has hurt an awful lot of good people.'

Christian Science Monitor, July 15, 1997.

SAME DAY - RETURN TO THE COTTAGE

A CLOUDLESS DUSK was closing the day when I reached the dirt drive that leaves U.S. Route 1 and winds among pines and oaks a third of a mile to my cottage. I would face an empty place; Lucinda was flying back to New York.

A northeast wind was blowing through the trees from the marshes, but the smell was of something burning and increased as I arrived at the cottage. My dock was ablaze; my old but reliable Hewes drift boat was launching black clouds of smoke that spiraled from the dock and caused my eyes to burn.

"Where is the county fire department?" I wondered. But who would have called it in? Someone at the nearby Princess

Estate, worried that a woods fire might spread? Soon sirens disturbed the silence. I drove back, unlocked the gate, and waved the procession of assorted vehicles down my drive. First and noisiest was a hook and ladder truck—sufficient since my dock is at most two feet high. Following was a pumper—I hope with extensive hose since the nearest hydrant is miles away. Next was an emergency van and finally, bringing up the rear in the safest position, were three sheriff's office cars—a little excitement for our finest after sitting in a police car all day where some county road was being repaired. Oddly, one of the police cars was flying orange and blue Gator flags above each rear door window.

My flats boat has a 70 hp Merc. Jimmy Jennings was to fill the gas tank and leave the boat at my dock. The boat's gas tank must have exploded, starting the fire that was consuming both the boat and the dock.

I ran down as close to the dock as smoke permitted. The burning fiberglass produced an irritating smell as noxious as when a new boat comes out of the mold.

The fire crew, after using portable chemical fire extinguishers on the boat, searched the adjacent woods for signs of burning embers cast off the dock. But the ground beneath the spreading pines had been saturated as a three-day season-ending tropical depression sat a hundred miles off St. Augustine pummeling the fragile, receding beaches. Nevertheless, I appreciated the effort of the firefighters. Considering the few forest fires in the county over the past few excessively wet months, they need the practice.

It was a joint effort with no doubt about who was in charge of fires. A hefty fifty-something firefighter, made even more portly with his cumbersome gear, drew the attention of every other firefighter present. He stood watching the flames for what seemed longer than needed for a decision to go put out the fire.

"You the guy who lives here?" he asked after the flames subsided largely on their own.

"I am."

"Sorry about your loss."

"You did what you could," I said, thinking it could have been more.

When the wind shifted and blew the remaining smoke away from us we walked together closer to the dock.

"I think you need a new boat. You insured?"

"Nope. It was old and due to be replaced. Soon. The motor has almost 3,000 hours. It has served its owners well."

"You got some repair work to be done on the pier. It may need some county permits. Damn! It stinks."

"That's not all fiberglass we smell," I said, looking more carefully at the remains. "There's a pile of charred something in front of what remains of the center console. It's . . . there's a little netting that didn't burn hanging over the side. And . . . Jeeze! It can't be! . . . That's not all netting. There's a hand sticking out. The whole pile has the shape of a person."

"It does," he concurred. "This is quickly moving out of my responsibility." He turned and yelled to where the three police were talking together by the steps of my cottage, oblivious to the fire. One looked up.

"Come down here," the firefighter called. "There's work for you guys."

There was indeed.

19

THE AFTERNOON LINGERS ON

"Y OU GOT A HEAP OF PROBLEMS, MAC," said a sheriff's deputy, his authority advertised by three chevrons on his sleeve, two more than either of the other two displayed. Above the three chevrons on the head man's right sleeve was a small, oval UF Gator logo. It was his car that was flying the two Gator flags.

"I do have problems. I need to replace the boat, the motor, and most of the dock."

"The hell with that. You have some *explaining* to do."

"The body speaks for itself. It's your job to decide why and how."

"That's a *murder*, mac," he said, not knowing my name. Apparently, everybody is "mac" to him. "You're the owner of this place and the most obvious suspect to have killed the guy."

"How did you conclude the person was a guy? And why do you assume it was a murder?"

"Don't screw around with me, mac. When the lieutenant gets here, I'm gonna throw cuffs on you."

I ignored him, took out my cell phone, and called Jen.

"Hi, Macduff. Did I clean your place OK?" she answered.

"As clean as always. But my boat burned. It looks like Hiroshima. Someone in the boat was burned to a crisp. Is Jimmy home?"

"He's here with me."

"Tom?"

"In Gainesville. Probably in the UF library."

"Thank God! I was concerned about Jimmy or Tom having an accident getting my boat ready for fall fishing."

"What's going on? Who's at the cottage? Who's in the boat?"

"I arrived forty minutes ago. Behind me was a cacophony of fire, emergency, and deputy sheriff's vehicles."

"Have you spoken with the sheriff's people yet?"

"More than I want. To a sergeant who looks comical in a uniform two sizes too large. Every other sentence from him ends in 'mac.' He immediately labeled me as the principal suspect. He didn't distinguish a suspect in a murder from an innocent bystander to an accident. And he assumes the unrecognizable remains are of a man. There's not enough left to tell the gender."

"You're talking about Deputy Turk Jensen. He's a three-stripe sergeant and a five-star jerk. At an earlier time he was a nice guy, until some junkie drilled a bullet into his brain. He's been a bitter, mean man since. The county keeps him around—he needs a couple more years before he can retire."

"I thought they did better to take disability."

"He's not smart enough to figure that out, and he doesn't take advice. Stay away from him. Tom said his professor of criminal science—I think his name is Christensen—wrote a mystery novel and used Jensen to develop a character in the book."

"Maybe I'll call Christensen and get a recommendation for a St. Augustine criminal defense lawyer."

"Don't do that. Christensen isn't a lawyer; he was a police officer years ago and worked with Jensen. Call Bill Muirhead, a prominent criminal defense lawyer in St. Augustine. He's different. Ponytail. Diamond in his left ear. Western boots. The sheriff's staff hates him. His record has got to be close to a hundred percent acquittals. And he's sued several deputies, including Jensen, for wrongful arrest, mistreatment while in custody, or failure to give a Miranda warning. Jensen will go ballistic if he learns you hired Muirhead."

"Let me hang up. I'll dial him right now."

After five minutes, Muirhead agreed to represent me and wanted me to refuse to say another word to the sheriff's people, unless he was present."

As I walked toward the house, Jensen stopped me.

"Brooks, get over to my car. I've got some questions."

"Not until my attorney's present."

"Attorney! What do you need a damn lawyer for?"

"I didn't like your attitude when we talked a few minutes ago. No more questions until Muirhead is here."

"Muirhead! You SOB. You can't hire him!"

"Why not?"

"He sued me. Three times. There's a conflict of interest between us. He can't represent you."

"I'll call him and ask his opinion."

"No, you won't. I'm placing you under arrest on suspicion of murder."

"What's your probable cause? You might ask the county attorney to explain that to you."

"Don't give me that crap. Anyway, I gotta Gator football game to go to tonight in Gainesville—starts at 7 p.m. National TV. I don't have time to screw around with you."

Jen had arrived in time to hear Jensen's ranting.

"Macduff, shall I call Muirhead back?"

"Please, tell him what Jensen just said."

"That's Deputy Sergeant Jensen to you."

"Jen, tell him *Turk* Jensen is about to arrest me."

"You do that, lady, and you'll be arrested, too."

"Ignore him, Jen. Call Muirhead."

Jen turned away from us and lifted her cell phone and dialed. She looked back and said, "Turk, you want to talk to Muirhead? He's on the line."

Throwing his hat on the ground, Jensen kicked it three feet, cursed, picked it up, and walked away without another word, muttering something about missing the kickoff.

I didn't go and sit in Jensen's car. I didn't answer any questions. And I wasn't arrested. Red faced and visibly angry, Jensen drove off down my dirt road faster than anyone else I've ever seen. I listened, thinking I would hear car-metal challenge tree-wood. No such luck.

That evening I sat with Wuff on the porch, looking over the marsh that gradually replaced backlighted green and gold with gray dusk. A pink reflection high in swirling clouds to the east over the Atlantic was the last measure of a sunny day. Best of all, a welcome southwest wind was blowing the smoke and stink away from the cottage.

Momentarily, I thought of sitting on the pier swing, but all that was left were the chains. Plus, the idea of sitting on the swing alone wasn't appealing.

It took three glasses of Gentleman Jack to put me to sleep.

20

Several fish houses were constructed about a century ago sitting on pilings in the water of Pine Island Sound. In the 1980s they were placed on the National Register of Historic Places as examples of early 20th century commercial fishing.

The Ice House at Point Blanco sold in 1980 to private owners. It burned on July 1, 1995, just after a state constitutional amendment went into effect banning the use of entanglement nets. Today only the tops of the pilings can be seen at the southeastern end of Punta Blanca, slightly charred, and often crowned by pelicans and cormorants.

Newsletter of the Friends of the Randall Research Center, March 2014.

ALONE AT BREAKFAST THE FOLLOWING DAY

THE SMOKE VANISHED, but during the night the wind shifted back to the northeast and returned the acrid smell of the combined remains of my boat, part of the dock, and portions of the dead body that couldn't be scraped off and sent to the morgue. Wuff and I remained inside the cottage, but the smell had no trouble finding its way in.

I slept no more than hour stretches. My thoughts jumped back and forth between the fire and losing Lucinda. I called her at midnight, but to no avail. She didn't answer, and I didn't wait to leave a message.

When the sun rose, I was exhausted, but I ground beans and brewed coffee and then realized there was little else in the house for breakfast. Twenty minutes later I was at a restored 1930s Pure Oil gas station turned breakfast and lunch stop. I smelled bacon sizzling in the kitchen, but guilt caused me to heed Lucinda's nutritional naggings, and I opted for an assortment of melon, pineapple, and mango; a small bowl of some relative of granola; and a poor substitute for the coffee I had made earlier. Lucinda's haunting me. I can't order what I really want even when she's not here.

On the way home, I stopped and parked in a friend's drive on old A1A and walked Wuff on the deserted beach. She frantically dug into ghost crab holes—with no success—while I sat on an old telephone pole that had made it to the beach in a recent storm.

I started thinking of the time I met Lucinda, searching for what I might have done to date that so troubled her. The worst likely was agreeing to kill Isfahani and now there's also the presence of Elsbeth and whether she's better alone with me.

Dan and I *had* discussed killing Isfahani, but I told him I was reluctant to do another shooting or anything I couldn't talk about with Lucinda. Apparently she had taken my "yes" answer to mean Dan and I were not merely discussing what to do about Isfahani; secretly we had made conclusive plans to assassinate him.

Lucinda doesn't have any idea about the depth of his intended revenge. Nor does she know I killed his brother in Khartoum three years before she and I met. Ironically, it was during the time that Isfahani was my student. I've never found the right time to tell Lucinda.

It was my only killing for the CIA. At least my only successful killing. My botched attempt to end Isfahani's life several years later in Guatemala was a disaster from the beginning. It started when Lucinda walked down to my Montana cabin and found me practicing with my CheyTac rifle. Ten minutes later she saw the drawing of a target superimposed over the face of Isfahani when she discovered my music room and went downstairs before I could stop her. I have to concede she has reason to mistrust me.

It's time I called Dan and told him about the Montana death. I value his friendship and the reassurance of his advice, but not enough to destroy my relationship with Lucinda. Dan has a one-track mind about Isfahani, even more so than about Juan Pablo Herzog. For good reason. Herzog's not a political terrorist bent on killing thousands of Americans; he's interested only in power and wealth and gratuitously will kill without mercy anyone in his way.

I don't know if Lucinda has left for good. If so I'll work with Dan to take out first Isfahani and later maybe Herzog. If there's any prospect that Lucinda might return, my participation in CIA dirty tricks is over once Isfahani and Herzog are memories.

Will Dan understand?

21

The constitutional amendment that bans nets is an example of how voters can take the reins of government into their own hands when elected officials fail to act in the state's best interests, says Ted Forsgren of the Coastal Conservation Association in Tallahassee, Fla. 'There needs to be something in the constitution to remind the government that the power does reside with the people,' he says.

Christian Science Monitor, July 15, 1997.

THAT AFTERNOON AT THE COTTAGE

I WAS SURPRISED BY KEN RANGLEY'S PHONE CALL from the Park County Sheriff's Office because I thought it might be Lucinda calling. In my excitement I dropped the phone on a rug, and it bounced under the sofa. Ken was patient with my clumsiness.

"Macduff, how was the drive to Florida? Did Lucinda get to New York for a few days? How's Elsbeth doing in Maine?

"Never ending, yes, and fine."

"I want to talk to you about the body you two found in Mill Creek. Is Lucinda listening in?"

"No, I'm here alone with Wuff," I answered, hoping he would not interrogate me as to why Lucinda wasn't present.

"What's up with Elsbeth? Hear anything from her?"

"I got back yesterday from Maine. She's doing fine. She has a kooky roommate but has made a good friend she met in one of her classes. They'll room together in the spring and maybe both will transfer next year. Elsbeth said the student body is a little too provincial; most of them have never been outside Maine."

"She should talk!" Ken exclaimed. "She's been outside the state only the couple of months this summer she spent with you two."

"And one other time," I reminded him. "We forget she was born in Jackson Hole."

"I wish she'd come out to MSU. Bozeman's a great college town."

"She may. It's one of her final five choices."

"Ken," I asked, diverting him to answering rather than asking questions. "Anything more about Hendersen, the guy we found in Mill Creek?"

"Not much."

"Well, I have some information. I met him a year ago at the Fly Fishers of America Southern Council meeting in Helena, Georgia. The Southern Council covers Georgia plus five other southeastern states. Helena's north of Atlanta in the Georgia mountains, not far from the North Carolina border. Hendersen, who lived in Georgia, and I talked over dinner one evening about both the Florida gill net ban and the Georgia-Alabama-Florida Chattahoochee/Apalachicola rivers water dispute. Georgia won't concede a drop. Nor will it do any long-term planning about providing water to out-of-control Atlanta population growth. Florida's Apalachicola oyster industry is dying for lack of fresh water from the Chattahoochee—which becomes the Apalachicola when it crosses into Florida."

"Were you the only two at the dinner table?"

"No. Come to think of it, there were about eight of us. Mostly from Georgia. It was a big oval table. No one else said a word about the net ban, but they did jump in when the water issue arose."

"Did Hendersen express any opinions about the Florida net ban?"

"He sure did. Agreed that reforms extending the gill net ban are needed. But that's the view of most recreational fishermen"

"What did Hendersen do for a living?"

"Owned a fly shop and outfitter in Helena. He's head of the Southern Council of the FFA. Or he *was* head."

"What did *you* say about the gill net ban?"

"I don't remember. Maybe too much. Hendersen and I were totally in agreement."

"Did you learn what the other people at the table did for a living?"

"No idea. I don't recall any names or any mention of their work. I assumed they were all fly fishermen."

"Not much help. What other contact have you had with Hendersen?"

"None."

"Even less help. I don't understand why he was wrapped in a net. Nets aren't usual here in Montana. I doubt we allow net fishing on any rivers or streams, except by the state trying to get rid of undesirable species. But. . . ."

"But what?" I asked.

"I'm pretty certain Hendersen was murdered," Ken opined. "Erin has doubts. Someone took everything he was carrying and everything in his car that might identify him. That was foolish. We found finger prints and obtained dental records. The University of Vermont assured us that a Bill Hendersen graduated in 1972. But you know that."

"Any suspects?"

"Not one. No family—his wife died last year. No children."

"Anything in common with the Florida death of Clint Carter?" I asked.

"I've talked on the phone with the head of the Lee County Sheriff's Office in Ft. Myers. No success there beyond confirming the identity of the body. . . . Macduff, do you know any more about Carter? Now that we have two bodies wrapped in gill nets."

"We have three."

"Don't tell me I've missed one?"

"Yesterday. I arrived at my cottage to see my flats boat in flames, along with a body—not yet identified—wrapped in a gill net on the boat. Charred beyond recognition. Except some teeth. The county police are investigating. The county sheriff's office deputy who arrived here with the fire and rescue vehicles is named Turk Jensen. He's impossible to deal with. I learned he's the enforcer for two members of the county commission. Both make you wonder about our electorate. One's under indictment for bribery. The other's too dumb to know what a bribe is. Jensen accused me and was going to arrest me on suspicion of murder. I called my lawyer, and Jensen backed off. The lawyer mentioned something about Jensen wanting to avoid another embarrassment."

"And then there were three," Ken mused.

22

MILES AWAY ON A COOL SPRING DAY THREE MONTHS EARLIER

OYSTER BAY, FLORIDA, is a diminutive settlement plodding along the path to ghost town status. It sits forlornly a few miles north of Cedar Key on the state's west coast. The "bay" is little more than a bulge in the Soxahatchee River that winds south from the vast Georgia-Florida border-straddling peat-filled Okefenokee Swamp. Oyster Bay connects to the Gulf by a quarter-mile channel that contorts west through tidal flats fringed by spartina grass. The town is sagging from the consequences of the economic development adopted by its more creative neighbors. Oyster Bay increasingly is omitted on road maps.

The town is entered exclusively by a single road that meanders north from Cedar Key without any apparent goal, until it terminates at Oyster Bay. A century ago it had acres of cedar that were decimated tree-by-tree and sent to the New York pencil-making plants of Eberhard Faber. The cedars disappeared from the land as surely as Faber's pencils did when fed into a sharpener. When the cedar had vanished, the town turned to commercial gill net fishing, both towns supporting about a thousand residents. But when the gill net ban was imposed in 1994, they parted in development.

Oyster Bay gill netters had nearly exhausted the local mullet stock over the four decades preceding the 1994 ban. After it was in place, some of the local fishing families turned to farming clams, assisted by state and federal funds. Clamming declined when the U.S. renewed trade relations with Vietnam. In little time Vietnamese clam exports overwhelmed Oyster Bay clam production. Asian clams were cheaper despite the costs of transportation.

While some stayed with clamming, a few of those twice-bitten families turned to oystering. That became successful until a researcher at the University of Florida asserted in a much challenged report that oysters were linked to Hepatitis B.

Discussions that take place in Oyster Bay's few stores, the barber shop, and one remaining bar, not to mention between neighbors over backyard fences and at church suppers, are depressing. Such talk is discouraged at the two remaining restaurants that depend on out-of-town patrons and among the men who once sought mullet, clams, or oysters, but more recently have become fishing guides after snook, redfish, and sea trout, and some less tasty species. These men consider being a guide akin to being a servant and are conscious of behind-their-back references to them as "salt-water stewardesses."

Oyster Bay was once a proud community happy in its self-dependency and isolation from the outside world and having avoided the waterfront takeover by outsiders that occurred in other coastal towns. But no longer.

On a Tuesday morning two weeks before the death in Southwest Florida and destined to impose a three-figure heat index by afternoon, six residents gathered in the basement of the sole Baptist church that remained unshuttered. It was commonly called the "Old Baptist" church, in contrast to the six other Baptist churches that once drew large Sunday attendances. On one such bygone day, a Methodist resident muttered over a back fence to a neighbor's visiting guest that "There are more Baptists than people in Oyster Bay."

After coffee and donuts—brought from the new Dunkin' Donuts in Cedar Key—a rail thin resident of Oyster Bay asked the others to sit, took a last bite from a lemon-filled glazed donut, and addressed the group.

'We're a pretty crummy lookin' bunch," the donut eater exclaimed. "Oyster Bay's dyin'. We all know why: 'the damn gill net ban!'"

"Hear, hear," called someone with poor clothes and unkempt hair, sitting in a corner on a chair tilted back precariously against the wall. The "hear, hear" would constitute the speaker's sole contribution to the discussion.

"We all knows the town's dyin'," said a third party, dressed all in black as though in mourning for the loss of their town as they knew it for decades. "We need to do what we did back in '93, when the ban was being debated. We sure debated pretty strongly, if you know what I'm referrin' to."

"Don't talk about that," said the first speaker. "We been livin' with sealed lips ever since. . . . But I gotta admit we trashed a lotta boats owned by outsiders fishin' for fun, not to support their families like us."

"This meeting ain't gonna do a damn bit of good," interrupted a fourth person, showing a smirk that was intended to establish superiority. "We can't fight city hall. We can't fight the so-called Coastal Conservation Association. We can't fight recreational fishing money. But we can do somethin' by ourselves to teach all them a lesson."

"Can too," replied a fifth individual, adding nothing of substance for support.

After the five looked toward the sixth and last member of the group, one of them asked, "You got nuthin' to say?"

"Nope. . . . It's time to stop talkin' . . . and do sumthin'."

"What you got in mind? Pissin' on the state capitol lawn?"

"Don't be a smart ass. I mean sumthin' that sends a message that we ain't puttin' up with this crap no more."

"Meanin'?"

"Not pissin' on the capitol lawn. Hangin' some recreational fishermen somewhere, wrapped up in gill nets. I'll supply the nets."

The room fell silent. Suddenly, everyone had nothing more to say, and one by one each of these citizens quietly walked up the poorly supported narrow staircase, out of the church, and dispersed in a rusting pickup truck or car.

23

THE PRESENT — BREAKFAST AT THE COTTAGE

LAST NIGHT WUFF HOPPED UP ONTO MY BED, lay on Lucinda's pillow, and whimpered. Then she picked up the pillow in her teeth, jumped down, pulled the pillow into the living room, curled up on it, and fell sound asleep. She may have been trying to tell me that she'd rather live in Manhattan.

This morning, when I filled her bowl and set it on her small Oriental rug, she grabbed the bottom of the bowl by her teeth and a paw, flipped it upside down, sending the food spreading across the floor, and went and lay by the front door, staring at me with unhappy eyes. At times like this I'm glad she can't speak. But she certainly can communicate. When I left to run some errands, she refused to leave—the first time ever she wasn't first to the car.

"Wuff, you're not making this any easier," I said, walking out the door for a lonely solo morning.

My first task was to replace my charred flats boat. The blackened Hewes had served its time well, but since I spend only part of the year in Florida and am not a licensed Florida guide, I have no intention of spending $40,000+ on a new Hewes.

I can't expect to duplicate *Osprey*, my 16' ash, mahogany, and oak drift boat I built the first year in Montana. It has floated a dozen premier rivers in a half dozen Western mountain states. *Osprey* has never been east of the Rockies; it would feel out of place parted from the mountains. The boat has a feel and life only a wooden boat presents. But even in the West, fiberglass drift boats far outnumber wood. I have a fiberglass boat in my garage in Montana, a highly functional Clack-a-Craft. I use it regularly, saving *Osprey* for clients I know or who come with recommendations. Such clients will appreciate floating in a work of art—not wearing metal cleats on their wading boots and not putting out cigarettes on the ash gunnels.

Osprey is growing old along with me. It's been in some tight spots over the past decade. Initially, retired ambassador Ander Eckstrum was shot and killed on *Osprey*, two hundred yards north of the Deadman's Bar takeout on the Snake River in Wyoming. Later that season, *Osprey* was the site of another shootout on a different section of the Snake, again involving Park Salisbury, Eckstrum's killer.

Salisbury had intended to shoot me on the earlier float. The second time he disguised himself as a rotund, bearded Oregon fisherman interested in building a duplicate of *Osprey*, but truthfully he was planning to kill me, plus any other living beings in the boat, which happened to mean Lucinda and Wuff. Fortunately, it was Salisbury who was killed. But Lucinda, Wuff, and I were all struck by several of his final shots.

The following year no murders were committed on *Osprey*, but the mutilated bodies of three women were found waiting for us at the end of three floats. They were tied to wooden crosses laid across *Osprey's* trailer.

Osprey has become more than just another drift boat, more than just another piece of fishing equipment. It has gained a reputation of its own like Noah's ark, the *Mayflower,* and the *Constitution.* I am *Osprey's* protector, vetting its prospective occupants of all but the favored few.

A fiberglass flats boat designed for salt water lacks the persona of a wooden drift boat designed for fresh water. But my incinerated Hewes was a work of art in its own way. A Maserati on the water. Glossy white, as reflective of light as the water that gave it life, it was a maritime minimalist.

On a flats boats less is more. What I need should have at most six inches of draft, letting the boat ease along behind the edge of an incoming tide. The deck should be devoid of projections: meaning no cleats that don't drop flush with the deck and no push pole holders because I don't intend to stand on a poling platform and plummet onto an oyster bank. But I like the poling platform to lean against. I don't need a speedometer; a tachometer is enough. Trim tabs are a must because they help stabilize the boat on a plane. No VHF or radio, but I want a top-of-the-line chartplotter/fishfinder that has a large screen I can read on a sunny day. No anchor pole. I have spent decades tossing a small Danforth fluke anchor over the side of my boats.

In my case, tradition trumps technology. That leaves little more to add other than an electric trolling motor, which I may decline. I can't fly fish while operating an electric motor, and I like to let the boat float freely up the braided channels on incoming tides. An electric motor sitting on the bow is not complimentary to fly line.

I spent much of my lonely day looking in the yards of boat dealers between St. Augustine and Daytona Beach. At 4:45 I suddenly realized Wuff was alone. Her dinner was due promptly at five. When I reached the cottage at 5:30, I expected to meet a wild barking Sheltie, but she was sound asleep on Lucinda's side of the bed. She didn't lift her head as I entered the room, but opened eyes that stared at me disdainfully as I walked about.

"Wuff," I said, "I didn't walk out on her. *She* left me!" Apparently Wuff doesn't see it that way. I thought all was forgiven when she came up to me while I was sitting changing shoes and put a paw on my leg. Quickly, I realized it was a prod to get her dinner immediately—not a sign of affection. After she was served with her mix of salmon, duck, and turkey, plus some applesauce on top, and had been taken out for her post mealtime toileting, she trotted back to the bedroom and jumped onto Lucinda's side of the bed.

24

We need to understand that some of the old traditions, the old customs, need to be given at least some dignity as we change in a transitional mode from one thing to another. When you summarily take a simple fisherman's ability to make a living for himself and his family, you destroy his dignity and his self respect. And that's not the way to do things.

Living on Earth (1997). www.loe.org/shows/segments

THE FOLLOWING MORNING

WITHOUT LUCINDA, Wuff is my only conversation companion. She leaves much to be desired, focusing mostly on when she will be served her next meal and where she will take her next nap. But if she could converse, she might not want to have anything to do with me.

As much as I brooded and saturated myself in self-pity over losing Lucinda, I tried to focus on losing my boat and identifying the charred remains of someone found in it, apparently either wrapped in a gill net and then murdered or murdered and then wrapped in a gill net. Unlike in Montana, where I have good friends to contact, I've made no friends because I worried they would ask about my past. I don't consider my attorney Bill Muirhead a friend, at least not yet, while he tries to hold the testy local authorities at bay and keep me from the unpredictable fate of appearing before a local county judge.

I knew dozens of people in Gainesville, but not one as Macduff Brooks. Those I knew as Professor Maxwell Hunt have diminished in number. Some have moved away to other jobs, some retired, and some rest below granite markers, leaving only their statistics and a place for pigeons to disperse digested meals.

I suspected that by now the remains on my boat have been associated with a name. I was anxious to know it. Since I hired an attorney, I should be using him.

When I called Muirhead at his office, immediately I was presented with a curt, previously recorded message that all persons in the office were otherwise engaged and I was to leave my name, number, and purpose of my call. My call, whoever I was—apparently even a wrong number—was—according to an electronic voice—extremely important to him. The voice promised someone would get back to me, which hopefully would be soon if I were sitting in jail making one permitted phone call.

Someone did call back—Muirhead's secretary—four hours later. She quickly put me through to Muirhead.

"Macduff, what's up?" he asked.

"This is less about my issues with Jensen than wanting to know what's been discovered about the identity of the remains on my boat. Anything new?"

"Yes, made the front page in today's local newspaper. You're mentioned, but solely as the owner of the boat and property where the remains were found. No accusations."

"Who was the person?"

"Name's Hugh Bradford. Familiar to you?"

"No."

"Don't you read our venerable *St. Augustine Chronicle*?"

"Not if I can avoid it. A dreadful editorial page but an excellent weekly section on local activities. Like a lot of struggling, small-town papers."

"Well, Bradford was the editor of the editorial page, so maybe there'll be some improvement with his replacement."

"Nothing in the article about why pieces of gill net were found with the remains of the body?"

"Not a word," said Muirhead. "I called the state attorney's office this morning. The local assistant state attorney is a woman; she's a refreshing successor to a line of unimpressive appointees to that office. Keep her name in mind—Grace Justice. Intelligent, doesn't suffer fools gladly—which means she's already crossed swords with Jensen on a number of cases, even though the two are supposed to be pursuing the same goal—enforcing the law.

"Grace has an engaging personality. I told her about you, that you're in the county each winter for rest and recuperation after long days guiding on Western rivers. She was impressed. She said she likes being on the water and just came back from a fly fishing instructional week in Vermont."

"She sounds intriguing. . . . What did she say about Hugh Bradford and the net?"

"Bradford wrote a series of articles for the *Chronicle* back in the 1990s when the gill net ban was on every Florida fisherman's mind—commercial or recreational. His articles favored the ban, but in a cynical and disparaging way that infuriated commercial gill netters and their families. Bradford's car was broken into and spray painted, a brick was hurled through his home's front window, and his dog went missing. Its body was found wrapped in a small part of a gill net."

"They ever find who did it?"

"No, but there was no love lost between the newspaper and the county sheriff's office. . . . Macduff, I have to go. Call me any time. You have my private cell phone number. . . . I'll let you know about Jensen. He hasn't lodged any charges against you—yet."

I'm relieved I didn't know Bradford. I don't recall ever having been in the same room with him or at the same event. That should eliminate me from being linked to *any* of the three dead men. My relationships with the first two were hardly what I'd call links; I had only one brief meeting with each.

One lingering problem I dwell on is why Bill Hendersen's body was dumped into Mill Creek, if indeed it was dumped. He was from Georgia but owned a cabin near Livingston which meant Mill Creek could have been one of his fishing places. When we sat at the same table at the program in Georgia, I don't recall telling him I had a cabin in Montana or where it was. In fact, I may not have told him anything about where I guided in the West.

It seems to me it's hard to link Bradford's death either with that of Clint Carter in Southwest Florida or Hendersen in Montana. All three men may have drowned. Neither Carter nor Hendersen had any marks from a blow or a bullet or for that matter any evidence of foul play. Bradford's body was burned too much to tell. It's implausible that one person could wrap himself in a gill net and jump into the water! But one or two persons could overwhelm someone, wrap him in a gill net, toss him in the water, hold him until he drowned, and set him adrift. Or put him in someone's boat and start a fire. If all three *were* murders and related to the new proposals to tighten and extend the scope of the Florida gill net ban, the death in Montana makes little sense. Why wasn't Hendersen killed in Georgia? He fished there more than in Montana.

The first two deaths have some characteristics common to those a year ago in the West, when five people I knew better than Carter or Hendersen were killed as part of the wicker man and mistletoe murders. The wicker was a basket-like enclosure and the head wreath symbolized mistletoe growing high in trees, allegedly being the plant that grows closest to heaven. The deaths were a diversion and maybe a warning to me. If the gill net deaths were because of the victims' outspoken positions favoring new net controls, *these men* were the targets, not me. That would be a relief to me, but I still have to find out why Bradford was killed on my boat.

I hope Lucinda hasn't read about Bradford. It might affirm her concern about being with me. She approaches our problems with a different perspective, an intuitive perspective, one invariably closer to what ultimately proves to be the actual facts.

The music playing on my stereo didn't help my feelings about losing Lucinda. It was the Buena Vista Social Club's singer Ibrahim Ferrer, singing *Aquellos Ojos Verdes.*

Those green eyes,
peaceful as a lake,
into whose still depths I looked one day.
They don't know the sadness that was left in my soul
by those green eyes I can never forget.

Is it Lucinda I have loved all these years or her uncanny ability to solve problems and keep me out of worse situations?

25

THE SAME DAY IN OYSTER BEACH

THREE MONTHS AFTER the six local residents of Oyster Bay first met in the basement of the marginally surviving Baptist church, they gathered again. The six arrived separately, leaving their vehicles parked some distance from the church, slipping quietly through the pastor's narrow side door and descending the fragile, rickety stairs to the stuffy basement. The air was stale and warmer than it had been at the first meeting. It was the only basement in Oyster Bay any of them knew about. The church sat on the crest of the solitary hill that rose above the town. "Nearer my God to thee" was written in fading gold letters over the front entrance.

The six sat on the same chairs they had chosen at the earlier meeting. This time suspicion hung over the room as though they were all waiting outside the Pearly Gates for decisions on their admission.

The same resident who "presided" at the previous meeting opened the conversation.

"*It's been done.*"

"What you mean *it's done?*" asked the second resident, wearing the same black clothing as before. "I ain't done nuthin'."

The first spoke again, "*Two* bodies in Florida. One more in Montana. All wrapped in gill nets. Each of them recreational fishermen who wanted the net ban. And each spoke out favorin' a newer ban of *all* nets, plus controllin' our only friends, the black robed puppets we keep electin' to the bench."

Then a third, who had offered to provide the nets, added, "But I never got requested to give up a net. They weren't wrapped in any of *my* nets."

"We decided it had to be done," the first speaker reminded the group.

"Hear, hear," added a fourth, repeating the same words uttered at the first meeting.

"*It's been done,*" said the first, more loudly than before.

"Not by me," claimed the fifth, who previously had argued that they couldn't "fight city hall."

"That don't mean a tweet," said the first, perturbed at the increasing denial by the others.

"I ain't meetin' again'," said the one in black, who rose and with effort climbed the stairs as the remaining five stared dumfounded.

Following up the stairs ten minutes later was the third to have spoken, muttering words as he left unwelcome in a house of God, even in the basement.

"I ain't sayin' another word," sputtered the fifth, who also rose and quickly departed.

"Well," claimed the sixth, who when they first met had said it was time to stop talking and do something, "I guess we figured they would talk big and find excuses. . . . We need worry 'bout them talkin'?"

"Nope," answered the one who first mentioned self-help instead of relying on city hall and big money.

"Hear, hear," repeated the one who in three comments had managed to use only one word—"hear"—six times.

The remaining three got up and hugged one another, smiling. With some effort by two of them, they slowly climbed the stairs, left the church through the side door, and without another sound went their separate ways.

26

THE SAME DAY IN MANHATTAN

OUTSIDE THE CHRYSLER BUILDING rain streamed along the rooftop's aluminum art deco figures, dropping off gargoyles to splash hundreds of feet below where the water mixed with the dust and grime of the streets, only to be tracked into the very same building that was trying to shed it.

In an office on the fifty-fifth floor with large glass panes on the south façade, Lucinda Lang sipped a cup of bitter coffee made in the firm lounge. She longed for the coffee beans from the slopes of Agua towering above Antigua in Guatemala. She remembered Macduff telling her that a friend of his, Luis Ramírez, owner of a coffee plantation in Antigua, once discussed American tastes in coffee.

"Macduff, where would you go to buy the best quality Guatemalan coffee?" Luis had asked.

"To a gourmet coffee shop in Guatemala city?"

"No. To the store at the airport where travelers departing buy last minute gifts to take home. We want them to appreciate our very best coffee."

"Then the next best would be bought in the U.S.?" Macduff had asked.

"No, the next best is exported to Germany, where coffee lovers are very discriminating."

"Third is the U.S.?"

"Still no. The next best goes generally to the rest of Europe."

"So we're last?"

"Correct. Plus, in the U.S. consumers don't know our prime coffee is often mixed with poor quality lowland coffee from Brazil or Kenya. Remember that the best coffee is shade-grown at high altitude. The beans are fewer in number but milder."

Lucinda always bought her coffee beans from specialty stores in Manhattan that imported beans directly from Antigua coffee *fincas*. And she always ground the beans immediately before brewing. She had never been able to convince the frugal office manager at her brokerage to buy Antigua beans and never finished a cup her secretary brought her from the staff lounge.

She noticed her reflection in the mirror-like windowpane and approved her dress selection that morning. She wore a smart knee-length dress from Saks, a dark burgundy that appeared black from a distance but subtlety changed shade as she neared. Her light brown hair touched her collar. A single-strand, pale amber necklace matched similar earrings, both a gift three years ago during a life that now seemed a fading dream.

As she watched the slanting raindrops explode against her large windows, a single tear broke free from the corner of one eye, ran down to her chin, and dropped to be consumed by her dress. She absent-mindedly reached with her right hand to feel the fingers of her left and looked down to see a white band on her tanned ring finger where no ring reflected prismatic images.

Carrying the half-filled Styrofoam coffee cup to the staff lounge, she emptied it into the sink and tossed the cup into the basket, returned and sat at her desk quietly for several minutes. Then she moved her computer mouse to click onto the first of many client files. Within the first half hour, she had put aside any visions of a winding creek that ran down the Absaroka Mountains to join the Yellowstone River just below the tiny junction of Emigrant, where a solitary traffic light blinks at a nearly empty roadway.

Lucinda's Mill Creek ranch lay idle. Only two ranch hands remained employed. A middle-aged woman named Mavis had been her helper. This week she was cleaning the main lodge for what might be the last time. Lucinda had talked to Mavis on the phone the previous day and sadly told her there would soon be "For Sale" signs along the road that bordered the northern side of the ranch.

It was unlikely that Lucinda would ever again hike the trail to Passage Falls and dapple small dry flies in the riffles of Mill Creek, float the Yellowstone River when hoppers were jumping into the river to be snatched up by hungry brown trout, or cast from *Osprey* in an early morning mist to a rising cutthroat. She had become a competent fly caster and was proud of her skill in dropping a fly where Macduff suggested. She wondered whether the beautiful bamboo fly rod he had made for her seven years ago would remain forever in its cloth bag.

At lunch Lucinda took a company limousine to Sardi's in the Theater District, dining on a favorite meal she hadn't tasted in several years—*Spinach Cannelloni au Gratin*—a spinach and ricotta cheese filling rolled in a French crepe. For a moment she remembered discussions about the merits of spinach at a table in that small log cabin near her Montana ranch. But the memory passed.

She sat below the hundreds of signed caricatures of celebrities with three other women who also had burst through glass ceilings to be crowned with prominent positions in New York's most famous—now more infamous—investment firms.

That evening she remained at work until shortly before seven, when her roommate from college days years ago at Oberlin met her at the Metropolitan Opera at Lincoln Center. Lucinda had bought two orchestra tickets for Mozart's *Così fan tutte,* the premier performance of the season. She had treated her friend to seats that were $367 each, hardly affordable by her friend's job as Associate Director of the Hispanic Society of America, where "wealth" came to her not in salary but by daily association working among the renderings of El Greco, de Ribera, and Velázquez.

After the opera and drinks at the Algonquin's Blue Bar, Lucinda returned to her apartment on East 67th Street between 2nd and 3rd avenues, said goodnight to the concierge, and put on a pair of worn denims sent to her with her ranch belongings, plus a sweatshirt with "Montana State Bobcats" across the front in large, deep-red letters. She sat on the sofa in her living room, picked up a book on country homes in Tuscany, and remembered the night not so many years ago when she walked into this room, where on this very sofa there was a male figure she thought was sleeping soundly, but in truth was watching her silhouetted in the window in her transparent, silken nightgown. In the darkness she had taken his hand and guided him to her bedroom.

She dropped the book, slipped off the sofa onto the floor, and began tearful convulsions that endured until the antique grandfather's clock quietly struck three a.m. Finally, she slept, waking at ten and immediately realizing she had client meetings beginning at 9:30. Twenty minutes later she was gulping down a cinnamon bun at a Starbucks near her office, while apologizing to a client on her cell phone, stammering through unconvincing excuses for her tardiness.

When she reached her office, she sat in her desk chair, looked south over a day with the prospect of a rare blue winter sky, and thought to herself: "I cannot live this life." But then she opened a file and called one of her best clients about some investments her firm was pushing but which she thought excessively risky. Even if they were, they would bring the firm prodigious fees. Any losses would, of course, be the problem of the clients.

Lucinda wondered whether she should send Macduff the ring with the distorted setting and replacement diamond. Would that be a prudent way to end their relationship as though all matters were settled?

She opened a drawer, lifted a silver flask, took a sip of expensive vodka, and pulled up another file on her computer.

27

Before the net ban amendment, the mullet resource was extremely over-fished in all regions of the state. With the amendment and rule in place, we are on the road to full recovery of the mullet resource.

*Manley Fuller of Florida Wildlife Federation (March 31, 1999).
www.earthjustice.org*

TWO DAYS LATER AT THE COTTAGE
IN ST. AUGUSTINE

IF YOU ASKED ME WHAT I ACCOMPLISHED over the past few days, I would be hard-pressed to remember anything noteworthy.

Yesterday morning I received an encouraging call about a three-year-old Hell's Bay drift boat that might be for sale by the estate of a guide who committed suicide. Plus the return of a call I made to my real estate friend Janet who brokered the purchase of my cottage the second winter of my new life years ago—this time responding to my question about what my cottage and land might bring if I decided to sell.

The most memorable call, however, was from Erin Giffin at the Park County Sheriff's Office in Livingston, Montana.

Our conversation became a mixture of my obliquely articulated responses and devious answers to her questions, with moments when I put my hand over the phone to gain composure because of where Erin was taking me.

"Macduffy," Erin asked, "I intended to call you and fill you in on Hendersen's death. More importantly, I've been calling Lucinda in Manhattan every few hours for three days with no response, other than a recorded 'I'll get back to you'. . . . What the hell's going on?"

"Nothing," I replied, truthfully. "What about Hendersen?"

"I'll tell you. Then you tell me about Lucinda. Deal?"

"Try me," I answered.

"We've learned embarrassingly little about how Hendersen came to be wrapped in a gill net under the bridge at the Passage Creek Trailhead. But we did learn he had received several letters postmarked Cedar Key, Florida. You know where that is?"

"I do. It's a small fishing-dependent town on the Gulf due west of St. Augustine, all the way across Florida past Gainesville. Cedar Key is a charming place. Good seafood restaurants, high demand for waterfront real estate. Three or four of my former colleagues at the university in Gainesville had weekend places there. What about Cedar Key?"

"All we know is the letters were sent from there."

"What did the letters say?" I asked.

"We don't know; we have only the postmarked envelopes. Apparently Cedar Key is one coastal town where the gill net ban had a drastic economic impact."

"That's right. A few small coastal towns north of Cedar Key were—for the most part—made extinct."

"Macduffy, we haven't ruled out murder. Nor have we ruled out an accident. The net might have been rigged illegally across Mill Creek, and Hendersen, fishing upstream, could have fallen in and became entangled."

"That sounds like fiction, Erin. I sense you're not very actively investigating the Hendersen death."

"Between you and me, the answer is we're not. We're short-handed and dealing with a fifteen percent budget cut and a seven percent increase in crime. We think Hendersen's death is more Florida's or Georgia's problem than ours. You folks have more resources."

"You wouldn't say that if you were here, reading about the county commissioners' rantings, attorney's office requests, police and fire services unions' threats, and the school system's demands. I guess we're not so different. . . . Do keep me posted on your progress. I'll talk to you soon."

"Wait just a minute, Macduffy. Now it's your turn to fill me in on Lucinda."

"I can't."

"What does that mean?"

"I haven't talked to her in ten days."

"I don't believe that. You two talk every day."

"We did. No longer."

"Why?"

"She walked away from me at the St. Louis airport on our way to Florida. Without a word of goodbye. One of the last things she said was she didn't know how long she'd be in Manhattan, but that it might be quite a while. I've come to understand 'quite a while' meant permanently."

"Doesn't she answer your calls?" Erin asked.

"No. But she flew to Jacksonville a few days ago and surprised me when I was coming back from visiting Elsbeth in Maine. We talked for a half hour without success, and she took the next flight back to Manhattan."

"What's the trouble between you two?"

"A combination of things. One, she doesn't think she should interfere with my getting to know my daughter. But I tell her Elsbeth loves being with her. She's also concerned about my activities with Dan Wilson in D.C. Last is what I can't help her with—she feels cut off from a city she likes, a challenging and rewarding job, and, *mostly*, having an identity other than being Macduff Brooks' companion."

"If companion meant wife, it would be different."

"I don't understand why, but maybe."

"Does she need time to think about it and talk with you?"

"I hoped so, but I think she believes it's over and wants to get on with reconnecting with Manhattan, her clients, and her colleagues. She's put her ranch up for sale and asked Mavis at Mill Creek to move all her belongings from my cabin and leave them at the ranch. The same here. She asked my housekeeper Jen to send all her things to Manhattan."

"She still has her ring?"

"I guess so, but it may be tucked away somewhere."

"That's incredible, Macduff. It doesn't make sense."

"Erin, the last thing I want is to have her unhappy. If what that requires is the end of us, it has to be."

"Don't be so noble. What are you going to do with your life? No impulsive changes, I hope."

I've asked my real estate friend here about handling the sale of my cottage. I'll do the same about the cabin on Mill Creek. Too many memories in both places not to make a change."

"But this will have a terrible impact on Elsbeth. She's had enough trauma recently."

"She's my remaining link to sanity. I suspect I'll buy a place in Gainesville. When El was pregnant, she carried Elsbeth around Gainesville for eight months before the tragedy on the Snake. I think Elsbeth would like living in Gainesville. She's talked about transferring from Maine after this first year. On her list is UF."

"You'll get yourself killed in Gainesville. You won't last long with Herzog and Isfahani on your tail, closing in. You're aware I know about them, Macduff. Remember, I was around when you were delirious after the shooting on the Snake, and I heard what must have been your life's story."

"I know. Isfahani will be dealt with in the next few months. Herzog is mostly interested in another try at the Guatemalan presidency. I'll be OK. If I can make it until Elsbeth finishes college and is settled, that's enough."

"Are you going to kill Isfahani? Is that one of the issues that bothers Lucinda? She hasn't told me much. In fact, she hasn't told me anything for at least a month."

"If I could tell you, the answers would be yes and yes."

"Then I don't blame her. Who the hell do you think you are? A one-man SEALs team after the next bin Laden?"

"You're pretty close. We've learned that Isfahani is bin Laden's nephew. He's in Khartoum planning a major terrorist attack. Somewhere in the U.S. We think it involves chemical weapons and D.C. We can't let that happen."

"And you plan to stop it?"

"I can try. I messed up the last time."

"When are you going to learn that you have two special women who love you—four adding Wuff and me—and you can't expect us all to hang in there while you traipse around the world trying to assassinate a terrorist? Patriots—like Mel Gibson—are for movies."

I heard a click. Erin was finished with me.

28

THREE WEEKS LATER AT THE COTTAGE

They say work has a cathartic effect on tragedy. *Maybe.* My work list includes numerous questions I must find answers to: Who caused the death on my boat? How long can I put off meeting with Dan Wilson about a second attempt to assassinate Isfahani? Do I agree or refuse? What do I tell Elsbeth at Christmas about Lucinda not being here? And when should I list my properties here and in Montana and move to Gainesville? As usual, the hardest issues get the last attention.

Glancing at the calendar a few days later, I was shocked to see Thanksgiving was only two days away. Elsbeth is going to Jackson Hole with her friend, Sue. On my one attempt this noon to reach Lucinda, I tried her office landline and, surprisingly, the phone was answered. It was her secretary, Carmen, whom I knew from better times.

"Miss Lang's not available, Mr. Brooks," she said, coolly, and began to hang up.

"Please, Carmen, I've tried to reach her for the past month. To no avail. I guess it's time for me to stop trying. . . . I won't call again."

"I shouldn't interfere, Mr. Brooks. Miss Lang isn't herself. She doesn't relax for a minute. She's at some fancy dinner and then a play, an opera, or a symphony. After that there's a party. *Every* night. She gets home late to her apartment and the next day she's here at the office early. She doesn't look good. She's short with me, like I was just now with you. I'm sorry. She's affecting me. I worry everyday she's going to fire me. To be truthful, I've been interviewing at Goldman Sachs. . . . Miss Lang needs to talk to you."

"I've tried," I said, confused. I'm in no great shape from the attempt and worse for the failures.

"Lucinda left for the holiday an hour ago. Maybe she'll be able to rest. But I think it'll all be partying."

"Is she going to Montana? *If* she hasn't sold the ranch by now."

"Not to Montana, although the ranch hasn't been sold. She's going to Peter Island in the Caribbean with a half dozen colleagues. It's terribly expensive, but she's been spending a lot more money than normally. She was a very frugal lady until she came here from Montana a month ago. Now she's a spend-thrift. She's even looking for a weekend place to buy in North-west Connecticut. I think she said Salisbury."

"Salisbury's a little like Southampton," I commented, "but less glitz and more class. It *is* expensive."

"That's not all. Yesterday she made some reference about buying a convent restored as a home in the hills north of Sienna in Italy. I'm not saying she can't afford it, Mr. Brooks. It's just not like her to spend the way she is. . . . I really shouldn't be talking to you about her."

"I understand. I'll let you go. Thanks for telling me what you did. Good luck in your job search. Things won't be the same around Lucinda's office without you. I hope you have a good Thanksgiving, considering."

Closing my cell phone, I poured an early Gentleman Jack. I'm at a loss to explain what's happening. With Wuff reluctantly plodding along behind, I took the drink to my rebuilt dock. I didn't replace the two-seater swing. I substituted a single-seat Adirondack chair bolted to a corner of the dock, facing east across the marshes, away from the cottage of good memories.

I enlarged the dock to hold kayaks as well as my new flats boat. Not actually new. I finally decided on a sixteen-year-old 17' Hell's Bay hull that was damaged ten years ago in a hurricane that passed over the beaches at Sarasota. The boat was damaged and the motor destroyed. The owner had it in a garage on Siesta Key and had restored the hull so it looks new. But he had a crippling stroke three months ago and needs to sell the boat. I've added a new four-stroke 90 hp Honda outboard, and installed a smaller center console, specifically limiting the seating to one. I don't plan to have anyone sitting beside me.

Admiring my restorative work on the dock, I looked up to see Jen drive in with some vegetables from her garden. She had something else for me.

"Mr. Brooks, when I came by yesterday, you weren't here. By the time I left and got to the gate, there was a UPS delivery man with a package for you. He said someone had to sign for it so I did. He said it was insured—for a lot."

I took the small package, talked a bit to Jen, and she departed. The package was post marked New York City. Opening it carefully, I slumped down on my cottage stair. The package held a small black velvet box that had seen better days. I know what from. Inside the box was an exquisite emerald cut diamond in a twisted setting. There was no note; the sender knew I didn't need an explanation.

It was the ring I first planned to give Lucinda the evening after we finished the float with Park Salisbury that nearly cost us our lives. One bullet had hit the box in my pocket. The diamond was dislodged from the setting, dropped overboard, and lost. I replaced the diamond and later gave it, damaged box and all, to Lucinda. It was a confirmation of our engagement. She wore it on special occasions and always when she was away from me; otherwise, it sat in its battered box in a safe at her ranch or apartment.

I put the ring back in the velvet box and placed it in the bottom of the box I had just filled with all the photos that reminded me of Lucinda and had hung on every wall in every room in the cottage. With some irony Lucinda had sent the ring back two days before the anniversary of our meeting Thanksgiving Day in Montana nearly a decade ago. I didn't want the emerald cut diamond ring back. As Shakespeare wrote in *Julius Caesar,* "This was the unkindest cut of all."

Thanksgiving morning I called Elsbeth in Wyoming while watching the Macy's Thanksgiving Day Parade in New York City on TV. Seeing the parade wasn't a good decision. Several times the camera scanned to show the Chrysler Building, and I found myself trying to locate Lucinda's office.

Elsbeth was enjoying Jackson Hole. Sue and she walked along the Snake River to where she thought El died seventeen years ago. It was where the Carsons found El, pregnant with Elsbeth, floating in the river after our guide crashed his drift boat into a pile of trees that had fallen into the river during the spring's surge of melted snow.

29

ON THE FLATS NEAR THE COTTAGE

WHEN I WOKE FRIDAY MORNING feeling relieved from a Thanksgiving day and night without an after-visit from my friend Gentleman Jack, I surprised myself by making a healthy breakfast and decided to postpone some work on the cottage's stairs and fish the flats. I hadn't set a foot off my dock to fish in months.

My flats boat wasn't ready; I had some wiring to install on the new center console. From off the new rack on the rebuilt dock I pulled a kayak, slid it into the water, and loaded a couple of bottles of water, my salt water fly box, and an L.L. Bean 9 foot 7 weight rod I've kept ready under the cottage and often used to practice casting in the yard. The line wasn't ideal; although I liked the size 7, the line was a pale yellow floating line. I prefer a slow sinking dark green line that I came to favor gradually because I always use floating lines in fresh water. I may be wrong, but I sense that—unlike freshwater trout—the fish on the salt marshes tend to feed almost exclusively below the surface. But sea trout often hit a fly as soon as it lands on the surface. Perhaps what I'm failing to add is that there are so many more variations of fish in salt water than trout, and many, such as redfish and flounder, are bottom feeders.

After my sudden urge to fish, I was more interested in getting out on the flats than rigging a more appropriate rod. The tide was ebbing, and I didn't want to walk home pulling the kayak.

It took only two or three paddle strokes before I realized how much I missed being out on these flats.

Sitting in a kayak means sitting within a couple inches of the surface level, well below the tops of the marsh grasses lining the channels. I usually stand when I fish from a flats boat, and my head is above the top of the grasses. I prefer the kayak when I'm alone. Once I've rounded a few bends, I lose sight of the horizons that tell me where I am. It's a world of peace induced by silence. With the tide heading out, I almost assuredly won't see another boat fishing its way back from the Intracoastal Waterway to the land where my cottage sits nearly hidden among the pines.

Sometimes I round a bend and encounter a group of shore birds that were not expecting me. Herons, scarlet ibis, oystercatchers, roseate spoonbills, and the ubiquitous gulls and terns scatter at my entrance, which disrupts their feeding, bringing momentary screeches of panic and warning as they vanish.

One time I turned a tight horseshoe bend and lying on the tiny piece of shore ahead was an alligator I knew to be too large to defy. Alligators tend to shun salt water, but food often trumps salinity. But only for short periods because gators lack the salt-secreting glands found in crocodiles. This gator was basking in the sun, a cold blooded reptile doing nothing more than letting its leathery coat absorb some warmth and raise its body temperature to put behind a particularly frigid January night. It moved its tail, turned its head toward me, and opened a mouth that sent me a signal I was unwelcome. For years I had thought such a heavy cumbersome beast could not match my skills in propelling my kayak. But one day a gator, ignoring my passage, spotted or sensed something that apparently was higher on its list of foods. It thrust its heavily scaled body toward its prey and moved with unimaginable speed through the grasses, appearing to be racing across the tops without disturbance of the thinnest blade.

There would be no alligators in my path today, but on one horseshoe bend in the marsh, I approached a pair of American oystercatchers standing—appropriately—on an oyster bank. They were opening the bivalves on the ebbing tide. It's a favorite bird that I enjoy watching. The two ignored my presence, using their long bright reddish-orange bills to pry open the namesake bivalves. Their eyes are yellow, edged by orange orbital rings. Pinkish legs support a black head and breast, gray-black back, wings, and tail, over a white underbody. In flight more white is seen along the rear edges of opened wings.

I favor the oystercatcher as much for its striking color as its monogamy. Some have been seen together defending the same oyster mounds for twenty years. Lucinda is less a fan of the bird because they are known for egg dumping, laying their eggs in sea gulls' nests and allowing the gulls to raise the young.

After slipping past the birds and rounding another bend, I stopped paddling and dropped the small anchor over the stern. The outgoing tide left my bow pointing downstream. I replaced the leader, using 9' 5X knotless fluorocarbon. The 5X tests at about five pounds. For a fly I chose a Lefty's Deceiver tied on a size 2 stainless hook, partly because I had left my box of Clousers in my kitchen where I was counting Clousers to decide if I needed to tie more.

The Deceiver does not take second place to the Clouser. It was designed by casting icon Lefty Kreh and is a must for salt water fly fishing. The Deceiver or Clouser I prefer liberally uses chartreuse white bucktail. My Clouser adds a little silver Krystal flash, the Deceiver the same flash in red. The Deceiver adds a red with black pupil eye a third of the way back from the hook's eye; the Clouser usually goes without an eye, favoring a buildup of a head just behind the eye. I wonder if the fish can tell the difference, or is it like judging whether red wine is *Pinot Noir* or *Malbec*. I like both flies and both wines.

I let the current carry the fly nearly seventy feet, stripping out line that was not wound tightly on the reel. Looking at the reel to see when to stop, the line suddenly pulled hard and the rod bent when I instinctively raised it and set the hook. Something had slammed the Deceiver and was on its way out with the tide. I had a choice: pull up the anchor and drift with the tide or play it and hope it didn't break off. I was sure I'd fumble with the anchor and probably have the kayak float onto an oyster bank. Oyster shells are not kind to fly lines. I chose to fight, doubting the fish was more than 2-3 pounds. It didn't jump, but it never stayed still. Fortunately, for me, there were no places along the hundred feet in front of the kayak that might favor the fish. Marsh grass lined the banks, and there was not an oyster bank in sight.

Patience and I would have it, I thought. But the line went slack. Never a slight glimpse of the fish. As though nothing happened. But when I reeled in, the fly had a chunk out of it, and the hook was bent. Chances are it was a bluefish. Disliked by many, I welcome a blue in the water or on the dinner table.

I grew up in Connecticut where the spring arrival of the bluefish from the south drew hundreds of boats. But when El and I moved to Gainesville almost thirty years ago, we discovered to our surprise that bluefish were reviled. Disliked by fishermen searching for something to eat rather than losing a lure to the formidable teeth of a blue, the fish was equally disliked by restaurants as too oily to serve. But to a catch and release fly fisherman, the blue is a prize. The late John Hershey, author of *Blues*, would be pleased to know someone likes it Down South.

Time is not recorded on the marsh flats in terms of minutes. Watches don't belong on a fishing boat; one goes home when one goes home. But tides do not wait.

I had drifted with the tide, lost in the coolness of the light breeze and the smell of the flats as the tide uncovered mud banks. I had been out long enough for the tide to tell me I was under its spell, a half mile from my dock in water that would reach its low in twenty minutes. My channel was rapidly draining. I spun the kayak around and began aggressively to paddle home, making only a hundred yards before I began to scrape, sometimes on sand, sometimes on oyster banks.

An old pair of sneaks gave some protection to my feet. They proved a lifesaver. I slid out of the kayak, tied a line to the bow and towed the kayak. By the time I reached the dock, the tide was starting its flood. The creek was never fully emptied, but the last fifty yards required pulling the kayak over bottom.

The day's tally was three or four painful cuts on the oyster banks and no fish landed. One Deceiver and two Clousers gone. An old pair of sneaks of little further use. Sunburn where I missed with the zinc block.

Would I have traded the day for a little better score? Not a chance.

30

Some of the changes these [family-owned commercial fishing] *businesses experienced* [after the ban] *include:*
The number of families in the fishing business ... decreased by 25 percent.
Following the net ban, 25 percent of the individual fishers retired.
Family income from fishing ... decreased by 31 percent.
An increased dependence on non-fishing income ... [was] *provided mainly by wives.*
The number of fishers targeting mullet, sea trout, and pompano decreased.
The number of fishers targeting blue crab, stone crab and grouper increased.

Since the Net Ban: Changes in Commercial Fishing (January 2000).
www.flseagrant.org

A WEEK LATER

The county hadn't released any further details about Bradford. Nothing in the local rumor mills has helped establish reasons for his death. Anxious, I accepted that facing some abuse from Deputy Turk Jensen was worth extracting any information from him.

"This is Sharon at the St. Johns County Sheriff's Office," a pleasant voice said when I called the Monday after the holiday.

"Is Turk Jensen in?" I asked.

"No. May I leave a message and tell him who called?"

"I wanted to get an update on the fire that killed Hugh Bradford."

"Who is this?"

"Macduff Brooks. I own the prop . . . ."

"I met you the day of the fire. I stayed in the background. I heard Jensen go after you. He's something else."

"He is," I replied, remembering the plain Jane redhead who appeared to be making a lot of notes, but never moved away from where the police cars were parked.

"Mr. Brooks, do you know Grace Justice, the assistant state attorney who's assigned to this case?"

"I know of her, but we haven't met."

Attorney Muirhead had told me about Grace soon after Bradford's death. She had been to a fly fishing school in Vermont.

"I talked to her an hour ago, Mr. Brooks. She'd be better to talk to than Turk. You want her cell phone number?"

"Sure, thanks."

I dialed Grace Justice. She answered, but background music made it difficult to hear. "Whoa!" she said, "I'm trying to juggle my cell phone in my left hand, turn down the music with my right, and keep the car steady with my knees."

"Where are you?" I asked. "I want to avoid driving in that area."

"Who is this?"

"Macduff Brooks, I'm . . . ."

"I know well enough who *you* are," she interrupted. "Stirring up things in our quiet little village? Not that they don't need it. . . . What do you want with me?"

"Sharon in Turk Jensen's office said to talk to you instead of dealing with Turk."

"The best thing about Turk is that soon he'll be put out to pasture. We all hope he moves to some golfing retirement community near Disney World. . . . He's a pompous, incompetent, ugly, misfit bastard—no other way to put it."

"That puts it pretty well," I stated.

"I suppose you want to know about Hugh Bradford?"

"I do. There's been nothing new in the paper, and I don't know many people in this area."

"You know enough people on the county staff to irritate the hell out of most of them."

"All misunderstandings."

"Please don't try to irritate *me*. I have faced enough already today. I need someone to be nice to me for a change."

"OK. How about going fishing?"

"Fishing?" There was a long moment of silence, then, "I heard you were a guide in the Rockies in the summer."

"You heard right, but I'm backing off a bit. Old age is not coming gracefully into my life."

"From what I know, you aren't old. At least not *that* old. . . . Where do you fish around here?"

"Close to my cottage by Pellicer Creek. Choice of flats boat or kayaks. I just picked up a flats boat to replace the one that served as Bradford's funeral pyre. The new one is not really new but restored so you wouldn't know the difference.

"The Pellicer Creek area has a ton of fish, and few people know the channels to get back there. There are no markers, and if you don't know where the deep water is, you end up sitting out the tide on an oyster bank. That's not much fun. . . . kayaks are good to fish from, but I wouldn't be able to help you cast."

"Help me cast? I think I know how."

"With a fly rod?" I asked.

"That's right."

"But I heard you took a course on fly fishing in Vermont. Beginning fly fishing?"

She laughed. "Not beginning. It was called Advanced Fly Fishing for Competition. Ever heard of the FFF?"

"Yes, its headquarters are a few miles north of my cabin in Montana. I hope to pass the CCI—that means Certified. . . ."

"I know what it is. I passed the Certified Casting Instructor level five years ago. Last year I passed the MCI test. That's Master. . . ."

"*I know what that is*. I withdraw my offer."

"To teach me casting or take me fishing?"

"Only the teaching part. How about fishing with me off my dock—spin casting with live shrimp?"

"I don't do spin casting. And I don't do live bait. Artificial flies only."

"You tie?"

"Don't have enough time. Don't have enough patience. And don't have enough space. I have a one-bedroom condo at Camachee Cove. I prefer displaying art to mounted fishing flies."

"My offer stands. As to both. But *you* teach me."

"From what I hear, you may not be easy."

"Try me."

She took my offer—set for Saturday. She sounded intimidating, strong willed, professional, and challenging. What I realized ten minutes after I closed my cell phone was that we didn't talk about Hugh Bradford, which was why I called her, not to suggest she go fishing with me. But I could use Saturday to learn more about Bradford.

I haven't fished the flats much the past two years. With the problems of the Shuttle Gal murders and then the wicker man and mistletoe "sacrifices," I didn't relish being on the water when Lucinda and I were in St. Augustine for the winter. But my day alone in the kayak made me want to go out more often.

When I do make time to fish the flats, it's rare to see anything other than spin or bait casting. Very few locals fly fish around St. Augustine. When I'm on my boat, I count how many people are fly fishing and write figures on a small pad. My notes indicate that of the last 177 fishing boats I've seen—between the 207 Bridge in Crescent Beach south about fifteen miles to Palm Coast—over a three-year period, only two boats had people casting fly lines. Doing so takes more practice, more skill, and more focus than dropping a hook, dangling a live shrimp or shiner, putting the rod in a holder on the boat, opening a Bud, and waiting for something to tug.

I've not yet seen one woman fly fishing in my area. My experience in the West is that women who are learning to fly fish, in contrast to men, are more patient and more attentive to lessons. When they cast, they don't look like they're trying to throw a hammer at a track meet. And they look much better.

Two Orvis Helios 9' 9 weight rods and two $70 Clearwater reels for 7-9 weight lines seemed a good choice for us for Saturday. Those two reels have worked better than the one $300 reel I bought, which kept coming apart even after it was "repaired." I keep several spare spools for the reels because I try to match the line to whatever fish I'm after. In the West it's always trout. On the salt water flats at the edge of my land, we hook up with sea trout, bluefish, yellow jacks, occasional snook and tarpon in the warmer months, and, my least favorite but popular, bottom feeding redfish. Bonefish don't come close to

Northeast Florida, but provide a good excuse to fly to the Bahamas, Belize, or Cuba during our winter.

I've loaded the reel I plan to use with a 9 weight intermediate line that sinks moderately below the surface. I'll load the other with a general purpose floating saltwater line, also a 9 weight. I've been using hard to see—by the fish—fluorocarbon leaders and tippets. Fluorocarbon sinks more than nylon. As in my freshwater fishing out West, I'll use 9 foot leaders in a size 5X, which generally tests at about five pounds. I break more leaders fishing in Florida waters than in Montana, where a five pound trout nears lunker status.

For flies, I have a larger than needed selection—a common trait of fresh or saltwater fly fishers—but usually fall back to some form and color of Clouser. Bob Clouser developed this minnow look-alike. I'll stick with the colors that have worked for me—chartreuse and white.

Many salt water flies, including some of the Clouser minnow variations, have fairly large dumbbell eyes. That makes for a heavy fly, especially compared to my old fresh water standards—the Adams and the elk hair. At some point I know I'm no longer casting only the line; I've added a lure. A small lure, but it's a lure all the same. I feel I'm *casting* artificial lures with a fly rod rather than casting the fly line.

I wonder what rod Grace will bring. I'm glad we'll be in channels where short 30- to 40-foot casts are the usual range. I don't want to try to match the distance she must reach with her Master Casting Instructor certification.

It should be an interesting day. I admit I'm curious to discover what she looks like.

31

WASHINGTON, D.C., IN EARLY DECEMBER

DAN WILSON CALLED ME SUNDAY NIGHT while I was finishing tying some flies for Saturday's fishing with Grace Justice.

"Dan, before you called, I made some notes about what I expect to accomplish around here this week. I suspect that after this call, I can throw them out and book a flight to D.C."

"Don't book it. One of our jets will be at the St. Augustine airport in the morning to pick you up. Be there at 8 a.m."

"Wait a minute. I haven't made any promises."

"You will. Be on that plane. We'll meet for lunch at the Army and Navy Club. Ever been there?"

"You're kidding! I was there the night before I flew to Guatemala at your request—if you remember."

"Now that you mention it, I do remember. We'll try to do better this time. I don't want you flown back here from where we're sending you, beat up and ready for another identity change and a new address. That sure would confuse Lucinda."

"No, it wouldn't."

"She expects you to come home beat up?"

"I don't think she expects anything from me. We've split."

"Sorry, Mac. But that means you can do even more work for us. I've got some ideas about. . . ."

"Don't even dream of my working for you," I interrupted, irritated at his attitude, "beyond agreeing to help take out Isfahani. I'm willing to talk now *only* because Lucinda is history. Working for you was one of the issues she had strong feelings about. She didn't want me earning a gold star in your lobby after being flown home in a body bag from who knows where. If things hadn't changed, I was planning to tell you my work with you was over. Finished! Done! Understand? Now, I'll postpone telling you that until Isfahani is dead."

"Maybe you'll make more sense in person. See you tomorrow."

If I could have walked away from Dan as easily as Lucinda did from me, I'd be typing an email to him right now. The Agency is no better than the New York Mafia. Once a member there's no way out. Especially if you're in their protection program. Maybe I can convince Dan to make me an exception.

The flight to D.C. was uneventful. No one, like the Village People who pose as security in airports, was at the CIA jet to pat me down. My stewardess on the jet was all business; she looked and walked down the aisle like a Manhattan fashion model.

Dan was waiting for me at Langley with a smile and almost a hug that would not be standard CIA protocol. Kill but don't touch.

"Good to see you, Macduff. Before we talk about Isfahani, tell me about Lucinda. Are you really no longer that inseparable elysian couple I knew?"

"This member of 'that couple' is not too cheery. Or maybe it's that I don't understand what's happened. But I have to move on. Starting Saturday—when I have a date with a lady to fly fish near my cottage."

"Not giving Lucinda any chance to reconsider?"

"I could only take so many rejected phone calls and unanswered letters."

"Maybe she's been ill."

"She spent Thanksgiving on Peter Island partying with colleagues. That's the Caribbean island those same friends went to seven years ago after their last-minute cancelation of an invitation to join Lucinda for Thanksgiving dinner in Montana. I didn't think she ever spoke to them again. I've always been thankful for their incredibly impolite action; it left me as the only guest at her dinner party. I was mesmerized the moment she opened her front door. Advance forward seven years, and now *I'm* the target of a cancelation."

"I hope fishing Saturday works out for you."

"One thing is clear. If I ever have another relationship, the lady won't be told any facts about my prior private life. Lucinda knows too much about me."

"Isfahani's last plastic surgery to correct the damage from your shooting him in Guatemala wasn't successful," Dan informed me. "He's in some discomfort that isn't going to change. He looks terrible. We know he's gone to Khartoum. We have reason to believe he's organizing and leading a terrorist attack in D.C. It could chemical, biological, or nuclear—we simply don't know.

"You weren't told at the meeting years ago with Malcolm Whitney that Isfahani was related to bin Laden. You had no need to know. I think you know it now. Isfahani was a favorite of bin Laden, and Isfahani idolized him. He would give his life to revenge bin Laden's death. We hope he can give his life without the revenge. That's where you come in."

"How?"

"It's time I told you everything. Well . . . everything you need to know."

Over the next few hours he told me more than I wanted to know.

32

AT THE COTTAGE THE FOLLOWING DAY

WHAT HAVE I GOTTEN MYSELF INTO I wondered over sausage and eggs back at the cottage. Dan promised that this would be the last time his dirty tricks group made any demands on me.

There's little time to prepare, mainly because the Agency wants me settled somewhere near D.C. for two weeks before I leave for Khartoum. But I put them off because I intend to give Elsbeth my full attention during the Christmas break.

I can't practice with my CheyTac on my St. Augustine property; Dan has made an arrangement with their firing range head to work with me. It's been five years since I fired the rifle at Isfahani in Guatemala.

The single bullet I sent toward Isfahani's head hit the target, but a couple of inches below the spot for a sure kill. The bullet went in at the lower corner of his nose and passed through his head missing the brain stem and passing beneath his cerebellum. The expansion of the slug destroyed his nose, split his lip, and crashed through some teeth. He survived only because a local doctor driving through the Guatemalan highlands came across his prostrate body beside the road in a rapidly spreading pool of blood. The doctor stopped the bleeding and rushed Isfahani to a local clinic, where he was stabilized and flown by helicopter to a hospital in Guatemala City and then to a more fully equipped facility in Zurich. His facial damage was extensive; repeated plastic surgery has only made him look worse.

Dan has followed Isfahani's track ever since, but there are gaps. He's been mostly in Khartoum, but Dan knows he's also been to Pakistan and Afghanistan four or five times. One trip was immediately after his blood relation, bin Laden, was killed by Navy SEALs Team Six.

The best intelligence Dan has access to tells him that Isfahani is the leader of a planned attempt early in the new year that would devastate the population of the D.C. area. That could be accomplished with a small nuclear weapon, a chemical attack, or some form of biological infusion in the D.C. water supply.

A biological attack likely would produce the fewest and most uncertain results. There isn't much experience anywhere with large scale biological warfare. Furthermore, nuclear weapons constructed by Islamic terrorists thus far have proven to be unstable. Dan thinks the attack will be with chemicals.

The Agency doesn't know which chemicals will be used or how they will be delivered. Or exactly where. Or. . . .

33

Oak Hill [southernmost coastal town of about 1,800 persons in Volusia County, Florida] *residents never were wealthy; the 1990 census showed that the average household income was little more than $19,000. But after the net ban, some say their incomes dropped by as much as half. Health insurance became a luxury. Evidence of the town's poverty can be found in the narrow, deteriorating mobile homes. . . . At the Family Crisis Help Center, about 20 people come in each day for free bread and canned goods.*

Orlando Sentinel, May 15, 2000.

CHRISTMAS BREAK AT THE COTTAGE

After a warm hug when she met me at the luggage conveyor, Elsbeth looked around and then at me. "I thought Lucinda would be at the airport with you. Dad, where is she?" Her tone demanded an immediate response. She stared at me as she settled into the passenger seat of my new SUV. I didn't want to have the holiday start with an argument. Or receive a scolding from my daughter.

"She's not here" was all I could get out.

"That's apparent. I assume she's at the cottage. . . . This is my first visit here."

"It is," I muttered.

"You're so articulate! What's wrong?"

"Let's get this over and then enjoy the holiday."

"Get what over?"

"Lucinda's no longer with us."

"Gone? She died? And you didn't tell me? She was perfect for you."

"She didn't die. She left. Right now she's in London for Christmas holiday with friends from New York. Living well. Staying at the Connaught. Afternoon tea at the Ritz. Shopping at Harrod's. Opera at Covent Garden. Symphonies at Prince Albert Hall. Theatre in the West End. Not to mention meals at five-star restaurants.

"I don't give a damn about all that. Why isn't she here?"

"I can't answer that. It was her decision. She left me weeks before Thanksgiving."

Elsbeth has been my daughter for nearly eighteen years, but only half a year knowing I was her dad and living with me. For three months of that brief time, she was away at university in Maine. . . . This is the first time I've seen her shed tears of sorrow.

"I need to explain. Let me start from the beginning. At least from when you joined us."

During the remainder of the drive and the first two hours at the cottage, not diverted by a single sip of Gentleman Jack, I tried to tell her everything about my relationship with Lucinda. Every conversation. Every silent communication.

"What are you going to do? She'll be back from London in a couple of weeks. You *have* to get together."

"I can't."

"Meaning you won't?"

"I can't," I repeated.

"What *do* you mean?"

"I've scheduled some things with Dan Wilson. I have to move ahead with my own life." I haven't told Lucinda about my commitment to Dan to deal with Isfahani. I don't plan to tell her.

"What's more important? Doesn't Lucinda count?"

"She does. But her actions tell me as much as she's going to convey."

"You're a wimp, Dad."

"What do you suggest?"

"Fly to London. At *least* meet her plane in New York when she returns. Make her sit down and talk. At least *know* why she's left you. I don't believe it's living in Manhattan and making lots of money. Or that she can't deal with the risks you two have taken. It's more. What are you up to that may have caused her to leave?"

"I'm going to do something for Dan that Lucinda doesn't like."

"What?"

"Assassinate a terrorist named Abdul Khaliq Isfahani."

Elsbeth looked at me as though *I* were the terrorist. She got up, took my car keys from the table by the door, and left. I heard the car start and roar off.

34

TWO DAYS LATER AT THE COTTAGE

I was packing when Elsbeth returned. She came in the door and saw me placing books in cartons.

"Now what are you doing? Selling your favorite books?"

"Not selling. I'm packing my things to make it easier for you."

"What on earth do you mean?"

"I can't talk about it."

"It's Dan Wilson, isn't it?"

"Yes. . . . I won't say anything more."

"So I'm supposed to be prepared to come here on school break in February and dispose of your things because you haven't come back from wherever you're headed?"

"It'll make it easier for you."

"I don't want *easier*. I want you. I need you. Don't you understand that?"

"I think I do. But I've agreed to do something. It's already in motion. I can't stop it."

"You can walk away."

"If I do, thousands of people may die. And Dan might drop my protection. I'll be at risk. Lucinda as well. And you."

"Dan wouldn't do that. He's a friend!"

"True. But he puts his country ahead of my interests."

"Then he's no friend. He's using you. Don't you understand that?"

"I do. . . . I don't have much choice."

"Of course you do. When do you leave?"

"Soon after you . . . the day after New Year's."

"When will you be back?"

"I haven't thought about that."

"Well, you'd better think about that. You may come home to an empty house."

Elsbeth left, again taking my car.

I'm to fish with Grace Justice in the morning. Fortunately, Grace is driving here. When we talked, I offered to pick her up, but she said it made more sense for her to come here.

Elsbeth hasn't returned this evening. Nor has she called. She must have turned off her cell phone. She knows no one in St. Augustine, so I don't know where she'll stay for the night.

Things are not going well.

35

THE FOLLOWING DAY FISHING ON THE
SALT WATER FLATS

GRACE ARRIVED AT NINE. I suggested the time because the high tide was due about eleven. More or less at
eleven because my sources didn't list "The Brooks' Dock" as a
point of reference for high and low tides. I had to look at the
tidal times for more commonly known locations and add or
subtract so many minutes. I got a rough estimate by occasionally checking the actual high or low at my pier with the tide listed
for St. Augustine Beach. If I remembered correctly from last
year, my dock's high and low tides are about three hours after
those at St. Augustine Beach.

Normally there's not enough water for my flats boat to get
out between two hours on either side of the low tide. I don't
determine when it would be possible; lunar idiosyncrasies are
more powerful than my wishes. A full moon at a solstice or
equinox, plus a strong northeast wind, can raise the tide a foot.

Grace and I planned to start about 9:30 and fish the last
hour and a half of the flood and the first hour or two of the
ebb. I like following the tide through the channels in the marsh.
I've learned where the holes are that hold fish. I suspected the

flood would be better to fish than the ebb. "Suspected" meant I didn't really know. What I've most enjoyed is nothing more than being on the water.

She drove up in a five- or six-year-old red Land Rover that she must have had washed on the way. A cloud of dust from my road followed her. The car's wet surfaces were a magnet to the dust, and by the time she stopped, the car was a dirty gray and ready for a revisit to the car wash.

When she reached the top of the stairs to my porch, I judged her to be a few inches short of six feet and have the movements of an athlete. Or a hunter. She came up like a tiger after prey. Her face was hidden behind large, black wrap-around sunglasses.

Grace was wearing white sneaks, gray shorts, and a super-light-weight faded yellow shirt with the sleeves rolled up and buttoned. It was insufficient cover to disguise the presence and abundance of her breasts and the fact that she'd left her bra at home. A long-billed gray cap covered her head, advertising a fishing camp in Abaco in the Bahamas. When she was close, she dropped the sunglasses so they hung on a line around her neck, took off the cap, and shook her head, letting auburn hair tumble out and settle on her shoulders. She reached out to shake hands. She was by far the best looking Master Casting Instructor I've ever seen. I'm not sure she has any students who concentrate as much on their casting strokes as on her.

"I'm Grace. You have to be Macduff. Who's the little lady behind you wagging her tail?" she said in a low sultry voice that sounded like Lauren Bacall's.

"That's Wuff. She doesn't fish. She came out because she thinks you came to play with her."

"How do I tell her I'm here to play with *you*, without hurting her feelings?"

"A treat from a can on my kitchen counter will speak more than any words of explanation. Come in."

"This place is cozy," she exclaimed as she walked in, stopped, and surveyed the living room. "Have you lived here long?"

"About a half dozen years. I'm gone in the summer."

"Where?"

"Montana and Wyoming and a sliver of Idaho."

"To fish?"

"And guide. It's different there. Those three states are all trout country, unlike the treasure trove of variety around here."

"Do you fish salt water much?"

"No, and I really don't know why. I'm here about five months—more or less early to mid-October through March. But when I get here in the fall, there's usually maintenance to do. Plus, I'm often bushed by the combination of too many floats in the West for a guy my age and the lethargy accumulated crossing the boredom-inducing Great Plains."

"Those are poor excuses," she said with a smile that covered doubt. "You should be recovered by Thanksgiving and have four and a half months to fish."

"I'm hoping to do more this winter."

"You have friends you fish with?"

"No. I don't mind being alone."

"When you want company, give me a call."

Grace was curious about the cottage. She gave Wuff a treat and wandered around looking. She didn't ask about the packed boxes. But she was curious about something else. Probably because female clothes were in evidence.

"You don't live here alone." she asked, meaning it to be taken as a question.

"I have a daughter in her first year at UM in Orono. She's here for the holidays, but she's off with friends for a day or two." I had to say something because there's no car around the cottage.

"Maine? Not many Florida kids go there for college. Did she go to high school here? Pedro Menendez High isn't far."

"She went to high school out of state." That was true. I didn't want to explain Elsbeth's life to Grace. Especially El's death and what I did before becoming Macduff.

"Does she like Montana?"

"She does. She might transfer there next year," I replied, struggling to change the subject. "We have time for coffee on the porch. I want to hear your thoughts on the Bradford death, and anything you know about the first gill net death near Ft. Myers and even the death in Montana.

Three wooden rocking chairs line a narrow porch wrapped around the cottage, allowing the sitter to move according to wind and sun preferences. With fresh coffee, we settled into two of the chairs facing the marshes.

"So what about Bradford?" I started. "He died not thirty yards from here when my boat was incinerated."

"Bradford was burned so badly we don't know if he was wrapped in the gill net, but we think so," she commented. "The autopsy was brief and inconclusive. We can't tell whether he died from drowning or the fire. Or strangulation. Or shooting. There wasn't enough left to allow any reasonable speculation.

"He had a lot of enemies because of his often caustic editorials, especially when he wrote about the city and county commissions. . . . Did you know him?" she asked.

"Never met him. I haven't read more than two or three of his columns."

"We've gone through his columns, as well as response letters to the editor, and made a list of about forty-five people who had reason to be mad. But killing is another matter."

"Is there any doubt about it being murder?" I asked.

"How would he have died otherwise? Wrapped himself in a gill net, leaving his arms free to ignite a fire? Suicide? It was not an accident. Fire doesn't leave much. . . . The first gill net death near Ft. Myers—Clint Carter—is also a puzzle, but the police had a body to examine. No sign of foul play with Carter. No strangulation. No blows. But I have reservations; I don't see Carter's death as an accident. Especially because it involved a gill net."

"And, finally, there's the out-of-state death of Hendersen not more than a mile from my Montana cabin."

"I know. You found him. You were fishing with a lady friend," she added with a hint of curiosity.

"I was. The local medical examiner in Montana did an autopsy on Hendersen. I have some friends in the county sheriff's office there. Hendersen's death is more like Carter's than Bradford's. Like Carter's there were no signs of any blows to Hendersen. No strangulation. No poisoning. Of course, there was no sign of *anything* with Bradford. . . . The folks in Montana don't buy the idea of an accidental drowning, but Hendersen *might* have fallen into Mill Creek and floated into someone's gill net. . . . But I've never heard of anyone using a gill net in Paradise Valley."

"Macduff, you probably know that most suspicious deaths go unsolved. If we're assuming the three were murdered—and I tend to agree with that line of thinking—I'm not convinced they involved the same killer. Maybe copycat murders?"

"For Hendersen? Perhaps. He died only four to five days after Carter, three-quarters of the way across the country. It doesn't seem likely the killer crossed the country to Montana if he knew Hendersen was soon to return to Georgia. "

"There was time enough to learn about Carter's death in Montana and decide to get rid of someone you didn't like, using a gill net to have the police believe it was the same person responsible for the Florida death."

"Conceded," I responded.

"There is something you haven't raised," she noted. "The link between *you* and each of the three."

"I met Carter *once* at a fly fishing program in Ft. Myers, met Hendersen *once* at a different program in Georgia, and *never* met Bradford. What link?"

"You were *with* Carter and Hendersen on separate occasions when they each criticized the way the net ban wasn't achieving its intended goal. You agreed with them. Bradford wrote several columns with the same critical focus. And he died on *your* dock."

"Sounds circumstantial to the extreme. I bet there were people at the Georgia meeting who also were at the Ft. Myers program and who had read some of Bradford's columns."

"That's stretching reality, Macduff. Do you seriously think a person from Ft. Myers and another from near Atlanta routinely read the St. Augustine *Chronicle*? Do you believe Carter and Hendersen read Bradford?"

"I don't know the reach of his columns, but with the internet, anyone going online to search about the gill net ban could have read his pieces."

"That's something I should check, and I will. . . . No matter how you view the three deaths, Macduff, *you* had a link. Different links granted, but they exist. . . . Enough! Let's fish!"

"We should get started. The tide's a little over an hour before high. We can talk more on the boat."

"What can I carry?" she asked, slinging a bag over her shoulder and taking two rod tubes from her Land Rover.

"Just bring your gear. I took water and sodas down before you came. The boat's in the water. Fueled and ready."

I started us off in little more than ten inches of water, with the engine tilted because we were going to be in shallow water until the tide came in. Grace sat on the seat atop the cooler in front of the console. I wondered where she would have settled if there had been room next to me. The single seat means I don't have to think about that anymore.

She sat down, got up again, and opened the cooler. After looking in for a few seconds, she pulled out four bottles of Coors from her gear bag, and added them to the water, soda, and lunch already in the cooler. Two beers for her and two for me? All four for her? Should be an interesting day.

"We'll start fishing a couple of hundred yards from the dock, along the edge of some twisting channels lined with oyster beds and spartina sea grass. There's a good hole I want to revisit—discovered it last year—that probably hasn't been fished much since. We can cast and drag flies back over the hole."

"What fly do you suggest?"

"Let's start with some Clousers I tied. In all white or chartreuse and white. . . . Choose yours," I added, handing her one fly of each color.

"I like all white," she said. "I see you added a little tinsel-like flash to the body. Good idea."

"Bob Clouser's idea. Not mine."

Any special knot you suggest?" she inquired. I wondered whether her asking about the fly and knot choice was a test or a sincere query.

"I like to let the Clouser wobble as I retrieve it. I use some form of loop knot rather than drawing the tippet tight against the eye, like you would with a clinch knot. I prefer the clinch knot fishing for trout in the West. But a loop knot gives the fly more natural movement. At least according to its advocates."

When we reached the hole, I continued beyond it twenty-some yards and dropped anchor.

"Let's sit a bit and let the fish resettle in the hole we passed. Then we'll cast about 45-50 feet. After a half dozen casts, I'll haul the anchor, leave the engine off, and drift with the incoming tide a few yards. Doing so repeatedly, we'll be at the hole after about five drifts. That's where we're most likely to find fish."

As Grace moved to the stern to cast, I stayed by the helm, keeping low to avoid her back casts. She was careful to use roll or sidearm casts to avoid hitting me with the fly.

She turned her head as she stripped in line and asked, "We were talking about Elsbeth and her liking Montana. Does she?" She was shifting the conversation from the techniques of fishing to Elsbeth and our family history.

"I think so, considering she. . . ." I caught myself about to say Elsbeth had spent a total of only a few months in Montana. I knew—if I said as much—Grace would ask where she had been the previous years. I don't want to discuss that.

"You were saying," she asked.

"I was distracted by some movement on the surface off the stern to the left. Near the bank where that three- to four-foot clump of grass is disappearing under the tide. Try casting a foot this side of the grass."

She did, with an easy motion, using a Spey cast adapted to a one-hand rod. It's a good way to change direction, and it immediately confirmed she is a fine caster. With no further suggestions on my part, she set the fly down about three feet to the right of the spot I mentioned and then cast-by-cast worked her way across the channel. On her last cast just off the right bank, something pulled hard on the Clouser and quickly exploded through the surface film in the first of several attempts of desperation to rid itself of the foreign object tugging at its mouth. It surfaced once more and abruptly decided the bottom was a safer place to hide. It was not to be; Grace never allowed the line to slacken so the barbless hook could be shaken out and never kept it so tight as to break the line.

The fight was over in three to four minutes. A spotted sea trout lay curled deeply in my boat net, breathing heavily with nowhere to go in a foreign world.

Not admitted to the trout family, the spotted sea trout is related to the salt water drum, which neither tastes nor looks as good. I grew up in New England calling the trout a weakfish, which is actually a close relation. It's also called a speckled trout.

Grace turned, smiled, easily withdrew the barbless hook, lifted the fish from the net, and flipped it over the side where it lay still on its back. I winced at her tossing the fish; survival after an exhausting attempt to break free is more likely if the fish is held under water until it regains strength and won't do what Grace's trout did, float away on the tide bottom side up. While we watched, unsure it would roll over and swim off, I didn't say a word. Finally, it turned over slowly and disappeared.

We moved the boat ahead in the channel three times to new water. But with no more takes, we moved again where I wanted us to be, about forty feet from the hole.

"Grace, your long casts here should be beyond and over the middle of the hole. The two oyster banks on each side slope down into the channel. Imagine a line between the banks. I'd go right to the middle twenty feet beyond and let the Clouser sink—it should be about six feet deep there now. Then bring it back in with short strips. Don't let it hit the sides of the channel—too many oysters."

This time there was no waiting. Grace was patient to perfection. When she gave a short tug as soon as she sensed the fly was near the bottom of the hole, something pulled. She set the hook, and the fish immediately tried to run with the first minutes of the outgoing tide. It barely missed tangling in my anchor line. Grace had moved to the bow, keeping the rod bent, and screamed something in glee I couldn't comprehend. My worry was oyster banks, which are unkind to fly line tippets. But she kept the fish in the channel's center, and I pulled the anchor, started the engine, pointed the bow with the ebbing tide, and moved barely fast enough to hold in the channel, letting her crank in line until the fish was twenty feet off our bow. I shut down the engine and tilted it so the prop was above water.

"That's a good fish, Grace. It's a red with its signature random spot. You're playing it great. I've got the net."

Two minutes later I scooped up a thirty-four-inch redfish that dwarfed the boat net. Not a keeper, beyond the slot limits of 18 to 27 inches.

"Take a photo, Macduff; it's my best red for several years, even better when I consider I've been using bigger tippets than this one. Mine have been ten-pound breaking weight. The one you gave me is half that and much less visible to the fish. This red must weigh fifteen pounds. We have to let it go."

"I don't often keep one," I added. "Only when I want one for dinner. The more we throw back today, the more will be here tomorrow. Especially if they're females."

"Do you object to throwing out *all* females?" she asked.

"Nope, just the ones that are fish."

After a short rest, a sandwich, and a beer for each of us, she said, "We've been here two hours. I've made something over a hundred casts. You haven't made one. Your turn."

"I like watching people enjoy their fishing. You obviously do."

"At least toss your Clouser in that hole. Let's see if the added chartreuse helps. But I can't imagine your fly doing any better than mine."

We were on the beginning of an increasingly fast ebbing tide. I stepped up onto the bow deck and, with a couple of false casts, dropped the fly onto an oyster bed. A couple of tugs loosened it. When I tried again, I was too anxious, dropped my rod tip, and placed the fly at best fifteen feet in front of the boat and the same distance short of the hole.

As I prepared to back cast again, she said, "Let me show you something that should help. You're starting with a good back cast, but you bring the rod forward too soon, and then to add to your problems, you drop the rod tip. You'll snap off the fly at the worst, make a wind knot at the least."

I've often gone against my own advice when working with beginners, who usually drop the rod tip on the back cast and start the rod forward too soon. I try to get them to take the rod back only to two o'clock at the most, stop the rod quickly, and wait a moment before starting with the forward cast. I tell them it's not cheating to turn your head and look at your back cast.

Grace is right. If I start the rod forward too soon and the line hasn't yet straightened out in back, the line and fly heading forward may contact the last of the line still heading back. The result is a knot deftly tied solely by the wind. Appropriately called a wind knot. Another problem, as she mentioned, is just like snapping a whip. The tippet may break and send the detached fly dozens of feet into the marsh grass.

Before I could say anything, she was standing behind me, without her fly rod. She turned me more directly forward than sideways, stood close enough behind me that I had sensory proof she was amply endowed, and wrapped each arm around me to "adjust" my rod.

I never made another decent cast the entire time we remained. But I received a lot of "hands-on" help.

"You smell delicious," she commented after several casts. I can't pinpoint it. Pine?"

"Sage soap and sage shampoo," I answered. "Courtesy of Wyoming."

When the tide had been running out for an hour, I said, "If we don't get back within thirty minutes, this outgoing tide can leave us short of the dock with nearly a four- to five-hour-wait before we can float again. We can both get out and drag the boat back, but that's not part of a good day on the water. Or we can sit high and dry in the afternoon sun. Both are agony. I know. I've been stranded here once and promised myself never again. I didn't admit the stranding had been *very* recently."

We made it back to the dock with little to spare; I had to tilt the engine up a fraction below the point where the water intake would suck in only air. That's unkind treatment of a water-cooled engine.

As we walked toward the cottage, I looked at her and asked, "Drink on the porch?"

"I was waiting for the offer," she replied, with a smile that affirmed I hadn't needed to ask.

"It's a small cottage with a big bar. What's yours?"

"Anything with bourbon, Scotch, or whiskey. I like the dusky drinks."

"I'm having Gentleman Jack," I said. "Short glass. Over ice. Splash of soda."

"The same," she replied. "But a tall glass. No ice. No soda. Double bourbon." I remembered that she had downed three Coors while I sipped one."

I made the drinks, filled a small silver dish with bleached almonds amid tiny cut pieces of rosemary, and we settled in rocking chairs on the porch. It was approaching four. I had an hour before Wuff would be announcing her interest in being served her evening meal—promptly at five.

"Macduff, why were you so nervous fishing?" she asked. "It was obvious you can do it. You finally settled into a rhythm casting beautifully."

"Only after you gave me the lesson. I'm a slow learner. I like hands-on instruction."

"I've got a lot of other things to teach you."

"I could use some work on the double haul."

"I wasn't thinking about casting," she added.

At five, I left her sitting for a few minutes while I fixed turkey, salmon, and duck with a little omega oil. It wasn't a dip for us; it's what Wuff expects for dinner as long as it's topped off with a large spoonful of chilled applesauce.

I refilled our drinks, and as I set her drink in front of her on a small table, the last of the December sun slanted through the pines, spreading ochre shadows across the porch from the final light of day.

"This is a special place, Macduff. Do you sit here often?"

"Every day when I'm living here. I'll miss it."

"Miss it! Why?"

"I'm thinking of selling and moving to Gainesville."

"That's strange. You're a water person."

"I have been. Maybe it's time for a change."

"Let me show you a different water view. My condo at Camachee Cove is on the third floor, overlooking the yacht basin. A couple of condos are for sale. There's a lot of activity with boats on their way in and out. . . . I have a suggestion: Let's go and have a last drink on my porch. The night lights in the harbor are beautiful."

"Dinner first at Kingfish Grill?" I thought some food would be wise before we started on more drinks.

"Sounds like a perfect ending to the day," she exclaimed.

"I like the idea, but I don't have my car. Elsbeth took it."

"I have mine. I'll bring you back."

"OK."

Her condo was as she described, but she didn't mention she collected Indian art, mainly miniature paintings she's acquired online from London auctions. The paintings were mostly egg tempera done in the 18th century, several of Lord Krishna and Radha. There must have been twenty in a group on one wall. The condo's single bathroom had more miniatures, *all* of them erotic. Some very erotic.

Grace made the drinks this time. Mine tasted a little stronger than when I poured the first two at the cottage. We sat close on a two-seat outdoor wicker sofa. I could feel her warmth, and the drinks made her increasingly alluring. Hundreds of tiny lights flickered in the marina, sending vivid colors across us, like prisms of jewels.

When we'd drained the bourbon bottle, it was apparent to me she was in no condition to drive me home and return by herself. She's the assistant state attorney for the area, and she doesn't need a DUI charge.

"I don't think you should drive," I said. "I know I shouldn't. Can I crash on your couch? I'll buy you breakfast in St. Augustine on the way back to my place."

"Thanks," she mumbled, the drinks taking their toll on any bedtime explorations. "I know I shouldn't drive anymore, Macduff. I probably shouldn't have driven here. I'll get you some sheets and a blanket."

She went into her bedroom and hadn't come back in five minutes. I looked in. She was sprawled across her bed fast asleep; the sheets and blanket she was getting for me were on the floor. I took them and went back to the living room couch. The sheets never made it to the couch; I was so gone I managed only to get my shoes off and pull the blanket over part of me. The last thing I remembered in the morning was watching strands of light from the yacht basin discharge fluttering shadows across the condo's ceiling.

I wasn't sure whether the lights actually were fluttering or my brain was functioning like a kaleidoscope.

36

Recently released findings show that families with emotional problems such as depression rose from 24 percent before the ban to 44 percent afterward. It found more marriages were strained as men coped with losing their traditional roles as breadwinners.

Orlando Sentinel, May 15, 2000.

THE FOLLOWING NOON AT THE COTTAGE

GRACE DROPPED ME OFF at my cottage at the same time Elsbeth returned with my car. I didn't know where Elsbeth had spent the night—I wouldn't ask. She didn't know where I had spent the night—I hoped she wouldn't ask. Over the next few hours, she gave me some looks-could-kill glances. Things weren't going well, especially with Christmas coming in three days. Finally she spoke her piece.

"Dad, where were you last night?"

"I don't think you should ask. I didn't ask the same about you."

"I'm not engaged. You are."

"I received the ring back in the mail. I'm not engaged."

"But you're in love with Lucinda."

"And with your mother, El."

"She's been dead for nearly twenty years. You have a new life, with a special woman. And now you're being unfaithful."

"Unfaithful? Faithfulness presumes a relationship. That's over."

"It's not!"

"Lucinda seems to disagree."

After a few minutes of silence, she said, "Dad, I won't be here for New Year's."

"Going to Sue's in Jackson Hole?"

"No."

"Back to Maine early?"

"In a way, I'm stopping in New York for a few days."

"Joining friends gathering at Times Square to watch the clock bring in the New Year?"

"I may see it, but I won't be with school chums."

"Do you have a place to stay?"

"Yes, a great apartment on 67th Street."

"You know that's the street where Lucinda has an apartment."

"I know."

"Will you try to see her?"

"I'm staying with her."

"You invited yourself? Was that a good idea?"

"I didn't invite myself. Lucinda called me yesterday from London and invited me. I don't know Manhattan. She wants to show me. She's getting some tickets for Broadway shows."

"Oh! . . . Well . . . that's nice."

"Anything you want me to say to her?"

"No. It wouldn't do any good."

"Why not? You love her. She loves you."

"That message hasn't reached me."

"It's your fault. Maybe you should put her ahead of Dan Wilson."

"Let's not go into that again."

"Sorry to press you. Will you be OK here alone?"

"I won't be here."

"With *that* woman who dropped you off?"

"No. I haven't been in Cedar Key on the Gulf Coast since El was alive. I have good memories of our evenings there."

"What's the attraction in Cedar Key?"

"I want to visit some of the coastal towns from Cedar Key north. They're mostly old fishing villages. They've all undergone periodic declines. The fishing families are dying out, and many are moving inland because they can't afford the property taxes anymore and they have opportunities to sell their houses to outsiders. Enough money to buy a doublewide somewhere away from the water and have a modest nest egg left."

"Dad, I read an article in one paper—I don't remember which one—about some of those towns. One is Oyster Bay. It's a few miles north of Cedar Key, accessible only from a road out of Cedar Key. You might like to make that one of your stops."

"I will."

Christmas was a struggle. Elsbeth and I were alone. She was visibly concerned about leaving me, not because she'd miss whatever we might do together, but because she was afraid of what I might do to myself. She knew one thing I wouldn't do—eat decent meals. Or eat at all. She didn't raise this issue because she didn't want to provoke an argument.

The day after Christmas, while I was working on the dock, Elsbeth answered my cell phone I had left on the kitchen counter.

"Macduff, this is Dan Wilson."

Elsbeth knew the voice. "This isn't Macduff, Mr. Wilson. It's Elsbeth. Dad's down at the dock, rigging some lights for night fishing. I can go get him."

"Don't bother him. I just wanted to say Merry Christmas—a day late. Give him my regards and tell him I'll see him here in D.C. in two weeks."

"I'll tell him," Elsbeth said glumly, knowing what Dan was talking about, but not wanting to raise an issue with her dad that to her was not negotiable.

Two days before New Year's, I drove Elsbeth to the Jacksonville airport for her flight to New York. After her plane lifted off and disappeared into a cloud bank, I rode the escalator down to the baggage level and sat on the bench where Lucinda and I last saw each other almost three months ago, when she'd met me on my return from Maine. But after an unpleasant half-hour, she abruptly flew back to Manhattan.

My life was puzzle pieces that had come apart and scattered. There was no reason now for me not to work with Dan on the Isfahani matter. Elsbeth had her life under control. I had no one to come home to. Lucinda seemed to be adjusting quickly to her former role of a successful, handsomely compensated, and much-in-demand Manhattanite.

It was time I turned my full attention to Isfahani, after a short break relaxing on the Gulf Coast. I decided to stay at the old Island Hotel in Cedar Key and the following day head north along the coast.

My first stop would be as Elsbeth suggested—to see Oyster Bay.

37

OYSTER BAY THE FIRST WEEK OF THE NEW YEAR

NEW YEAR'S EVE PASSED unevenly for me in Cedar Key. After a delightful seafood meal and solo walk through town came a lonely, sleepless night.

I checked out on New Year's Day to start my first visit among the fishing towns to the north—Oyster Bay—wearing old worn jeans that were a size too large and looked to have come from Goodwill, a stained shirt with a frayed collar, and an aging pair of shoes with laces knotted from multiple breaks. I might not blend in with the locals, but I wouldn't stand out. I hadn't shaved in a week, and my green John Deere hat looked like it had been run over by a harvester.

Compared to Cedar Key, Oyster Bay is a town of enigmas. Years ago several public accesses opened to the bay, but when the town was nearly bankrupt, it sold most public waterfront land to outsiders who quickly installed fences to protect their privacy facing the bay. I sat on the edge of the lone public bench, worn and rotting and soon to collapse under the weight of an unsuspecting sitter.

Around the bay sat twenty-seven houses with little space between. Fifteen obviously had been rejuvenated recently, assuming they had once looked like the other dozen aged houses that seemed to be waiting for a purchase offer from an outsider.

Children were playing in yards, and two women were talking over a fence dividing their backyards. Many homes had an old pickup parked alongside, and one had a rusty RV missing all four wheels and sitting on cement blocks. The common color of these twelve homes was a variation of faded and chipped white; the cedar siding showed through along the edges where Gulf winds had frayed the wood.

The most significant contrast with the resurrected houses was that the latter showed no signs of habitation. Apparently their owners had drawn shades and returned to inland homes to resume daily schedules as lawyers, doctors, and assorted business owners.

These "outsiders'" houses had new roofs, new paint—though they remained white—and lawns that would make a golf course supervisor proud. Fertilizer residue was quickly flushed into the bay and on each outgoing tide challenged the remaining sea life. Not one of the outsiders' homes had a pickup truck or rusting auto in the yard. Most had been planted with bushes and trees, including some young cedars reminiscent of the town's past.

The panorama of the bay reinforced my sense of the considerable economic disparity between the outsiders and the locals. The outsiders had money; the locals did not. The outsiders had employment; the locals did not—at least in the commercial fishing industry that had once paid for decent schools, assured police and fire services, and instilled pride among the residents.

After sitting for nearly two hours, someone—I assumed either a local resident or homeless—sat down on the opposite end of the bench. Long, scraggly hair and unkempt, frayed edge clothes. But the homeless would not stop in Oyster Bay. Most of the diminishing number of long-time home owning residents live not far from the edge.

"You from outside?" the person asked, without turning to look at me.

"From a little farm in North Dakota," I offered, preferring my choice of homes to be one where the Florida gill net ban would not be something I would know about.

"That's a long way."

"It's a good place to get out of in the winter."

"How'd you git *here*?"

"Wrong turn out of Cedar Key."

"Not much here . . . because of the damn net ban."

"Net ban?" I asked.

"Gill nets. State banned 'em back in '94. Had a public vote. Ban killed the town. One time there was fishin' families in all the houses you see 'round the bay from here."

"Why the ban?"

"Pushed by stinkin' recreational fishermen who wanted all the fish for themselves. Pose as 'conservationists'. . . . Ain't that a hoot? They don't know what conservation means."

"Why did the legislature pass the ban?"

"Weren't the legislature. We had them in our pockets for years. We gave lobbyists a lotta money to keep it that way. . . . It were the people that changed the law. Called a referendum. Voted on all over the state, even inland. Makes no sense. We been here for generations. Families here got rights."

"Anything you can do about it?"

"Yep. Already been done. Maybe now the ban will be done 'way with."

"What's already been done?"

"You don't need to know, young feller. We take care of our own here."

I wondered what "already been done" meant. I suspected this resident—unlike most other Oyster Bay locals—was closer to advocating irrational action. A strong smell of whisky enveloped the bench, encouraging a loose tongue.

"Now that you mention it, I think I read in a paper as I came through Tallahassee that there was new trouble in Florida about ignoring the ban and using gill nets to fish again. And that somebody was killed wrapped in a net."

"Three people kilt. Two here and one out West. Hey! It were Montana. That ain't far from Dakota. Know about the Montana killin'?"

"No, Montana and the Dakotas are big. We get mostly local news where I live—near the border with Canada. . . . Tell me about the deaths in Florida."

"First one down south in the Clewsahatchee. Fishin' guide. Got what he deserved. Ended up wrapped in a gill net hung up on a channel marker. He were a damn fly fisherman."

"They fly fish around here?" I asked.

"Hell, no. Ain't part of our culture. Pussyfootin' 'round with those fancy rods from that stupid movie 'bout a river runnin' through something. With that bleached blond Pitts in it."

"You mean Brad Pitt?"

"That's the feller. . . . Usin' a bunch of feathers on a tiny hook! We do real fishin' here. *Bait* fishin'! Fishin' ain't a sport. It's a job. The way we feed our families."

"What about the other death in Florida? Like the first one?"

"Yeah. Another pussyfooter. Don't know much about him. I weren't involved wit . . . I mean I don't know much about the second one. From the other side of Florida. Some kinda newspaper guy. Can't trust 'em. He weren't a Florida guide. But he talked and wrote 'bout makin' the net ban easier to enforce and even havin' it cover all kinds a nets. We ain't got much left to fish with. They ain't takin' the gill nets we got left in our garages. Over my dead body. Gotta take me first."

"What kind of nets are you using now? Cast nets?"

"Nope. Still usin' gill nets. We ain't exactly in the line of fire over here. Don't get a fish warden around here at all. They don't like us. Ain't safe here for the police. . . . I better go, young feller. Got chores at home."

"Let me ask one last question about this ban." The resident had been sipping from a bottle that was returned carefully to a pocket after each swallow. "You said the people here have taken care of their own. Can other towns do the same?"

"Nope, ain't likely. We got saved by a hurricane."

"Hurricanes usually don't *save* people."

"Don't know why not. This one did. I'll tell you a little that's not to be passed on. . . . When the fight over passin' a ban started, four fishermen from here got together and started burnin' recreational fishermen's boats. Trashed their cars and, if they had flats boats in their yards, trashed their houses. Burnt down two of them. Then one day a guide who had lost his boat, car, and house, was found stuffed under a pier wrapped in a gill net. He'd been speaking out favorin' the ban."

"Was anybody tried for his murder?"

"They was goin' to be. But just before the trial, a hurricane come through and wiped out the public offices, includin' all the records and stuff for the trial. The matter got dropped. One of those four local fishermen was my daddy, rest his soul in peace. He died two years ago from cancer."

The resident sat there quiet, not uttering another word. I could see a lower lip trembling. Then the person got up and began to walk away.

"Well, it was nice to talk a bit," I offered, overwhelmed by the comments. What did 'already been done' mean? "I hope you folks come out of all this alright," I called out, watching the resident shuffle off.

"Hear, hear" was all I heard.

38

Some former commercial fishermen . . . have gotten into the guide business. For about $250 a day [a guide] takes sport fishermen into the river's hidden nooks. 'There's a lot of them that don't like the sport fishermen [said one guide], they blame them with what happened, and they say they're not going to take them out there and show them anything.'

Orlando Sentinel, May 15, 2000.

THE FOLLOWING TWO DAYS

THE REMAINDER OF THE DAY and the following two added nothing to what I learned from my conversation with the single resident of Oyster Bay: that there were strong negative feelings about the net ban along the Gulf Coast of Florida from Cedar Key north around the bend.

While numerous multi-generation commercial fishing families were desperate and living on food stamps and other aid, the northern communities, such as Steinhatchee, looked more like Cedar Key than Oyster Bay. New restaurants on pilings along the water's edge, condos nearly dangling over the rivers and beaches, old houses restored with some converted to B&B's, and new marinas dotted the landscape with the smell of money. The boats at the marinas were not twenty footers loaded with nets, but $40,000 flats boats, $100,000 offshore deep-sea fishing boats, and personal water craft that outnumber the mosquitos but are more irritable.

My drive back to St. Augustine seemed shortened by my inattention to the road while I struggled to reconstruct the conversation I had at Oyster Bay. When I arrived at my cottage, I called Grace Justice at her office.

"Hope you had a good New Year's holiday."

"It would have been better if you'd called. I spent New Year's Eve alone at my condo."

"I needed time with my daughter. When she left, I went to Cedar Key." I didn't add that Elsbeth celebrated the annual event in Manhattan—that might lead to more questions and give Grace unfulfilled ideas. I'm not in the market for a long-term commitment.

"Doesn't Elsbeth date?"

"Oh, yes. But at school in Maine. She went back the day after New Year's," I added—truthfully but deceptively. I didn't include "from Manhattan, not from here."

I need to remain friends with Grace. She's rumored to be the next State Attorney. That means being selected from among eighty assistant state attorneys throughout Florida. Considering my encounter with Turk Jensen and my inability to find anyone in this county's administration who makes sense, Grace may be the only person in government likely to help keep me out of trouble. But apparently that's going to come at a price.

"Why don't we get together after work. You free?" I asked.

She jumped at the chance. "Pick me up at my condo at seven. I'll take you to one of my favorite places. It's beautiful for a warm January evening. We can be outside for dinner. One condition. I drank too much the last time. Keep me honest."

"We can discuss that at dinner."

We parked by the Plaza, and she walked me to the A1A Ale Works, where she chose a table on the second floor balcony overlooking hundreds of thousands of tiny white lights decorating the city. Pushing both ends of the Christmas holiday, they're turned on soon after Halloween and remain on until the end of January.

I sipped one Gentleman Jack. Grace had one Old Fashion. We dined sharing a house specialty—Grilled Seafood Paella.

"Grace," I started after we were finished, "I need to tell you about a couple of days I spent on the Gulf Coast. I thought that sometime you and I might trailer my flats boat to one of the small coastal towns to fish. We'd see a different part of Florida."

"Name the date."

"It will have to be the end of February."

"You tied up that long?" she asked.

"I'll be away."

"Fishing the Keys?"

"Don't I wish! Casting crab pattern flies to tarpon alongside the Seven Mile Bridge. . . . No. I'll be in D.C."

"I wouldn't wish that on anyone. Politicians are not exactly my role models."

"Better to blame the lobbyists. They're the ones who have destroyed Jeffersonian democracy. . . . I'll be with people I've worked with at the State Department."

"What does a fishing guide do at the State Department?" she asked, adding, "I don't know much about you, Macduff, other than you live here for most of the winter and in Montana the rest of the year. Plus you have a daughter at the University of Maine. And you *had* a companion. Who are you?"

That's a question I don't welcome. One that brings on a defensive façade. I've become adept at avoiding going deeply into the matter. But this time it's with someone I've quickly become attracted to.

"Nothing unusual about me," I answered. "Grew up and schooled in New England, including college. Visited Florida once in college. Thought it would be an attractive place to live—*in the winter.* At about the same time, I went fishing out West, loved Paradise Valley just north of Yellowstone Park, and decided Montana would be a nice place to live—*in the summer.* I wondered how I might make a living and spend summers in Montana and winters here."

"Why here? Why not further south in Florida where the fishing's better? Miami? Or maybe the Keys."

"Too crowded. Miami's an asylum without walls."

"Guiding's a tough way to make a living. It hardly supports living in this cottage or your Montana cabin."

It was an open-ended question. I wanted to close it.

"I had a modest inheritance; then my only sibling died without leaving any descendants, and I inherited his estate. I intended to live comfortably for a few more decades and spend my last dollar on my last meal. But I have Elsbeth to think of," I added, not mentioning that I've only known about my daughter for less than one of her eighteen years.

"Grace, enough about my boring history. I want to tell you about a conversation I had with a resident of Oyster Bay."

I did the best I could to recreate sitting with the resident in Oyster Bay. Notes I made in the evening during my brief trip helped; I had written close to the exact words we exchanged. I held off telling Grace the last comments the resident made about the gill net deaths.

"What's your concern?" she asked calmly.

I was surprised she didn't react as I had, even without knowing more.

"You told me not long ago that nothing significant had developed with the two murders in Florida. Doesn't my conversation raise any suspicion?"

"Not really. Some cranky old-timer frustrated with life, combined with a little drink and a little bravado. That doesn't mean murder. Are you possibly suggesting that this person or a group of commercial fishermen in that dumpy little town conspired and committed murder because of the gill net ban? How old was this resident?"

"Probably mid-sixties. . . . Now let me tell you the last thing said when I asked if the residents of Oyster Bay could do anything about the net ban—'It's already been done.'"

"Now I am concerned," Grace said looking down and holding her chin with one hand like Rodin's *Thinker*. "But there's a problem. You said the records were lost in the 90's. I know the town no longer has a police department. Governance was shifted to Cedar Key. It sends a sheriff's car through Oyster Bay only on call. Those two towns have gone in opposite directions since the ban, though Cedar Key was also hit hard. But people worked to make it better. Not so in Oyster Bay. . . . What you heard could have been the ranting of a disgruntled old codger."

"Maybe. I thought I should run it by you. Let's forget I ever raised it."

"No. I'm glad you did."

Afterwards, we walked along St. George Street to the Café de Hidalgo, a Spanish named store that sells the best Italian gelato in town. Grace had *cannoli,* and I ordered *tiramisu.* She moved against me and slipped her arm into mine as we walked back to the car.

At her condo, when she unlocked and opened the door, I assumed she was inviting me in. But she turned in the doorway shaking her head and said, "I have a very difficult day tomorrow." I stepped back as the door was closed.

On my drive home, I recalled the last time I had eaten at the A1A Ale Works. It was several years ago, with Lucinda, also with the holiday lights sparkling. Also on the balcony. We had been seated for fifteen minutes when an old Gainesville neighbor, whom I knew when I was Professor Maxwell Hunt, sat down with friends at the table behind Lucinda. I slipped on sunglasses and did my best to avoid the woman's attention. Lucinda was not pleased. As Grace had started to do this evening, Lucinda had begun to prod me with question after question about my background. Sometimes it doesn't seem worth all the trouble to maintain my life as Macduff Brooks. I could have continued as Professor Maxwell Hunt at UF; there was no certainty Juan Pablo Herzog or Abdul Khaliq Isfahani would come after me.

But there was no assurance they wouldn't.

39

LATE THE FOLLOWING WEEK OUTSIDE WASHINGTON, D.C., AT A CLOSELY GUARDED MILITARY FACILITY

DURING THE PAST FIVE DAYS, I've worked on becoming reacquainted with my CheyTac sniper rifle. It's a formidable weapon, more a complex assassination system than a mere rifle. It includes a tactical ballistic computer with a linked laser rangefinder, plus a telescopic sight and muzzle break and suppressor. The .408 or .375 caliber rounds can travel up to 2,500 yards. That's 7,500 feet or nearly a mile and a half.

I've used the rifle twice. One cartridge each time. First was during the time between El's death and my entering the CIA protection program. I was increasingly reckless during those years, doing the bidding of the Agency without question.

That first shooting, about which I've told Lucinda nothing, was in Khartoum. I took a single shot from nearly a half mile that killed the leader of a ruthless Islamic terrorist group who had made two attempts on the U.S. ambassador's life. I couldn't identify the target from that distance; I was guided by a member of our Khartoum CIA mission who pointed out the person as he spoke at a rally on the same steps where, in 1884, British General Charles George Gordon was killed. He had been sent to the Sudan to evacuate the British garrisons that were under constant attack by Mahdist rebels who claimed dominion over the entire Islamic world.

My shot, taken as Professor Maxwell Hunt acting under an assumed name, came a century later. It was accurate, entering the target's head between his bushy black eyebrows. The Islamists went into frenzy, slaughtering anyone who didn't look Arabic. The day before the killing, the U.S. had airlifted the last Americans from the country. Along with a few remaining embassy personnel, I left in an unmarked CIA chartered jet within an hour of the shooting. The U.S. and Sudan didn't renew relations for months.

I started target shooting at ten, won the U.S. national junior rifle competition at fifteen, and had the best scores for rifle as an ROTC student in college. After college and naval service, I missed the shooting competitions and so I joined a local gun club. Happenstance brought me to the CIA; a former shooting competitor who had never quite been able to outscore me had joined the CIA, but was in too public a position to use his shooting skills in Agency sanctions. He got in touch with me while I was teaching at the law college at UF. In a state of depression after El's death, I was easily convinced to "do my patriotic duty." That's how I ended up in Khartoum with a Chey-Tac provided by the CIA. The Agency let me keep it as a reward for my deadly shot.

Three years after being relocated to Montana as Macduff Brooks, I was coerced into killing Abdul Khaliq Isfahani by unspoken indications that, if I refused, my protected status could end. Along with Juan Pablo Herzog, Isfahani was trying to learn my new name and location so they might pay me a final visit. I decided I would get to Isfahani first and agreed to kill him when the CIA convinced me he was a major participant in a planned attack on Manhattan, which would kill countless people by destroying two icons of American architecture: the Empire State Building and the Chrysler Building. My new lady friend Lucinda Lang had an office high in the latter.

Regrettably, my shooting succeeded only in disfiguring the face of Isfahani enough to make him all the more determined to kill all Americans. If possible, starting with me. Not killing Isfahani has troubled me ever since. It's a part of the reason I've been listening to Dan Wilson explain the Agency's current interest in giving me another try. But I'm more convinced because Isfahani is allegedly the leader of a terrorist attack that is intended to decimate Washington, D.C.—all the people if not all the buildings. I've asked Dan to give me more details this afternoon.

He's promised to tell me after a final session on the firing range.

40

THE SAME PLACE AND SAME DAY IN THE AFTERNOON

D AN DROVE OUT TO THE BASE FROM D.C., and we
met under a pergola in the garden of the base command-
er. It was the only part of the small facility that did not smell of
gunpowder. Being outside, we were reasonably certain no one
would hear us. But we checked the structure for bugs other
than those feeding on the green leaves of the wisteria. We were
a depressing sight, two middle-aged men wrapped in overcoats,
gloves, scarves, and hats. I came wearing a pair of my cold
weather knitted fishing gloves, which lacked covering for the
fingers so the wearer could tie on flies. I wore the gloves in-
tending to take notes in the cold, but Dan made it clear at the
beginning that "*any* note taking was not advisable," which was
Agency-speak for "not allowed under any circumstances."

"Mac," Dan began, his breath turning into a white fog that
quickly dissipated, "where would *you* like to begin? I'll fill in
after I've answered your questions."

"Let's talk about Isfahani's plans. I don't want the job if
he's not a serious threat to the U.S."

"Does your definition of a 'serious threat' include the death of everyone in D.C., meaning 630,000 residents, plus who knows how many tourists, including school children from all over the U.S. who swarm into the city each year like bees to a hive. There will be hell to pay if every state in the country loses hundreds of their children."

"A little melodramatic?"

"Not a bit."

"How's one terrorist going to pull this off?"

"He has help, but he calls the shots."

"How's he going to kill that many?"

"Depends on his methods."

"You don't mean nuclear weapons?"

"We don't think so. He may have access to those weapons but not a reliable delivery system. We believe it will be chemical or biological. Or both."

"How's he getting them?"

"First, the biological. Germs disseminate from where they're released. If that's in D.C., it could mean widespread infection before it could be brought under control. Meaning, at worst, it would spread globally. People carry infectious diseases across state lines and across national borders. There could be outbreaks anywhere."

"Even in Isfahani's Sudan?"

"Yes. We don't think that would bother him. He could become infected, which wouldn't deter him since he views this as a religious suicide mission."

"How would he release biological weapons?"

"Carefully. Remember that they're living organisms. But there's uncertainty using them. They take days to become effective. That helps them spread beyond the target. That means out of control.

"Chemical and nuclear weapons are effective immediately. But they're different. Nuclear weapons leave radiological residue for years. Hiroshima occurred nearly seventy years ago. The city may be safe now, but cleaning up has been measured in decades rather than weeks. Chemical weapons are primarily limited to the area where they're introduced. The dosage can be controlled. When the chemicals spread, like in a water supply, they're diluted. They can be controlled more so than biological weapons."

"Who has these weapons? Can their ingredients be bought?" I asked.

"Many are easy to make. Anthrax is an example. *Bacillus anthracis* forms spores. They can be dispersed in aerosols. The aerosol particles must be a certain size—too big and they don't reach the lower respiratory tract; too small and they're exhaled back into the atmosphere. Using it at specific locations, such as in the Senate and the House, within various department agencies, and on military bases, could bring the country to a halt. But we don't think that would be the way chemical agents would be used. We think the targets would be schools, hospitals, and crowds, such as those at sporting or musical events or popular beaches. But anthrax isn't the only chemical agent that might be used."

"Is ricin a possible toxin to use?"

"Probably not. Ricin has to be inhaled, ingested, or injected. Remember in 1978 when Bulgarian dissident Georgi Markov was injected in London by means of an umbrella tip? He died an agonizing death.

"Unfortunately, ricin comes from the castor bean plant which grows naturally in some states. It may be the most poisonous nature-based toxin. No treatment exists for the general public. Castor beans are used to produce castor oil. The waste material—a kind of mash—has about five percent ricin content. If ricin is ingested, it enters cells and prevents them from producing proteins. No protein and the cells die.

"Ricin could be made and stockpiled easily. But it has to be delivered. That could be done, but we don't see it as a weapon of *mass* destruction. Like the London attack on Markov, usually its use is for specific individuals. But it could terrorize a community and disrupt the economy if many people were separately targeted, and no one knew who might be next. Creating widespread fear by random deaths might be more effective than widespread killing."

"Dan, aren't there international agreements covering chemical and biological weapons?"

"There are two: the 1972 Biological Weapons Convention and the 1993 Chemical Weapons Convention. Most nations around the globe have signed or ratified both. But, for example, Syria and South Sudan have done nothing with the chemical convention. Syria has signed but not ratified the biological convention. Israel hasn't moved fully on either. But terrorists like Isfahani do their dirty work in several countries. Sudan may be where he is now, but he may be planning and making weapons elsewhere. You can't punish the Sudan for something Isfahani does unknown by the government."

"Isfahani can't do this by himself. Do we know anything about who's assisting him?"

"Yes. There's a lady who was educated in London and has been linked to numerous biological weapons activities. Her name is Dr. Lydia Hussein—she's better known as 'Dr. Germ.' She was a major player in Saddam Hussein's biological weapons, helping to design anthrax and *botulinum* weapons. We lost track of her for several years. But now we know where she is. Khartoum!"

"Working with Isfahani?"

"With his terrorist group."

"Is she dangerous?"

"Extremely. She's believed to have been responsible for the recent death of three British UN weapons inspectors working in Iraq."

"This is all a bit perplexing. You don't know what kind of weapon will be used. You don't know what kind of delivery system will be used. And you haven't named anybody other than Isfahani and Dr. Germ."

"It's the way things work these days. Are you in?"

"Do I have a choice?"

"Not really."

"When do I leave?"

"Tomorrow."

41

ARRIVAL AT KHARTOUM IN THE SUDAN
TWO DAYS LATER

DAN WASN'T KIDDING. I returned to my room, and twenty minutes later a young man knocked on my door. He was tall and gaunt and carried an expression of complete disdain for his "being here" and what he had come to do to me. That was hardly a positive bedside manner. I barely had time to ask him who he was when he brushed by me, pushing a gray metal cart with a tray that held assorted vials and syringes.

"You're James Smith?" he asked, looking at a chart on his tray. Not waiting for an answer, suggesting he didn't care who I was, he ordered, "Roll up your sleeves—both arms," took the cap off the first vial, filled the syringe, and held it up to the light to assure that liquid rather than air would flow into me, and jabbed it deep into my upper right arm.

"I know you're not really James Smith," he finally explained. "We get mostly Smiths and Joneses through here. With all the shots you're getting, I assume you're headed for some tropical, third-world basket case. Don't tell me which one. I'm not supposed to know, and I don't much give a damn. . . . I've got six more shots for you." He was finished in another three minutes.

I estimated it was about thirty minutes later when another knock came, but I wasn't sure because both my arms hurt and I was a little dizzy. This time it wasn't a medic because he wasn't wearing blue scrubs. He carried a briefcase of old leather. As befitted an Agency employee, he wore the trademark dark rumpled suit—always a variation of black—mostly covering a wrinkled white shirt and an out-of-fashion narrow tri-color tie. His shoes needed shining, if not replacement.

"I'm Alex Jones," he offered. "Dan Wilson sent me with some papers you'll need. Plus some foreign currency, several passports, and some sales literature for Smith & Wesson. You'll travel in the Sudan as Curtis Wainwright, a Canadian citizen. Can we sit and go through them? . . .

"Let's start with your itinerary for getting you to Khartoum. You'll leave here by a U.S. government jet from Bolling Air Force Base . . . tomorrow at 10 a.m. You're going with a group—a trade mission to the Sudan— that was scheduled to go on to Egypt, but is now going to Libya."

"What am I trading?"

"Something familiar: a new Smith & Wesson pistol that claims to be better than a Glock or Sig Sauer. You're familiar with it; the same model you've been practicing with here. You'll be an S&W demonstrator. There'll also be someone from the factory who heads up sales to foreign police and security."

"Where do we fly to? Directly to Khartoum?"

"Not directly. No U.S. or Canadian airlines fly there. You'll first go to our Ramstein Air Base in Germany, deplane at the passenger terminal, and shift to a Lufthansa flight out of Frankfurt."

"Won't we be searched at the Frankfurt airport?"

"Of course."

"Weapons?"

"Yours will be delivered directly to the embassy at Khartoum, using diplomatic pouches."

"Will I be met at the embassy?"

"Yes. You'll be given further documents there as Wainwright. You'll split from the group and stay at the U.S. ambassador's residence. The group will be told you picked up a virus and won't be touring with them any further."

"How long will I be there?"

"I don't know."

"How will I get back to the U.S.?"

"I don't know."

"Who's my contact at the embassy?"

"I don't know. . . . He or she will find you."

My confidence didn't increase. . . . I was merely one of a stream of people with false names who are processed through this facility on their way to carry out clandestine activities for the Agency.

Like all flights, mine was boring. I sat with the factory rep from Smith & Wesson, an average looking forty-year-old with less than average intellect. He let me know he was in charge and that I wasn't really needed. I feigned a need for sleep and managed to neutralize him for most of the flight.

The transfer in Germany was without incident. I asked for a window seat to Khartoum and on the descent recognized the two rivers, the Blue Nile and the White Nile, which merged at Khartoum to become the Nile. It had been nearly two decades since my last visit. I hope this brief visit is as successful.

Our trade mission entourage was dropped at the Burj Al Fateh Hotel, but it had been arranged for me to go directly to the ambassador's residence within the embassy grounds. A woman met me at the residence gate where security was thorough. She guided me to the ambassador's office.

When the current residence was constructed, an escape route was built, allowing the ambassador to cross under the compound's walls and come up on an adjacent side street in a shabby building the U.S. rented. A nondescript but armored vehicle was in the garage.

Memories remain of the 1973 murders of then Ambassador Cleo Noel and his Deputy Chief of Mission Curtis Moore by "Black September" Palestinian terrorists. U.S. relations with the Sudan have since been off and on. When the terrorist killers were released to Egypt in 1974, our ambassador was recalled for several months; economic assistance was withheld until 1976. The embassy staff was reduced in 1985, an embassy employee was shot in 1986, and embassy staff departed the country for six months. In the 1990s, Osama bin Laden, Carlos the Jackal, and other terrorists were living in Khartoum. Also in the 1990s, Isfahani—the man I've come to assassinate—resided in the Sudan.

Relations between the two nations haven't significantly improved. The Sudan wants our aid, which is considerable but doesn't appear to have brought any visible economic development. The Sudan plays the game of being a friend only as long as the checks keep arriving. I often speculate why we waste our time with countries like this. But if we acted rationally throughout the world, what would we do with all the career foreign service people who would come back to the U.S.?

On my last trip to Khartoum, I was driven around the city with the ambassador in his official car with the U.S. flag fluttering. No more. The ambassador asked me to go to lunch with

him and see some sights. He drove an old and battered SUV
with no flags and no diplomatic license plates. But he carried
his diplomatic passport. We went over the bridge to Omdurman, past the remains of the fortifications where General
Kitchener overwhelmed the Mahdist forces and avenged the
1889 decapitation of General Gordon at what is buried in British military history as the Battle of Omdurman.

We drove slowly past the silver dome of the Mahdi's tomb,
saw traditional wooden boat building along the Nile, and entered the camel market. A serviceable camel—complete with
hump and a nasty disposition—brought $1,200. I'd rather have
three more Shelties. Camels do not emit a pleasant fragrance.
There are so many at the market it's a wonder anyone remains
long enough to buy one.

Escaping the smells of Omdurman was not unappealing.
We drove back over the traffic-challenged bridge to Khartoum
for a late lunch at Tangerine. I didn't order camel liver, which is
a popular dish in the Sudan, but went to the buffet where the
ambassador helped me identify foods. I sat down with a plate
of many colors, jasmine rice topped with food that didn't look
like liver.

The smell of the camel market will linger long in my
memory.

42

THE SECOND DAY IN KHARTOUM

THE AMBASSADOR EXPLAINED to our group that I was ill and would remain after the group departed for South Sudan. It was formerly part of the Sudan but gained a variation of independence in 2011 that hasn't resolved the differences between the two regions that led to a thirty-year civil war. Sudan is Arab/Muslim—South Sudan is Black/mixed religions with a minority Muslim. Sudan does not have oil—South Sudan does. That all spells dissention, a synonym for trouble.

Isfahani is known to be in Khartoum, undoubtedly staying in a safe place across the Nile River in Omdurman—considered part of greater Khartoum. Because he is Osama bin Laden's nephew, he's increasingly a target of the free world and has steadily gained the status of a hero in the Sudan and much of the Arab world.

Dr. Germ is staying at the Fundak Al Kabeer, along with fourteen other Islamic terrorists who make up the U.S. list of the twenty-five most dangerous persons in the Islamic world. I don't know why the U.S. wouldn't be better off delivering a couple of missiles to that hotel by air, rather than having *me* eliminate only Isfahani. Everywhere he speaks, his disfigured face further enflames Muslims and enhances his prominence. I hate to think what his death at my hands will do to induce retaliation against the U.S.

Several matters remained to be explained to me. When and where would I shoot Isfahani? How would I get away? I had no doubt about my shooting ability. In Guatemala I missed a sure killing of Isfahani by less than two inches. I attributed that to his running. He jogged with an up-and-down movement, rather than a professional runner's glide. I've been assured that this time he will be seated or standing. But the distance will be significantly greater.

After the trade delegation went to the convention center for the day, I joined the ambassador and met the thirteen CIA people working in Khartoum, either on a normal, several-year assignment or present only for the final planning and fulfillment of my assassination attempt. I was surprised when I scanned across the group and saw sitting quietly in the middle—Dan Wilson.

The ambassador remained in the background. His is not an easy job, especially when the CIA enters the city with plans that often bypass the ambassador. He is burdened by complex, conflicting views about assassinations held by the State Department's Foreign Service and the CIA. He had told me at lunch yesterday that if the killing of Isfahani was linked to the U.S., his career was over. But he was willing to take the risk and, if necessary, pay the price for being in the wrong place at the wrong time.

A slightly built man with a moustache and glasses rose from the seated group, stepped to the front of the room, and spoke.

"Gentlemen, most of you know me. I am Luis Cardozo, head of Clandestine Operations. I succeeded Malcolm Whitney who retired two years ago and within a month passed away. He desperately missed his work and was depressed."

I knew Malcolm Whitney, the iconic CIA figure who talked me into the first attempt on Isfahani. Cardozo was present at that meeting but had not spoken a word. Now he had much to say.

"Four of you know the man seated next to the ambassador." All but Dan's head tuned to my direction and stared expressionless. I felt uncomfortable. "You four were at the planning meeting for the failed attempt to kill Isfahani. He was about to fly one of two small jets into the Chrysler and the Empire State buildings. Although not killed, he was badly injured, and the planned attack in New York was aborted. The jets never left the ground. So while Isfahani survived, our mission, nonetheless, was a success."

That sounded to me little more than labeling my role a failure, nevertheless reassuring all in attendance that somehow the Agency had performed well.

"Isfahani has risen close to the top among al-Qaeda leaders. We are certain he is planning an attack in the U.S. intended to decimate the population of a major city. Killing Isfahani will both remove him from a role in the planning and end his personal attempt to find and kill the person who once shot him.

"Isfahani is in Khartoum along with more than a dozen Islamic terrorists from various countries. Especially troubling is the fact that Dr. Lydia Hussein—better known by free world governments as Dr. Germ—also is in Khartoum. Most of the terrorists and Dr. Hussein are staying at the newly renovated Funduk Al Kabeer. Isfahani is hiding somewhere in Omdurman. We lost track of him in Zurich, but our sources say he arrived in Khartoum by private plane several days ago.

"The assassination is set for the day after tomorrow shortly before noon. Isfahani, Dr. Hussein, and the other terrorists will be at the Al-Nilin Mosque in Omdurman. Also called the Mosque of the Two Niles, it's on the western bank of the Nile more or less at the confluence of the Blue Nile and the White Nile. The mosque is a striking piece of architecture, one of the most admired buildings in the Sudan. The entrance is twenty-some steps up from the surrounding flat tiled area, providing an open view for the shooting.

"Just over three thousand feet away is the Al Mogran Amusement Park. It's been closed for six months for rebuilding after the main Ferris wheel collapsed. At one end of the park, along a main thoroughfare—Nile Street—is a prayer tower, commonly known as a minaret. It's closed because of damage during the civil war. But it's soon to reopen. From the top of that prayer tower is an unobstructed view of the Al-Nilin Mosque across the White Nile."

"Three thousand feet is a very long shot. Can it be done?" asked an agent.

"Yes. The rifle to be used can shoot a mile, perhaps a mile and a half."

"That's what the gun can do. What can our shooter do?"

"Like an all-pro field goal kicker going for a fifty yarder. Pretty routine for a practiced shooter."

"Is there wind on the river?"

"Yes, but the windy season ended in February. It's much diminished from a month ago."

"Assuming he makes the shot, how does he get out of the city—and the country?" asked the persistent questioner.

"Down the stairs, out of the tower, over a small fence that parallels Nile Road, and into the waiting truck."

"That's a busy street," noted one of the resident agents.

"It is. The truck purportedly will be broken down."

"What if some thoughtful policeman stops to help?"

"We'll deal with that if it happens," Cardozo answered, without further explanation.

"Will the shooter be taken to the embassy or the ambassador's residence?"

"Neither. If the Sudanese authorities think the shooter's hiding out there, we want to invite them in to see he is not."

"Then how does the shooter hide and leave the country?"

"We think we have it covered. I'd rather not talk about that."

43

TWO DAYS LATER IN KHARTOUM

I HADN'T SLEPT WELL because of concern about the wind affecting my shot. I couldn't make the shot if it hadn't abated by morning. But when I finally fell asleep and woke a few hours later at 8 a.m., I was greeted with a dead calm. Breakfast was delivered to me at 8:30, and I ate alone on the private walled patio outside my room.

Dan was at my door at nine, pulling a large suitcase. Behind, carrying a small bag, was an insipid middle-age woman with bushy eyebrows and clothes a size too small. Inside Dan's suitcase was my CheyTac, broken down into two pieces. There was a clever nylon harness that Dan placed around my head and then showed me how to tuck in the rifle, with one part hanging under each arm. Four .408 cartridges were in elastic shell pockets like you see on a bird hunting jacket.

"I can't walk around like this," I proclaimed.

"You won't. Get bathed. Then we'll get you ready."

"In the shower I tried to imagine what Dan planned for me to wear. He'd also brought a shirt, pants, socks, and shoes, all looking like purchases from the local *souk*. I slipped them on and then put the gun harness back on.

Dan next handed me a Sudanese style, slate colored cotton *dishdasha* with wide, loose sleeves for ease of movement, under which I would hide the CheyTac. The sleeves were buttonless, but there were four down the front top that let me access a document pouch without disclosing my weapon. Adding a classic Arabian *shora,* nothing more than a white head scarf for men, further disguised my non-Arabic features. Finally, I wore an *egal,* the adjustable headband common to Bedouins.

When I looked in the mirror, I thought of Lawrence of Arabia, but more was needed to keep me from looking like Peter O'Toole. That was the role of the woman. She took off my glasses and handed them to me, shaved off my moustache, and darkened my skin with something from a small glass jar that smelled more like camel dung than sage after shave lotion.

At Dan's suggestion, I reached under one sleeve and discovered a pocket for my glasses. Without them I might look more like a local, but I wouldn't be able to hit even the side of the mosque with a bullet, much less hit Isfahani.

Inside the ambassador's garage was an old truck Dan said would take me to the prayer tower and pick me up on adjacent Nile Street. The driver looked Sudanese but was not. He was born in Brooklyn after his parents fled from their home in Tehran. He was later educated in Paris where he landed a job with the U.S. Embassy. Proving extraordinarily intelligent and unquestionably loyal to the U.S., he met a diplomat in Paris who was appointed ambassador to the Sudan. The ambassador brought the man with him. The man thought he had the best job in the world.

I might soon test that belief.

44

LATE MORNING

THE TRUCK HAD A COMPARTMENT below the back of the front seats. The space was padded and barely large enough for a man my size to lie down. A couple of cracks in the frame allowed a modest exchange of air. It's where I'm to hide after the shooting, heading somewhere they haven't told me.

For the drive to the prayer tower, I sat in the cab, wondering how Lucinda would feel if she could envision the sight of this old truck with its scrabble-faced Arab driver and me, joining hundreds of Sudanese on the roads. It would surely be one more foot in the grave of our relationship.

The day was thankfully windless, scorchingly sunny, and dreadfully oppressive. Traffic was horrific; gas-powered vehicles competed with and mostly ignored motorcycles, scooters, and a few crazed bicyclists.

It wasn't far to the prayer tower. The fencing around the reconstruction site had a single entrance. The gate was hanging off its hinges, the work of either construction trucks or Dan Wilson.

We parked next to a pile of roof tiles, beyond which we could see the tall, slender tower and its narrow door. We listened as the *muezzin* finished his *adhan*—call to prayer. He soon descended the tower steps and exited. The adjacent mosque had not been reopened, and the *muezzin* left the construction site to perform his own prayer ritual somewhere else, leaving us alone for my task.

Stepping down from the truck, I brushed some dust from clothing I hoped portrayed Muslim modesty and walked straight to the minaret. Entering a place that was off-limits to non-Muslims was discomforting. I had no desire to disrespect the millions of good Muslims or violate the Quran's dictate: "It is not for such as join gods with Allah, to visit or maintain the mosques of Allah while they witness against their own souls to infidelity. The works of such bear no fruit. In Fire shall they dwell" (9:17). I don't plan on dwelling in fire; my sole intention is to kill a man who is the enemy of the best interests of mankind.

The CheyTac was awkward to carry in the harness, so I removed it as soon as I entered the tower, put it together and carried it—unloaded—up the deeply worn stone steps. An outside open balcony ringed the tower's top. A balustrade had narrow vertical slits that perfectly suited my task. Prone, I could place the barrel tip on the bottom of one slit so nothing protruded. I wouldn't need the barrel tripod to steady the Chey-Tac. The distance was formidable, but I had a perfect line of sight to the already gathering group in front of the Al-Nilin Mosque on the far side of the river.

With my glasses back on, I could identity figures appearing through the scope. One man was without doubt the person who drew the attention of all the others. When I adjusted the scope to better see the figure, a chill went down my spine like a lightning bolt. There was no doubt: It was Isfahani. The scope enhanced his disfigured face.

I settled back against the wall of the minaret, holding the CheyTac in my lap, and carefully inserted into the chamber a single .408 cartridge. Only one shot could be taken. If Isfahani fell injured, once again I would have neither time nor a line of fire to try a second time. He would likely immediately be surrounded and protected by his adoring bodyguards. I lay back down, checked the rangefinder, and looked for signs of wind. A flag near the mosque drooped without the slightest flutter.

There was no time schedule for Isfahani's demise, other than not to delay until he and his colleagues split up and certainly not to linger until the next call to prayer when the *muezzin* would return to the tower.

Isfahani looked relaxed in the company of his terrorist colleagues. The group looked like the leaders of the American Mafia at the New York Apalachin meeting a half century ago—a gathering of the worst of the worst. Isfahani's location in front of the entrance was the perfect execution site. He stood facing me, while one by one the others walked up to talk to him for a few moments, nodding their heads in deference to this equivalent of a Cosa Nostra don. I noticed that one man who was a head shorter than the others was about to speak with Isfahani. I didn't want a head other than Isfahani's to come suddenly into my sight as I pulled the trigger. The time was perfect.

As my finger touched the metal of the trigger, I realized what was happening. I was about to kill a terrorist little known to the public in the West—much the same as bin Laden—but known within the free world's government security agencies to be a most serious threat to national security. I closed my eyes for a moment and thought of the population of D.C. suddenly exposed to a devastating chemical or biological weapons attack, opened my eyes, confirmed my target, and pulled the trigger.

One moment Isfahani was standing smiling to the short man nodding at whatever Isfahani was saying. The next moment he was dead, fallen at the foot of his disciples. Figures looked in every direction for signs of the shooter. Then they began en mass to move quickly to the safety of the mosque, leaving Isfahani's body unattended, worried more about saving their own lives than helping. The expanding stain of red around Isfahani's head spread a blot of death on the purity of the white stone of the mosque and terrace.

I had one more challenge to address: safely getting back to the U.S.

45

THE LAST DAY IN THE SUDAN

DESCENDING THE STAIRS as fast as I dared wearing the cumbersome *dishdasha*, I stopped for a moment, broke apart the CheyTac, and returned the two pieces to the harness. My driver had pulled the truck over close to the minaret's entrance.

"Forget walking to Nile Street," he said smiling as I joined him in the front. "I parked behind the construction debris. There hasn't been another person since the *muezzin* left." But suddenly the streets were filled with sirens.

"You'll have to get in the compartment behind the seat," he ordered. I did as told, losing any ability to know where we were. When we reached Nile Street and turned to take the nearest bridge north, I could hear various sirens and horns coming toward us. Somehow we'd been compromised, I thought, struggling to reach the pistol strapped to my leg. But the noise passed us by.

In five minutes we had crossed the Blue Nile into North Khartoum and soon were on the road that follows the Nile River north toward Egypt. I knew from a map the ambassador showed me that this road went either to Sudan's major port on the Red Sea, Port Sudan, or north along the Nile to Sudan's border town with Egypt, Wadi Halfa. After an hour of discomfort, the driver suggested I crawl out of the compartment and sit with him.

"Where're we headed?" I asked.

"Wadi Halfa," he said, as though I would understand as much as if he had said Cairo.

"That's a long way to drive?" I asked.

"Almost 600 miles. We'll be lucky to be there by daybreak. . . . I'm a driver. I go where I'm told."

"What's in Wadi whatever?"

"Wadi *Halfa*," he repeated. "There's not much there."

"Airport?"

"Yes."

"Flights to London?"

He laughed. "*Sometimes* there's a flight to Khartoum."

"Let's not do that."

"You'll go to Aswan from Wadi Halfa. You like boat rides?"

"Yeah. I've never been on a Nile *felucca*."

"You won't be on a *felucca*. There's a weekly ferry from Wadi Halfa to Aswan. We'll take that."

"Long wait?"

"Not if we make it by tomorrow's departure when the ferry leaves Wadi Halfa for Aswan. We'll make it. If we miss it, we wait another week."

"Let's not miss it," I pleaded, unfolding an old map that showed the route. "Wadi Halfa's on the border. Any problems crossing?"

"Yes. Sometimes the border's closed. At least on the road. But the ferry keeps running. I have a ticket for us."

"Private stateroom?"

"Ha! The boat's been around since the war. The Great War, in 1917. It's always crowded. Most people sleep on the deck with the cargo. We've got a tiny cabin. Not enough to be called a stateroom."

"So you're coming with me?"

"Of course. I'm an American citizen."

"U.S. passport?"

"Sure. Plus one from Sudan. Another from France. You use your Canadian passport; I'll use my Sudanese one."

"You taking me to D.C.?"

"Nope. Just where you'll be safe."

"My home in Florida?"

"Not a chance. To Aswan. Then we'll worry about the next step."

The road north was pitted and dusty. I didn't ask if he wanted me to drive so he could nap. He'd emphasized *he* was the driver. I dozed a bit, occasionally challenged by the crackly static and unfamiliar Arabic from a radio.

"Is it safe all the way to Aswan?" I asked, not sure I wanted to hear the answer.

"It's safe *to* Wadi Halfa. And it's so-so on the ferry. . . . It's not too safe *in* Wadi Halfa."

"What kind of trouble?"

"I didn't want to tell you, but I will. All the police we passed in Khartoum were on their way to the Afra Mall in a suburb. A group of terrorists carrying automatic weapons had entered when the mall opened. It's always crowded from the moment the doors are unlocked. The terrorists started firing, the way some did recently in Kenya. Ninety-some people were killed. Women. Children. Mostly indiscriminate killing, but they searched for anyone with light skin. Like you. All of those were killed."

"What happened to the terrorists?"

"The Sudan military killed every one they found. Six haven't been found."

"Does it affect us?"

"Maybe. We don't know how it will impact the border. The Khartoum airport is closed. The main port on the Red Sea is loaded with soldiers."

"And Wadi Halfa?"

"There's a small border group of military. We want to avoid them. I think we can do it, get around them, and board the ferry."

We didn't see Wadi Halfa until it was upon us. The tallest building can't be more than three stories.

"What are your plans?" I asked, as he slowed the truck and stopped near some piles of roadside trash that were our first signs of civilization. Plastic bags, Styrofoam chunks, and even bubble wrap.

"We have to get rid of the gun. Wrap it in your Arab clothing, he urged as we stopped for the first time in hours. "Shove the gun under some Styrofoam." I did as asked, keeping the small pistol and a silencer.

"Wadi Halfa is on Lake Nasser," the driver explained as we drove on, "surrounded by dunes of the Nubian Desert. It's the eastern edge of the Sahara. The town's depressed, like a small version of Detroit. It looks older than it is. The original Wadi Halfa was flooded when the Aswan High Dam created Lake Nasser. The residents resisted; Sudan's army forced them into the desert. Many died. Sudanese are not a compassionate people."

We threaded our way through side streets of Wadi Halfa, passing occasional donkeys, carrying poor and depressed looking people. My driver succeeded avoiding the formal border crossing by using sandy roads, and we pulled over within sight of the ferry five miles north of the town and out of sight of customs. It was too good to be true.

Both of us were famished. Fortunately, even at this hour there were food venders at the ferry dock where we bought bread and fried Nile perch. My driver produced a flask of whiskey, which, in a nation that prohibits alcohol, we sipped only when others weren't watching. In the distance the early morning light outlined the sculptured curves of the tops of dunes.

The ferry was tied at the dock. The driver had been accurate—it displayed its age. The boat looked like a larger version of the *African Queen*. We walked up the gangplank and stepped onto the deck where a crew member stopped us. The driver showed our tickets and asked if we could board. The crew member agreed after his hand was greased with a wad of Sudanese currency. It was good fortune for us; we would be ensconced in our cabin before the masses of passengers boarded. We wouldn't come out until Egypt.

Five minutes before the ferry departed, a customs policeman boarded. The border proved to be further north of Wadi Halfa than we thought. The driver went out and discovered that the customs official would remain with us until Aswan and then return on the same ferry. He was aboard because he was looking for the remaining terrorists from the mall killings. But he had little to go by, no photos and insufficient descriptions.

Regardless, I had to stay in our cabin out of sight. But sooner or later the agent might want to check this room.

A tattered guidebook to Egypt lay on the cabin table, the only thing in English to pass the time. I opened it to Lake Nasser and learned we would pass close to Abu Simbel, but not close enough to see it clearly from the ferry. UNESCO saved the site from submersing into the lake's waters by moving it a couple of hundred feet higher. It has a Temple of Ramses and the apparently *de rigeur* smaller temple to his favorite wife, Nefertari.

Most visitors to Abu Simbel come from the north, not much more than a brief hour flight from Aswan, where our ferry will dock in another twenty hours or so. Abu Simbel has been on my bucket list for years. It will stay there a while longer.

When we finally arrived at the ferry dock a few miles south of Aswan, securely into Egypt, the driver and I came out of the cabin and bumped into the customs official.

"I've not checked your documents. Let me see them," he demanded, exerting all the authority of a minor official.

"We are in Egypt, not the Sudan," I responded. "You have no authority here."

"We have an arrangement with the Egyptian government that allows us to retain authority over passengers on the entire trip to Aswan. You are not under Egyptian control until you step off this ship here at Aswan."

Our safe haven was not thirty feet away down the gangplank.

The driver showed his papers. The agent gave them back, turned and looked at me, and thrust out his hands, touching my chest, waiting for my papers.

"I have a diplomatic passport," I stated.

"I must see it!" he demanded.

"I've lost it," I confessed.

"Then you must stay aboard and go back to Wadi Halfa."

"I grabbed his arm with my left hand, pushed him into our cabin, drew my pistol from its ankle holster, and thrust the cool barrel against the side of his sweating head."

"You won't get away with this," he whined. "If you shoot, the noise will bring soldiers aboard."

The face of my driver expressed terror. He was holding the official and had taken his pistol.

"No one will hear the shot," I promised, screwing my silencer onto the end of the barrel.

"Tie him up," I instructed the driver, who tossed the official's pistol under the bed. "And make sure he can't yell."

The driver wrapped the official so he looked like an Egyptian mummy. He would be found after we left the ship.

I had a diplomatic passport—in a deep pocket along with four other passports. My chances had been only twenty percent of pulling out the right one. I might have presented my forged passport from the South Sudan, which remains at odds with its northern brethren.

The driver pushed the official into a chair and we left him there, looking terrified at what might happen to him when his superiors discovered we had slipped into Aswan.

At the gangplank we were slowed to a shuffle, not because of another official, but the mass of people competing to get off with their bulky loads. Many had come to Aswan to sell Sudanese crafts, including protected ancient jade and gold. There was no way to get through the crowd. It was nearly thirty minutes before we stepped off onto Egyptian soil.

I was relieved. Isfahani was dead. My driver and I were out of Sudan. I turned to the driver, tapped him on his shoulder, and said, "We're safe."

"Yes, we are but. . . ." he started, but I didn't hear him finish because a shot from the ferry echoed off the walls behind us. The bullet went in my right shoulder and didn't come out. I dropped to the pier's wooden planks, as much to avoid a second shot than the consequences of the first. I didn't think the shot was serious, but when I got up, it proved bad enough to make me lean against my driver. He took off his torn jacket and covered my shoulder as we worked our way through the crowd.

All the attention on the pier from Egyptian police was directed at the ship and where the shot had been fired. I couldn't believe the Sudan official had freed himself. A crew member checking cabins to be certain everyone was disembarking must have found him while the driver and I were struggling to get off the ferry.

The driver flagged down a taxi, helped me in, and said, "*Old Cataract Hotel.*"

The *Old Cataract* room was better than our ferry cabin. In fact, the hotel was a 5-star Sofitel Legend luxury conversion of a 19th century Victorian palace on the banks of the Nile. Our room overlooked the river where *feluccas* sailed tourists around nearby islands.

In our room was a basket of fruit and a plain note card. Until I opened it, I assumed it was from the hotel. Inside was a second envelope containing a few brief words: "Good job. Relax and see Aswan and the High Dam. Regards to your driver. Would you like next to travel at our expense to Guatemala?"

It was signed "Enjoy—Dan."

46

ASWAN

A SWAN WAS PLANNED as a single night stop, with a flight after breakfast to Cairo on Egypt Air, then to Frankfurt to the Ramstein Air Base for a final flight to D.C. But I needed to be stabilized before any flight. Within twenty-four hours red was spreading outwards from where the bullet entered—a suspicious indication of infection. The bullet remained inside.

My driver found a local Aswan doctor and agreed to pay him handsomely to look at me but not report the bullet wound. He must have been into his seventies, his head and hands shook and he had trouble putting a thermometer into my mouth. I rejected his suggestion that he remove the bullet. He wanted me to be transferred to the local hospital, but I declined, worried it would be required to report the shooting. The doctor left me holding a handful of pills. He held a handful of dollars.

The next morning I was no better. Concerned, my driver sent Dan Wilson a coded email explaining my predicament and asking for advice. The response an hour later said to be at the

Aswan airport in three hours and go to the private aviation section where someone would meet us.

We waited two hours, checked out of the hotel, and were at the airport a half hour later. A man wearing the clothes of a mechanic was waiting by the entrance.

"Curtis Wainwright?" he asked, using the name on my Canadian passport.

I nodded.

"I'm Bill. Follow me."

We did, but the antibiotics and pain killers the doctor had given me were wearing off and I stumbled several times. Bill grabbed one arm, my driver the other, and they guided me to the plane. I was amazed when I saw a U.S. fighter jet parked behind Egyptian military vehicles.

"Is this yours?" I asked Bill.

"It is. It's your air taxi. I'm a pilot—a captain in the Air Force. I was diverted to pick you up and take you to my base at Ramstein. The plane only fits two." He turned to the driver and added, "You have tickets waiting at the Egypt Air counter. In about two hours a plane will take you to Cairo where you'll transfer to a direct flight to D.C. I'm told you did quite a job."

I shook hands with the driver with my left hand, adding, "I wouldn't be here without your help. We'll be in touch."

"Maybe. But I've never given you my name."

He turned and walked away.

47

AT RAMSTEIN IN GERMANY

THE MORNING I AWOKE AT RAMSTEIN, I opened my eyes and thought I was at the gates to Heaven. But I saw no "pearly" gates, only a dreary hospital room and three anything but colorless fuzzy visitors standing by my bed, named Big Bird, Oscar, and Elmo—in all their glorious colors. The Muppets had come to Ramstein to entertain injured troops back from their most current engagements.

When the Muppets left, a doctor wearing camouflage scrubs walked in. I was reassured by her stethoscope, but too groggy to see her very well. Anyway, I preferred the Muppets.

"I'm Greer. Officially Dr. Greer Goodwin, but please call me Greer."

"I assume I'm going to live," I mumbled.

"Most likely. I don't know why you're here. You're not military. But I was ordered to take care of you. I do what I'm told. You've been delirious."

I turned toward my right side to say something to her and received a jolt of pain in my shoulder.

"Hurt?" she asked.

"Wow!" I answered. I remembered being shot, but not much after that.

"You were shot. I extracted the bullet. It should have been removed much sooner. You had a dangerous infection. We thought we were going to have to remove parts of you one by one."

"Did you remove anything?"

"Not that I recall," she smiled.

"That's reassuring. How long have I been here?"

"Three nights. . . . Do you always talk in your sleep?"

"Not that *I* recall. Did I?"

"Constantly."

"Disclose any national secrets?"

"You made no sense. Mumbled about copper johns, some place called Arrowgate Ranch, and a guy named Juan Pablo. I've never heard of making a toilet out of copper. . . . But mostly you kept saying, 'I'm sorry, Lew . . .' and you never finished the sentence. You work for a guy named Lew?"

"No." I let it go at that. . . . "Am I ready to go home?"

"Not a chance. You've lost a lot of blood from the shoulder wound. I deal with infections from wounds. Your infection was acute. We analyzed your urine, blood, and sputum—coughed up mucus—cultures, plus spinal fluid, to be certain you had no brain infection. You were feverous, rejected food, sweated a lot, had chills, and weren't much fun to be around."

"I assume the infection was bacterial."

"Of course, a bullet wouldn't leave a viral infection."

"Every bullet doesn't cause infection. Why mine?"

"You probably don't want to hear the technical stuff. Your infection started when the bullet entered your shoulder. It opened access to your insides, and you were vulnerable to anaerobic bacteria. Everyone shot doesn't end up infected."

"What's my recovery period?"

"That's hard to say; it depends on your overall health, which seems OK. Plus, whether you're a diabetic or smoker—you are neither; depressed—we don't know about that; where the bullet went—did it break bones, damage tissue, or fragment?; how well your physical therapy goes; eating; stable vitals; and family support. You're missing the last; we haven't been told anything about your family or friends.

"You had a shattered humerus and clavical that required surgery. Bone healing takes three to six months. You'll wear a sling for at least one or two. You should be out of here in ten to fourteen days from your admission. Questions?"

"No."

"Good. Be positive, and you'll recuperate faster."

She turned and went off, scribbling something on papers on a clip-board.

"Three to six months?" I muttered.

48

THE SAME DAY IN NEW YORK CITY

THE 407 BEDS FOR CANCER PATIENTS at the highly rated Memorial Sloan Kettering Cancer Center in New York City were fully occupied. In the bed in a private room was a woman being treated for an infection that developed after a double mastectomy that otherwise appeared to have been successful. Her doctors were convinced that the infection was under control and that the patient would not be among those very few who survive an operation but succumb to a post-operative infection. But she was extremely weak from the consequences of both. The woman's name was on a card next to the door: Lucinda L. Lang.

Three months earlier, the week before Lucinda left Montana with Macduff, she had felt a lump in her left breast. She was busy with her move to New York and put off seeing a doctor. After she returned from Christmas in London, and New Year's with Elsbeth in New York, she began to worry about the lump and called her former general physician in Manhattan, Dr. Ruth Pennington, who set an appointment for the following day. At that appointment Lucinda was examined; Dr. Pennington affirmed a lump and ordered a biopsy. It came back positive. Then the choices began, with both Lucinda and Dr. Pennington agreeing on the next step—a bilateral mastectomy and reconstruction. She chose bilateral because there was a history of breast cancer in her family.

"Miss Lang," the doctor had asked, "Do you want me to schedule the surgery for here? Or since you spend much of your time in Montana, I could suggest a surgeon in Bozeman. Or Salt Lake City."

"I want it done in New York City. I don't want to bother my Montana friends with my problems."

"It's helpful to have friends for support. Do you have a significant other?"

Lucinda paused for a moment, making Dr. Pennington wonder about whether support would come from any relationship she might have.

"No," Lucinda answered, in little more than a whisper.

"I'll arrange a date immediately for the surgery at Sloan Kettering. You should have come to me sooner."

Lucinda immediately requested leave so the operation could be done in two days. Her boss thought it had to be important and didn't ask questions.

"Why don't I tell your colleagues that you've postponed your decision about staying in New York and working full time and are tying up some loose ends?"

"Good, I prefer that no one knows about this."

"One thing I should know—I won't share it with anyone—are you going to be OK?"

"We'll know better after the operation. Let *me* call you."

"Fine."

The mastectomy was successful, but, as infrequently happens with such an intrusive operation, Lucinda developed an infection. She wasn't released in the few days expected. It was another three weeks before she was discharged.

She didn't want to call her office for help getting to her apartment. Fortunately, Freddie, her building's concierge, picked her up at the hospital and saw her safely to her apartment. A year ago, when Freddie's mother was dying, Lucinda had paid for her care at a private hospice. Like everything in Manhattan, private hospice care is expensive.

For the next two weeks, as she regained her strength, Lucinda didn't leave the apartment. Freddie brought her food. When she finally felt strong enough, she asked her doctor about flying to Montana so she could recover at her ranch. Although there was an interested buyer, the ranch had not been sold. Her doctor agreed the quiet setting in Montana, without all the stress of her Manhattan life and work, would be a sensible place to recover. Records of the surgery were sent to an oncologist in Bozeman.

Lucinda thought she'd book a flight for Montana to leave in about three weeks. She called her friend Erin Giffin in Livingston.

"How are you?" Erin shouted into her phone. "It's been more than a month since you left. I don't have your Manhattan number. . . . What's up? What do you hear from Macduff? Have you talked to Elsbeth in Maine? How's Wuff?"

Erin was special to Lucinda. No one in Manhattan cared as much. That also was true of Ken Rangley at Erin's office. Plus her ranch housekeeper Mavis Benton. And Amy Becker, Bozeman judge and friend to Lucinda and Macduff. Also Wanda Groves, Macduff's lawyer, and Park County Prosecutor Will Collins. As well as John Kirby, Huntly Byng, and Juan Santander in Jackson Hole.

Lucinda thought how important these people had become to her—and how contented they were living in Montana and Wyoming. They meant more than all the museums, theaters, restaurants, and routinely boring dinner parties and weekends in South Hampton, even more important than the occasional long weekend in London or Paris. . . . And she thought about Macduff.

She remembered all he had gone through over the years—losing El and his identity and skills as a law professor, not to mention the tragedies that had occurred while guiding. When Lucinda was shot by Park Salisbury, Macduff was by her side throughout her coma and over the following months as she battled with amnesia.

Lucinda kept thinking that she might have communicated better. She acknowledged she was much to blame; there were so many calls from him she never returned, so many letters from him she never answered.

"Erin, I'm going to book a flight in about three weeks. The best connections arrive in Bozeman in late afternoon. Any chance you can meet me? I'll buy us dinner in Bozeman."

"Tell me the time, and I'll be at the airport. Can't wait to hear about you and Macduffy."

Erin was a very good friend, Lucinda thought. Too good to lose.

49

TWO WEEKS LATER BACK IN WASHINGTON

I RECOVERED ENOUGH to be moved across the Atlantic to Walter Reed in D.C. My return was almost two months from the day I left D.C. for Khartoum by way of Germany.

Walter Reed has a long and an inconsistent history of caring for military personnel, resulting in the firing of more than one commanding general and the resignation of a secretary of the Army. I was hoping my stay would be uneventfully brief.

Landing in D.C. was a spiritual and physical welcome. The cherry trees were in bloom and the floral work of First Lady "Lady Bird" Johnson in beautifying the city had endured. If my recovery from illness is enhanced by my surroundings, I should soon be back to my normal life.

Seasonal guiding in Montana was soon to commence with a week or two of spring fishing. I had little hope of regaining enough strength to make that realistic. June was a more likely time. Besides, I had to spend a week or two at my cottage in St. Augustine before I was mentally and physically prepared to confront the drive across country.

The day after I arrived in D.C. from Germany, I had a visitor. He stopped in the doorway, stared to make certain I was actually alive, and broke out into a broad smile.

"Hello, Dan," I said.

"You look like hell," he answered. "You did good."

"Do I get a bonus?"

"Yes, a new rifle. Like tools at Sears, CheyTacs are guaranteed for life."

"No thanks. Mine's in some landfill north of Khartoum, unless someone found it."

"If they did, it didn't make the papers. . . . What have you heard about the op, if anything?"

"I haven't seen a paper since I left here for Khartoum. No one at Ramstein said a word about the Sudan."

"The people at Ramstein didn't know about the Sudan," Dan asserted. "You know there was a shooting at the main shopping mall in Khartoum the day you shot Isfahani?"

"Yes, when we fled after the shooting, we heard the police heading south. We first thought they were after us, but they drove by. My driver heard on the radio that night, during the long drive to Wadi Halfa, that there'd been a shooting by terrorists at a Khartoum mall. Whatever it was, it may have diverted police from us. What happened?"

"It was a repeat of an attack on a mall in Kenya a few days earlier. Seventy-some were killed in the similar Khartoum incident, and an equal number are missing. It may have been the work of Isfahani and his friends who gathered in Khartoum. Your shooting may have disrupted plans for a similar attack in the U.S.; at least it's given us more time to try to stop it."

"You think you can stop it?"

"Between you and me, no."

50

THE NEXT DAY IN NEW YORK CITY

LUCINDA ROSE FROM HER SOFA where she had been napping, walked to the side table, and opened her ringing cell phone.

"This is Dan Wilson."

"I haven't talked to *you* in a while. Where are you?" she asked guardedly.

"In New York. Free for lunch?"

Lucinda thought carefully. What would Dan want? She felt better but didn't think she wanted to spend lunch with him.

"Booked, Dan. Sorry."

"Too bad," he commented. "How have you been?"

Lucinda was certain Dan knew nothing about her operation and maybe nothing about her changed relationship with Macduff. "I'm fine."

"Going to St. Augustine before you head for Montana?"

So he didn't know they had split, she thought.

"Not sure yet," she said.

"You *are* going to Montana?" Dan asked.

"I am. In a few weeks," she responded, without telling Dan she would be staying at her ranch and not at Macduff's cabin, *if* Mavis had transferred all her belongings at the cabin to the ranch, including all the photos she appeared in with Macduff.

"Have you talked with Macduff about his job for us?"

"Job?" she said curtly, knowing Dan was at the heart of Macduff's plans concerning Isfahani. "I haven't talked to him."

"Been reading the papers?"

"Not really. Been too busy at work."

"So you don't know anything about Isfahani?"

"No."

"He's dead."

Lucinda had been standing, wandering about her living room. She turned and dropped into a leather easy chair. "Can you tell me any more about it?"

"I can repeat what's been in the *International Herald* in Europe. Isfahani was shot in front of a mosque in Omdurman in the Sudan."

"Where's Omdurman?"

"Across the Nile from Khartoum. Isfahani was with a group of the U.S.'s most wanted terrorists from throughout the Arab world. We think they were behind the slaughter at the mall in Kenya, as well as the same kind of killings at a mall in Khartoum."

"Do the Sudanese authorities know who killed Isfahani? Was he caught?"

"Isfahani was killed with one .408 caliber bullet from a distance of a bit over a half mile."

"Were you involved, Dan?"

"Can't tell you."

"Then how did you know it was a .408 caliber?"

"Did I say that?"

"You did. . . . Don't play with me, Dan."

"You know there are things I can't tell you."

"Then why did you call me?"

"Then it's true you haven't heard about Macduff?"

"I haven't heard *from* him. What do you mean *about* him?"

"He's in Walter Reed in D.C. I visited him yesterday."

"What happened?" she asked as her voice broke.

"He was shot. Then the wound became infected. He'll survive."

Lucinda had trouble holding the phone steady. She set it down on the chair's armrest and tapped the speaker button.

"Who shot him?"

"I shouldn't tell you, but I will. It was a customs official."

"Customs official? Where?"

"North of the border town of Wadi Halfa. Actually getting off a ferry in Aswan on Lake Nasser in southern Egypt. The ferry had come from Wadi Halfa."

"Why was he shot?"

"He was apparently being sought by authorities."

"From Sudan?"

"Yes."

"For killing Isfahani?"

". . . Not sure. I've told you far more than I should."

"Damn him," she cried. "I knew he'd try that."

"This time he succeeded."

"How can he do these things?"

"I don't always know myself. Patriotic compulsion? But I think it's another reason."

"What?"

"You."

"That's absurd. Why me?"

"He couldn't live with the fact that Isfahani had tried to destroy your building in Manhattan and that he failed to stop it when he shot but didn't kill Isfahani in Guatemala. Additionally, Isfahani was heading a group that has been planning an attack in the U.S. We think D.C. Maybe using both chemical and biological weapons. Macduff threw a wrench into those plans, buying us needed time."

"So you think he's a hero?"

"Doesn't matter what I think. The President does. He's presenting Macduff with the Presidential Medal of Freedom, the highest civilian award the country has."

"When?"

"Tomorrow, at Walter Reed. In a quiet, private ceremony with no press or public invited."

"I guess that's great."

"It is. He's also going to receive, in another closed private ceremony, the CIA's Distinguished Intelligence Cross, their highest award."

Anything more?"

"He'd get a lot more medals from our friends abroad if they discovered who assassinated Isfahani. France wants to know who did the shooting so they can present the Legion of Honour. One more thing, the senior senator from Montana is on the foreign relations committee. He's the only member of Congress who knows some of the details because he's involved with oversight of the CIA. He wants Macduff to receive the Congressional Gold Medal. But he can't propose it because it would be a death warrant."

"*Every one* of those awards sounds like a death warrant."

"They could prove to be that."

After a long pause, Lucinda said, "Dan, I'll see you for lunch. I'm in no shape to keep my business luncheon date after hearing all this. . . . One last question—is Mac going to be OK?"

"No."

"Why?" she asked, barely audible.

"You."

"Me?"

"Yes."

"Why?"

"You can answer that better than I can. . . . Forget the lunch; give some serious thought to your future." Before she could respond, Dan had hung up.

They did not have lunch together.

51

On August 31, 2000, Bob and Damon Nichols [were arrested] for, among other things, violating the state's prohibition of fishing with gill or entangling nets made of monofilament material.

The jury found the [Nicholses] guilty of unlawful use of a gill or entangling net made of monofilament, and guilty of possession of mullet in excess of the recreational bag limit while in possession of a gill or entangling net.

[The county court judge found the ban's reference to "monofilament"' . . . to be "ambiguous," concluded that the statute was unconstitutional, and vacated the convictions. The First District Court of Appeals reversed the county court and reinstated the conviction and fines.]

State v. Nichols, 892 So.2d 1221 (Florida First District Court of Appeals 2005). Florida Fishermen Lose Net Ban Challenge. masglp.olemiss.edu

THREE DAYS LATER IN ST. AUGUSTINE

I STEPPED OFF THE PLANE AT THE JACKSON-VILLE AIRPORT into a sun that forewarned of the humid months of summer that would soon sneak in from the Caribbean. The last time I was at the Jacksonville airport, Lucinda surprised me by showing up from New York. She didn't remain more than a half hour when, after a strange, brief conversation that neither started nor ended well, she took the flight back to

Manhattan. It was the last time I talked to her. That was months ago.

I'd called Jen a few minutes before the plane took off in D.C. and asked her to pick me up. She was waiting at the baggage claim area. Wuff was with her and seemed to have forgiven if not forgotten me.

"Hello, Macduff, Jen said without emotion. She usually hugged me when I've been away.

"How was your trip?" she asked five minutes later, mainly to avert the silence.

"OK."

"You're favoring your right side. Are you all right?"

"Pretty much."

"What's that supposed to mean? Yes, you're OK. Or no, you're not."

"I'm fine."

You don't look it. You're thinner, you look pale, and there are wrinkles at the corners of your eyes."

"I'm getting old."

"Not that fast. Something you did caused it."

"I'm tired. I had some hard weeks working. Let's drop it."

The cottage looked better than her disposition. Walking up the outside stairs, I stopped on the porch, relieved to be back. A couple of weeks and I should be strong enough to drive to Montana. I wish Wuff could share the driving—I wish anyone could. . . . Maybe Grace Justice?

"Jen," I said as we walked in. "What have you done? It looks barren."

"Right after you left, Lucinda called. When I told her you'd be gone indefinitely, she asked me to pack her things and mail them to her apartment in New York. I did as she asked, but I didn't enjoy doing it. The place does look cold, like it did be-fore you met Lucinda and she began staying with you. She add-ed a touch of class."

I didn't say another word. After ten minutes of silence while I walked through the cottage confirming there wasn't a trace of Lucinda, Jen looked at me with a dozen questions in her eyes, said nothing, and quietly stepped out the door. Two minutes later I heard her car drive off.

Welcome home.

52

FOUR DAYS LATER IN MONTANA

LUCINDA LEFT HER MANHATTAN APARTMENT for her Montana ranch, looking forward to seeing Erin and buying her dinner. Lucinda was a little wobbly getting from the taxi to the plane at La Guardia and fell asleep in her first class seat.

The plane's descent to Denver woke her; she fell asleep again as soon as her next flight lifted off, bound for Bozeman. She awoke again when the turbulence that is nurtured in the Rockies began to shake the plane intermittently for the remainder of the flight. Even first class failed to alleviate that part of flying.

She walked through the arrivals corridor of the Bozeman airport and reached the top of the stairs overlooking the ground floor, a statement to visitors that they have arrived in the West. Shops line the halls selling bronze moose bookends, T-shirts promoting the MSU Bobcats and declaring "I'd rather be in Montana," and books describing the twenty worst Montana grizzly attacks of the last century. A distinguished gentleman carrying seventy years or more and dressed in tailored jeans, a pressed Western-styled shirt, a bison skin Stetson, and boots that said "Pure Country" brushed by her, stopped and tipped his hat, apologizing profusely. Lucinda thought: "I don't want to give this up. New York blood may still be in my veins, but Montana blood flows through my heart."

Erin was waiting at the foot of the curving stairs and met Lucinda with a ferocious welcoming embrace.

"Wow!" Lucinda exclaimed. "Do I owe you something or does the sheriff's office greet everyone like this?"

"Both. What you owe me is a dinner. Ted's 'Eat Great, Do Good' Montana Grill?"

"A good reintroduction to home. Bison steak is Montana gourmet."

Once they settled into the car, Erin asked, "I didn't want to say anything in the airport, but how's your recovery coming?"

"Recovery?" Lucinda said with a wondering stare. "What recovery?"

"From your mastectomy."

"No one west of the Mississippi knows about that, except one oncologist here in Bozeman. Who told you?"

"No one here. Remember, I'm a pretty good detective. I knew something was wrong the way you left Macduff in St. Louis without saying goodbye and then refused to take his calls."

"Erin! You're an irascible snoop."

"I thought you might have something wrong with you and called a detective friend with the NYPD in Manhattan. I asked him to check hospitals for a patient named Lucinda Lang. How did you like Sloan Kettering? Every bit as good as it's reputed?"

"Every bit. Who else here knows about this?"

"Only one person."

"Mavis?"

"You guessed it. I told her to take good care of you or the sheriff's office would arrive on her doorstep—in force."

Dinner at Ted's was uplifting to Lucinda, sitting on the front terrace and watching contented faces of MSU students walk past. Lucinda thought the students looked younger every year. . . . The later drive over the modest pass to Livingston went quickly as the two friends talked and laughed.

"To the cabin?" asked Erin.

"To my ranch," Lucinda replied quietly.

"I don't think Macduff's there," observed Erin.

"He's not," added Lucinda.

"Still in St. Augustine?"

"Maybe, if he's out of Walter Re . . ." she stopped herself abrupt.

"Walter Reed! The military hospital in D.C.?" asked Erin.

"Yes."

"Why?"

"He was shot. Then an infection set in. He was in critical shape for a while. He pulled through."

"Why aren't you there?"

"We're not together."

"What? That's ridiculous."

"It may be more than that," Lucinda nodded, and dabbed at moisture that ran down alongside her nose.

"Where was he shot?"

"In the right shoulder. In Aswan, Egypt."

"What on earth was he doing there?"

"I can't tell you."

"Lucinda, I know about Macduff's work years ago. Remember that I was the one who found him delirious in his cabin when you were in a coma in the hospital in Salt Lake City."

"Does Abdul Khaliq mean anything to you?"

"You mean Macduff shot Isfahani?" Erin asked.

"Yes."

"I know he's dead," Erin exclaimed. "It was in the papers weeks ago. Even in the *Livingston Weekly News*. Killed in Khartoum the day the terrible slaughter began at the mall there. . . . You said Macduff was shot in Egypt. That's not the Sudan."

"He was on a ferry going from a northern border town in the Sudan—Wadi Halfa—to Aswan in Egypt. I hope the article you read didn't identify the assassin."

"It didn't," Erin said with assurance. "Apparently neither the Islamic terrorists nor the Sudanese authorities want to admit that only one person was able to kill Isfahani."

"If Mac's name is disclosed, he'll be dead in a week."

"Sooner. . . . He was apparently willing to assassinate Isfahani and assume the consequences. . . . Is this related to you two?"

"Yes. I told him how upset I was with the idea of his assassinating anyone. He didn't have to do it."

"He apparently thought he did. I think there's more than you assume."

"Meaning?"

"I think he did it because of you."

"That's melodramatic."

"No. He's never forgiven himself for failing to kill Isfahani in Guatemala. Isfahani was going to attack your building. You would have been there."

"I would have. Macduff made me promise to get out. I left before the planned attack. Isfahani has never forgotten the shooting; he was reminded every day when he looked in a mirror."

"He would not have rested until he had retaliated," Erin claimed. "He would have killed you if he'd found you together. Now, Isfahani's terrorist colleagues will want to kill his assassin, if they know who to look for and can find him. . . . Macduff wanted to take all the blame. He may have thought that was easier with you gone."

"I've been selfish. I thought. . . ."

"I know what you thought."

"But there's another matter."

"What's that," Erin asked.

"I couldn't tell Macduff about my cancer. I didn't know how serious it was. I think I'm free of it. I've been told I should be OK. But it will take time to really know."

"Do you think that would matter to Macduff? He would have been by your side every step."

"I'm tired, Erin. And confused. Let's talk tomorrow or another day."

When Erin dropped her off, Lucinda walked alone into the elegant main house at her ranch. She stood in the darkened hallway looking into a barren living room where the stone fireplace was devoid of a single log or speck of ash—the room that was once full of life where Macduff and she had sat the evening they met. She walked into the room and stood next to where they had sat that evening. She wondered why things had gone so badly. . . .

After a half hour she went into her bedroom, emptied her carry-on bag on her bed, and put back her cosmetics bag and a few items of clothing. In a closet she opened a box that contained the photographs that Mavis brought from Macduff's cabin that documented their years together. She took out a favorite of Macduff and her standing alongside Deadman's Bar on the Snake River in Wyoming and put it in her bag, wrapped in some Western clothes she thought she would never wear again.

Lucinda left and locked her house, backed her SUV from the garage, and drove off. Her drive was brief—only to Macduff's log cabin. Because the last item returned between separating couples is often the first given—a key to the door—she was thankful she could enter. Letting herself in, she went directly to Macduff's bedroom, placed the photo on the bedside table, slipped out of the Armani clothes she had dressed in that morning in New York, tossed them into a corner, and slid under the covers—on Macduff's side. She put her face deeply against his down pillow and breathed heavily. She imagined she could smell him.

In five minutes Lucinda fell into a deep sleep for the first time in weeks.

53

Following jury trial in which defendants were found guilty of unlawful use of gill or entangling net made of monofilament and possession of mullet in excess of recreational limit, the Franklin County Court, Van P. Russell, [judge], granted defendants' motions for judgment of acquittal. State appealed. After quashing Circuit Court's order and reinstating appeal, the District Court of Appeal held that: (1) statute prohibiting use of gill net or entangling nets made of 'monofilament' material was not unconstitutionally vague. [The judge reversed] and remanded with directions that [the] conviction be reinstated in accordance with the jury's verdicts, [and] that the $250 fines be likewise reinstated.

State v. Nichols, 892 So.2d 1221 (Florida First District Court of Appeals 2005).

THE FOLLOWING DAY IN ST. AUGUSTINE`

I WANTED TO BEGIN THE INTERMINABLE DRIVE TO MONTANA, but I was leery about spending several days sitting in one position with pressure on my right shoulder. The decision was made for me by a telephone call from the St. Johns County Sheriff's Office.

"Is this Macduff Brooks?" asked a gruff voice.

"It is. Who is this?"

"Turk Jensen. I want to talk to you. Be here this afternoon promptly at one."

"No."

"No?"

"Call Bill Muirhead. He's my lawyer. If you want to charge me and arrest me, I'll be here at my cottage. Muirhead will be with me. It's always nice to have a third person to settle disputes."

"Damn it, Brooks. You'll be sorry."

"Probably not. I'll be leaving here in a few days. To Montana, where I work in the summer. I'll be back in October. I'll send you a postcard."

"Don't leave the state. That's an order."

"Whose order?"

"Mine."

"I'll listen to a judge."

"You'll listen to me."

The next day Jensen arrived with a warrant for my arrest on suspicion of murder. I called Bill Muirfield and went with Jensen, clasped in handcuffs in the back seat of his car. Muirhead joined me at the sheriff's offices.

"Macduff," Muirhead affirmed, "the warrant's signed by Judge Bennie Cortez. He's been on the County Court for decades. He's a golfing buddy of Turk Jensen. Wants desperately to move up to the Circuit Court. Been rebuffed every time and he's bitter and antagonistic. He hasn't a chance of being promoted. The Florida bar rates him unqualified. But he gets re-elected because he has an effective organization around election time. Turk Jensen is part of that organization.

"I've been to another judge, Shirley Hanson. You're released on your own recognizance. That means you don't have to post bail. One condition: You can't leave the area without the judge's permission. I don't have to add that judges Cortez and Hanson are not friends. It seems a quarter of her work is correcting his screw-ups."

"Bill, I want to leave for Montana soon. Any chance?"

"Give me a few days. I'll go back before Judge Hanson and ask her to allow you to leave. I'll emphasize the work you do teaching and guiding for Project Healing Waters. She's an Iraq war vet. And I'll remind her you own property in this county."

As I returned to the cottage in a cab, I tried to work through the killing of Bradford and why Turk Jensen has it in for me. I never met Bradford. I recall hearing about him, but I haven't been a devoted reader of the local *Chronicle*. It seems clear to me that Bradford and I had no dispute. I suspect he was killed on my boat either because the boat was convenient to where Bradford was taken after being drowned in the marsh or because the killer wanted to send *me* a message.

The police found no footprints leading from around my cottage to the dock other than mine and no sign that a body had been dragged there. The tides expunged any trace of whatever might have happened in the marsh. The medical examiner couldn't prove the cause of death because there wasn't enough left of Bradford. I'd like to think he was surprised while fishing in the marsh, was drowned quickly and wrapped in a gill net, and became part of a funeral pyre in my innocent boat. The fire apparently started by siphoning the full tank of gas into the bottom of the boat, dumping Bradford wrapped in a gill net into the gas, and tossing in a match.

I'll call a few Montana outfitters in the morning and have someone else take my April floats. I have none scheduled for May or the first week of June because the Yellowstone will be flowing too fast for safe floats; the water will not have cleared. Clearing occurs at different times, sometimes in early June, sometimes in July.

Since I'll be staying at the cottage for at least a few more days, I'll give Grace Justice a call and see if we can talk about the deaths.

54

THE FOLLOWING DAY

Ken Rangley called me in the morning from Livingston, asked Erin to join him on the line, and began, "Macduff, a lady named Grace Justice called me. She's an assistant state attorney based in your county. She said she's talked to you about the Florida deaths and wanted to know what we've learned about the death here of Hendersen.

"Macduffy," broke in Erin, "she also said you two were seeing each other."

"Let's keep focused on the murders," I said, coarsely. "Not my private life."

Ken interrupted, "Mac, Grace mentioned something you learned when you visited a town named Oyster Bay that might relate to the deaths. I want Erin and me to hear about it from you."

"I'll tell you exactly what I told Grace."

I repeated what I recalled I'd told Grace about sitting and talking with the resident in Oyster Bay, and added, "I've got notes I made after the conversation here in a file. What I'll tell you two that I didn't tell Grace—I don't know her that well, yet—is that the resident made some comments about the gill net death *on my boat.*

"The person in Oyster Bay didn't call it a death, but a murder. I thought it might be important. But since that conversation I've thought about it and tend to think Grace was right, suggesting it was the ranting of an old crank."

"I'd like to think about it," Ken said, "and talk to you when you get here."

"That might be awhile."

"Don't you have some floats in the next week or two?"

"Yes, but I can't leave here."

"Not up to the long drive?"

"I can't leave this county."

"Who says?"

"A local judge. I've been arrested for the murder of Bradford."

"You're joking! That must mean you haven't told us all you know about his death?"

"No, it means there's a deputy sheriff here who doesn't like me. I have a lawyer. I'm out on my own recognizance."

"Are they serious? You said they don't know the cause of Bradford's death."

"That's right. There wasn't enough left of him to tell much. The local medical examiner won't state a cause of death."

"Is this going to trial?"

"My lawyer assures me it won't. We have a different judge than the one who issued the warrant. I think the charges will be dismissed within two weeks. I've postponed some floats."

"Macduff, back to Oyster Bay. How old was the person you talked to?"

"Hard to tell. Sixties at least; maybe seventies."

"Male or female?"

"Female. Interesting, Grace didn't ask that. Possibly the wife of one of the commercial fishermen who lost his liveli-hood."

"When was the ban?"

"1994."

"That means the person was twenty years younger, in her forties or fifties."

"And?" I asked.

"An age when the ban may have been catastrophic to her family. And then it festered for two decades. . . . I think you ought to go back to Oyster Bay and snoop around."

"I'll try."

55

Cold fronts ... tell black mullet that it is time to spawn. The fish bunch up into schools and are easy pickings for poachers looking to make a quick buck. We have heard that they can make as much as $10,000 in a night. The illegal mullet trade is so lucrative that poachers will pay a 'spotter' $1,000 a night to stand on a bridge and raise the alarm if law enforcement arrives.

Huge Mullet Catch Seized, Tampa Bay Times, December 13, 2005.

THE SAME DAY IN APALACHICOLA ON THE PANHANDLE COAST OF FLORIDA

APALACHICOLA IS AN HISTORIC COASTAL TOWN with many old homes of distinction and a small center of town that is invaded by the exit of traffic from a concrete bridge that soars ungraciously over Towhead Island, turns abruptly north, and deposits confused motorists in the middle of town on Market Street. A block away on Water Street is the only fly fishing store in the area—Bay Fly Fishing Outfitters. Owner Tim Hicks worked for twenty years at the Orvis store in the company's hometown in Manchester, Vermont. He moved to Florida and opened the store in 1990, four years before the gill net ban went into effect.

Last evening just before closing, he had a call inquiring about guiding.

"Mr. Hicks, my name is Carl Hutchins. I live over in Eastpoint. Do you guide?"

"Yes."

"My mother and I fish together quite a lot. She's 74. Last month she watched a movie rerun on TV called *A River Runs Through It.* For some reason she told me last evening she wanted to learn to fly fish and go out with a guide. She's very good at using a spinning rod and artificial lures."

"Well, we could go out along the inside of Little St. George and throw streamers. I can work with her on casting, probably not to the extent of the movie, but enough to get her started.

"When do you have an opening?"

"Not for three weeks. But I have a cancelation tomorrow. That may be too soon for your schedule."

"That's perfect. What time?"

"Eight. Meet me here at the shop."

"We'll be there."

Carl's mother, who introduced herself as Gertrude, proved to be a charming client the moment she set foot on Hick's flats boat the next morning. Appearances are often deceiving.

At 9:30 that evening Glenda, the wife of Tim Hicks, became worried that he had not come home. He often stayed 'til dusk if he liked the client, but it was now well after sunset. At 10:30 Glenda called the home of Tim's employee at the shop, Bill Coombs.

"Bill, it's Glenda. Have you seen Tim? He had a guide trip today and hasn't come home. I thought he might have stopped off with you to have a beer."

"Nope. I didn't see him this morning when he left. And when I closed the shop at six, he hadn't come back. I assumed he went directly home."

Glenda waited until midnight to call the police and report Tim missing.

At seven the next morning, the police called Glenda and said they had heard nothing that helped, and an hour ago they had informed the Coast Guard about her husband.

The Coast Guard immediately began a search.

56

Poachers usually employ illegal gill nets because one strike will catch 100 times more fish than a single throw of a cast net. 'The new penalties helped get rid of a lot of part-time poachers,' said Ted Forsgren, executive director of the Florida Chapter of the Coastal Conservation Association. 'But the hard-core guys don't seem to care. There are plenty of them out there in full force.'

Huge Mullet Catch Seized, Tampa Bay Times, December 13, 2005.

FOUR DAYS LATER

THE MORNING *TALLAHASSEE NEWS* included a front-page article headlined MISSING APALACHICOLA FISHERMAN'S BODY FOUND IN BOAT IN GULF:

> *The body of Tim Hicks, owner of the Bay Fly Fishing Outfitters in Apalachicola, was found yesterday in his small boat sixty miles southeast of Apalachicola. The boat had run out of fuel and drifted. It was found during an extensive search by the Coast Guard. No official information has been released, but a man fishing where the Carrabelle River empties into the Gulf told this paper's reporter that he was certain that, when the boat was towed in and passed by near him, a gust of wind uncovered a tarpaulin over what appeared to be the body of a man wrapped in a net.*
>
> *Tim Hicks was active in conservation efforts and had spoken at numerous meetings and rallies twenty years ago when the gill net ban*

was proposed and enacted. Hicks was much disliked by commercial fishermen along the Panhandle Coast of Florida.

Hicks' death obviously was ruled to have been the result of foul play. I learned about it from a friend in Tallahassee whom I knew from Florida Council of Fly Fishers of America gatherings. I quickly forwarded his email to Grace in St. Augustine and Erin and Ken in Montana. Soon I had a phone call from Turk Jensen.

"Brooks, this is Detective Sergeant Jensen. Grace Justice sent me the news about the killing in the Panhandle. Where were you when it happened?"

"Here, at the cottage all day."

"Anyone to vouch for that?"

"Jimmy Jennings, the husband of my housekeeper, was working here all day *with me* doing some final work on my dock."

"You got a permit to do that?"

"Go read the county code, Jensen. . . . What the hell do you really want from me?"

"I'm going to check your alleged alibi with Jennings. You'd better not be lying."

"Why would I want to lie to such a fine and thoughtful deputy like you?"

"You smart ass. We aren't through."

Two days later the charges against me were withdrawn. I was free to go to Montana and made a note to send Turk Jensen a postcard from Paradise Valley. I'd promised Grace to take her to Gainesville, show her the town, and take in a Gator baseball game. I called her.

"Grace, now that I'm free of the travel restrictions, I need to leave for Montana soon. I promised you a day in Gainesville. Can you go with me tomorrow?"

"Yes. So you don't have to drive up here to Camachee Cove to pick me up, why don't I drive to your place and leave my car. I can be there any time."

"Around nine. No rush. We have no time restraints."

She arrived at 8:55 as I was sipping coffee on the porch.

"Coffee before we go?" I asked.

"I need it," she nodded. "Up late last night with a new case."

"Don't tell me about it."

Grace had never been to Gainesville. She was raised in Gloucester, Massachusetts, went to Harvard for her B.A. and then UConn law school. She clerked for a state Supreme Court judge in Connecticut after she graduated and then practiced in Hartford for fifteen years, the last seven as a full partner of the largest law firm in the city. Practice was financially rewarding, and living in a small apartment downtown, she saved a substantial amount. But she had some wanderlust and had always been intrigued with the idea of living in Florida. After all, so many people moved there *after* they retired. She thought: "Why not make the move before?" I agree with her; plus I've rarely heard of someone who spent a career working in Florida retiring to Connecticut.

Taking a year's leave of absence, Grace rented an apartment in Palm Beach and spent the time seeing Florida. Near the end of the year, she made a trip north along the coast following U.S. 1 from Melbourne to Fernandina. She loved St. Augustine. On the drive home to Hartford a month later, she composed and faxed her letter of resignation to the law firm. Reaching Connecticut, she packed her belongings and moved to Florida. She passed the Florida bar exam, put her name in the pot for an appointment as an assistant state attorney, and the rest—as they say—is history.

"Why have you never visited Gainesville?" I asked as we left the cottage. "You've seen most of the rest of the state."

"I never saw much of North Florida, especially the Panhandle. Once I had worked a few months as a state attorney and had some dealings with Tallahassee and places west, I began to think we'd be better off ceding the whole Panhandle to Alabama and Georgia. I thought Tallahassee especially was provincial and dull, and that university there—you know, the old women's college—appeared to be unplanned, unplanted, unattractive, and uninviting. Without ever being in Gainesville, I became an immediate Gator fan."

"But you've never visited Gainesville?"

"Happenstance. Nobody ever invited me until you. . . . What's the attraction to you, Macduff? You're not a Gator."

"How do you know?"

"I looked up your name on alumni and faculty lists. No Macduff Brooks."

"You're right. I guess I'm one of those many outsiders who adopt the Gators, as you have. But I follow up and go there often. . . . Are you up to an hour or so walk to see the campus?"

"I'm ready for *anything*, for the rest of the day."

I parked in the University Golf Course lot west of the campus. We walked through the campus, had lunch at the Copper Monkey with mobs of students, most wearing something that had "Gator" on it. Passing the tennis courts on the way back to the car, Grace tugged on my arm.

"I'm worn out. You walk so fast," she said. "Can we sit?"

"There are some seats around the law school. We can sit under the live oaks."

"So this is where I would have gone to law school if I'd come to Florida earlier."

"It is."

"I think I prefer the UConn campus."

"I know that campus. I liked it when. . . . " I caught myself from a path I've previously failed to maneuver. "I mean when I saw it sometime ago. It's a complex of restored old buildings, if I remember—a former seminary."

"When were you there? Maybe I was in law school and saw you. This handsome man walking across the campus."

"Not likely." I wanted the subject changed. "Ready to go on? One more place to show you."

I walked her through the Golf View residential area on the way to the car, passing where El and I had lived for ten unforgettable years before she died, and I remained for another ten forgettable years after she died. I didn't mention any of that to Grace.

It was a two-hour drive back to my cottage where Grace had left her car. As she drove she began to ask further questions.

"Mcduff, thanks for the day," she said as we passed through Palatka on the drive home. "You have such a passion for Gainesville. It's obvious. Why don't you live there?"

"I've thought about it, but I can't . . . I mean . . . I prefer the marshes along the coast."

"You have a great cottage. . . . but it's obvious you like Gainesville. . . . You're not a Gator? Where did you go to college?"

I was tempted to tell her I didn't. I didn't want to lie or get in trouble by not lying. "I went to UConn," I said, expecting surprise.

"My God, Macduff! That's *my* law school."

"I mean the undergraduate school in Storrs. You went to the law school in Hartford."

"You didn't tell me that when I said where I grew up?"

"I guess we got onto other things."

"So? Where *did* you grow up?"

"Farmington."

"Do you have family there?"

"No, they're gone, including my only sibling, a brother."

"Did he have children?"

"No, I'm the end of the line." Then I thought of Elsbeth and realized the line has been extended another generation.

We were noticeably quiet for the rest of the drive. At the cottage I parked the Jeep and walked her the dozen steps to her SUV. I thought of asking her in but didn't.

"I shouldn't pry about your family," she said as she got into her SUV. "You're leaving for Montana tomorrow. . . . When will you be back?"

"I don't know when, probably mid- to late-October.

"I'll call you first thing," she promised.

57

THE DRIVE TO MONTANA

WUFF AND I DIDN'T GET AWAY UNTIL NOON. I wanted first to cross the state and stop at Oyster Bay. Then we'd see how far we could drive until shortly after sunset.

One of the few businesses to have survived in Oyster Bay was a tiny single-chair barber shop near the town dock. Spiraling sun-faded stripes on an aged barber's pole were the only thing visibly in motion. The two remaining restaurants were not open, having collapsed their hours to dinners only. I assumed if you wanted to buy a breakfast or lunch you stayed in Cedar Key.

My hair needed trimming; the government hadn't cut it during my recuperation. Barbers are often centers of town gossip. Ben Thomas proved to be no different. Seated in the decades-old chair that squeaked when he turned it to start on the back, Thomas said, "I've been here cuttin' hair for forty-seven years, son. A lot's come and gone durin' that time."

"How's the town doing?" I inquired, "Surviving the changes to commercial fishing."

"We don't call them changes, son. We call them outrages. The state's supposed to help us, not drive more nails in our coffins. . . . But now that you've asked, we're more than sur-vivin'."

"How's that?" I asked.

"You heard of them deaths of fellers wrapped in gill nets?"

"Not much," I answered, hoping it opened a door to more information. If loose lips sink ships, they might also sink gill net boats.

"Those dead fellers were all ones who'd been lyin' about how gill netters were hurtin' fish stocks and catchin' turtles and dolphins. Not true. . . . Our folks got rights."

"What kind of rights?"

"Rights to fish, dammit. Been fishin' for generations."

"Weren't there studies that showed the numbers of fish caught were down?"

"More lies . . . the gill net ban killed this town, and some good people."

"Killed people?"

"Let me tell you, son. Not many people know. This town has been controlled for three generations by six families. Easy to remember; their names spell out 'mullet.' They're the Mur-phys, Unsers, Lowrys, Lumpkins, Edwardses, and Trents. They've controlled who did what in this town."

"How?"

"Anybody who went against them had their boats and gear—including their nets—stolen or trashed. . . . Even worse, their pets went missing, and their houses got painted with warnings."

"Are those the people you said got killed?"

"Nope, the ones that got killed weren't part of the six fam-ilies. . . . They were outsiders who deserved it. . . . You're all finished, son. Come back—Ya hear me?"

I was sure I would be back.

There was much to think about as Wuff and I drove on past dark until I was tired of staring at oncoming headlights. We stayed the night somewhere in the western part of Alabama, at a motel that wouldn't take pets, large or small, Pit Bull or Sheltie. Wuff stayed in the car and pouted. At midnight I walked out in the dark and carried her back to my room where she had a pleasant rest sleeping on the second bed.

The next day we angled northwest to the corner of Arkansas, and on the third day we were in endless Nebraska where I decided to turn west on Interstate 80 and confront the eighteen wheelers. Somewhere along the way—it's hard to distinguish when there's nothing implanted in your mind to remember—we saw in the distance something that seemed to be blocking the interstate. It looked like a huge railroad car set across the highway. But as we closed the gap, a sign urged us to stop at the Great Platte River Road Archway. It was Nebraska's version of Disney World and gave me something to muse about for the next several hundred miles, which finally took us out of Nebraska and into Wyoming where we stopped for the night at Cheyenne.

Five days is our usual crossing-time from Florida to Montana. I had no reason to rush once we were in Wyoming. We turned north in Rawlings and a few hours later watched the Wind River Mountains begin to surround us. A small motel that tolerated Wuff extorted more money than the room was worth, but I pulled a chair out in front of our unit and watched a priceless display as the sun set over a mountain with a name I didn't know.

We were firmly and pleasantly in the grasp of the mountains the next day. I stopped in Dubois, bought a Wyoming fishing license from a fly fishing shop and a sandwich from a delicatessen, and found a place to picnic along the Wind River. Playing the role of the tourist who fishes largely within sight of his car, I tossed into the water a Harrop's Green Drake I'd bought near Harriman's Ranch in Idaho the year before. It was the only fly attached to my vest that was accessible in the back of the SUV. Most of my flies were in the car-top carrier, the keys for which were "somewhere" in the vehicle. It was not exactly how I would like to select a fly, and it proved to be the wrong choice.

After covering a good bit of water and not seeing any sign of a fish, I bit off the fly, reeled in the line, and broke down my rod. While putting the gear in the back of the SUV, I took a last look at the river and mountains and watched four rises not fifty feet away.

Wuff gave a couple of barks as I was debating whether to rig up again. It was almost five, Wyoming time. Her supper was due. She's already adjusted to the time change. Her on-demand feeding is a small price to pay for her companionship, which I greatly value these days, even if she does head for Lucinda's side of the bed in my cottage. Maybe she won't do so at the cabin.

It was close to dark when we crested Togwotee Pass, bouncing through road repairs that were starting early in the spring so they might be finished before the rude onslaught of the following winter.

I knew I wasn't going the most direct way to Mill Creek in Paradise Valley. I wasn't looking forward to arriving at my cabin and finding it as desolate as before I met Lucinda. Grace Justice said she might fly out to visit if I wanted company; she had unused accrued vacation time. I interpreted her comment as soliciting an invitation.

Since I'd chosen to enter Montana using the South Entrance of Yellowstone directly north of Jackson Hole, I had to wait until the second week of May for the park road to open. Wuff and I passed the time by imposing on my Jackson Hole guide friend John Kirby for several days, two of which we spent drifting the Green and the Salt rivers.

Ultimately, Wuff and I had to push on to Montana. Yellowstone Park was quieted by a layer of late snow that softened sounds. Insufficient snow to delay opening the park roads, it discouraged all but a few drivers from entering. We had no trouble getting a room for a night at the cabins behind the Lake Hotel.

On the drive the next day north through the park, I pulled into the Nez Perce picnic area along Buffalo Ford. Not to picnic but to sit and enjoy the Yellowstone River flowing at the bottom of snow-covered hillside slopes. By the time we left the park at Mammoth, the snow had all but disappeared under a bright late-April sun.

Mid-afternoon brought us to Emigrant where I topped off our gas, bought Livingston and Bozeman newspapers, a few groceries, and a bag of charcoal for the grill. We could no longer delay arrival at my Mill Creek cabin.

I hadn't called Mavis about our expected time of arrival. I didn't know it, and every day on the drive I gave thought to turning around, going back to St. Augustine and looking for a place to buy in Gainesville.

My gate was locked, but there were tire tracks disclosing that someone had been at the cabin in the last twenty-four hours. I guess Mavis had sensed I would be there and started cleaning. But when I reached the cabin, there were tire tracks from two different vehicles. The best I could think of was that Mavis had her daughter or a friend along to help. The thought of having a clean cabin was pleasing. But however clean it might be, it was going to be empty.

58

The majority of those mullet [the 5-million to 10-million pounds per year sold in Florida] *are harvested by licensed commercial fishermen who use hand-thrown cast nets to capture their fish. 'There are probably about 55 boats who work it regularly during the roe season,' said Robert McCurdy, who works 11 months of the year as a boat salesman. 'It is hard work but worth it.'*
With roe mullet selling for $1.70 a pound, a cast netter such as McCurdy can still earn $9,000 a week during peak season. 'We start hurting,' he said, 'if the gill netters get to the fish before us.'

Huge Mullet Catch Seized, Tampa Bay Times, December 13, 2005.

EARLIER THE SAME MORNING AT THE CABIN

LUCINDA SLEPT SOUNDLY IN MACDUFF'S CABIN until nine, when a knock on the door woke her. Sleepily, she shuffled to the door. It was Mavis.

"I thought maybe you were still here. No one's been to the ranch other than you for the past few weeks. Every time I drop by I hope Mr. Brooks is here with you. You come to your senses yet?"

"I don't know, Mavis. I need some time alone. I don't think Macduff would mind my being here. I'll leave before he comes."

"That could be any minute. I just called John Kirby in Jackson Hole to see if he knew where Mr. Brooks was. He certainly did. Mr. Brooks stayed with Mr. Kirby for several days and left yesterday heading this way. He must have stayed in the park last night or changed his mind about coming to the cabin. Maybe he's with friends in Bozeman. That means he'll be here any time."

"I have to leave," she said abruptly. "I'll get my clothes and soon be gone."

"Are you sure that's best? Mr. Kirby said Mr. Brooks was not himself. Mr. Kirby thinks it's you. If you don't mind me intruding, I agree with him"

"I've gone too far, Mavis. I can't face Macduff now." In ten minutes she had dressed and picked up her keys from the table and pushed past Mavis and hurried out the door. In a minute her car was gone."

"What do young people do these days?" wondered Mavis out loud. "How did all this happen?" She left closely behind Lucinda, not even checking Macduff's room, where the bed covers were scattered.

As Mavis locked the gate and drove off, she saw a vehicle well behind her pull in and stop at the gate. It looked like Macduff's SUV.

She thought it best not to interfere and went home.

59

A FEW MOMENTS LATER

I WENT UP THE STEPS to unlock my cabin door. There were several footprints on the porch in the blown snow of late spring that had accumulated in the shade beneath the over-hang, avoiding the melting rays of the May sun. The prints were two different sizes. One set was made by smooth-soled boots, the other by non-skid sneaks.

Inside, Wuff ran immediately to my bedroom while I walked to the kitchen to see if there were any footprints on the rear porch. But any that might have been had melted. A sharp bark came from the bedroom. When I poked in my head, I was amazed to see the bed had been slept in. Perhaps Mavis was lacking room for a visiting family member . . . but she would have used my guestroom, not my bedroom, and not left my side of the bed unmade.

I called Mavis. "This is Macduff. I'm at the cabin. I should have let you know I was coming but I was uncertain when I would arrive. I guess you needed a bed for a guest. That's fine."

"Mr. Brooks. It weren't me. Or any guest of mine."

"A drifter? I see no signs of a break-in."

"You might say it was," Mr. Brooks, "but the drifter was beautiful and named Lucinda."

I should have known. Wuff had settled on my pillow. Not because I had slept there, but because it was where Lucinda had slept and left fragrant traces.

"Where is she, Mavis?"

"God only knows. When I arrived and surprised her this morning, she rushed by me, got in her SUV, and drove off."

"I'll bet she's at her ranch. I'll go there and look."

"Don't bother; I'm at the ranch, and no one's been here."

"Where would she go?"

"Anywhere. Away."

"I have to find her."

"Leave her be. She's not ready to be found."

Three days passed without a word from Lucinda. I called everyone I thought she knew in Montana and Wyoming. No one had seen or talked to her. I called her secretary, Carmen, in Manhattan. She had not heard from Lucinda. Erin called me back and pressed me about requesting an official missing person search. I asked her not to do that.

Mavis was right. If Lucinda is missing, it's because she wants to be.

60

THE FOLLOWING DAY

A DEEP CABERNET METALIC SUV that had never been outside Montana, showing tasteful signs on each door stating "Arrogate Ranch" and bearing license plates affirming the vehicle's Montana home, was in its fourth day of eastward flight. At dusk, showing the grime collected from eight states, like "I visited . . ." tourist decals, the vehicle drove in and parked at the historic Gibson Inn in Northwest Florida. The town was Apalachicola.

Lucinda Lang was tired from the fourth long day of driving. But most of all she was tired of being alone. Draped over the passenger seat next to her was the beige herringbone fleece shawl she had thrown over her shoulders when she left her apartment in New York. When she left Macduff's cabin, she wore it crossing Montana and Wyoming.

She took her small Gucci bag from the back seat into the inn; she had left Mill Creek hurriedly, confused and embarrassed, and stopped at a Target near Omaha to buy clothes and toiletries sufficient to allow her to pass inspection at a B&B or hotel lobby during her drive to Florida. The Gucci bag might help convince a desk clerk she was not as destitute as she both felt and assumed she appeared.

The next morning at breakfast in the Gibson Inn's dining room, she filled her plate from the buffet in a way more reminiscent of Macduff's preferences than her own—two fried eggs, bacon, sausage, hash browns, and a large butter croissant. Forgetting she was driving, she downed a double Bloody Mary, urging and convincing her to depart later than planned.

Lucinda opened the local weekly newspaper that had been slid under her door. She had brought the paper to the breakfast table more for companionship than enlightenment. The headline read NO RESOLUTION OF THE GILL NET MURDER OF LOCAL GUIDE TIM HICKS. It drew her close attention; she remembered a day last fall sitting at breakfast with Macduff at his cabin on Mill Creek and reading about a death on a southwest Florida river of a guide found wrapped in a gill net. Later that same day Macduff and she found another body wrapped in a gill net and lodged under a cross-beam of the bridge on Mill Creek. Macduff knew about both deaths but was not a friend of either person.

Lucinda hadn't yet learned about the death in St. Augustine on Macduff's boat, a body also wrapped in a gill net, but of a person Macduff had never met. The similarity of the Apalachicola incident to both that near Sanibel and that at Mill Creek, made her read further:

Nearly two months ago Tim Hicks, owner of Bay Fly Fishing Outfitters of this town, was found dead wrapped in a gill net in his flats boat sixty miles off the coast in the Gulf of Mexico. Detectives for this county have reported nothing that might identify anyone who participated in what is believed to have been a murder. One county commissioner, soon to face re-election, has publically criticized the county sheriff's office for suppressing the investigation.

Hicks had enemies. He was strongly supportive of the original gill net ban in 1994 and was promoting new efforts targeted against both commercial fishing interests and what Hicks called "improper judicial action" in this county. He alleged that some judges serving districts where there were many commercial fishing families, whose standard of living had deteriorated because of the net ban, had refused for one specious reason or another to enforce the net ban.

Only last week a circuit court judge in Leon County overruled the net ban, a decision that was purportedly effective throughout the state. The judge ruled that the ban wasn't fair to the families of commercial netters. An appeal was filed by the state, which automatically stayed the circuit court's action. Undaunted, the same judge lifted the stay, thus re-imposing her decision and allowing gill netting. Also undaunted, and unimpressed, the district court of appeal quickly intervened and re-imposed the ban.

By that time commercial mullet netters from as far along the Atlantic Coast as North Carolina were hauling in boatloads of mullet from the Florida coasts. The mullet roe would be shipped to Asia.

The police have not linked the judicial spat to Hick's death, but his murder has enhanced the net ban controversy and split voters' opinions in this county, as well as further along the Gulf Coast.

Using the guest computer at the inn after breakfast, Lucinda went online, searched "gill net deaths" and learned about a fire on a boat in St. Augustine, although the boat owner's name was not mentioned. She downloaded all she could find about the four deaths. None of the Florida deaths directly implicated Macduff in any reasonable way. The death in Montana remained mysterious because it occurred within a few miles of Macduff's cabin, even though the victim lived principally in Georgia.

After breakfast Lucinda checked out of the inn and drove past the sparse, deteriorating commercial docks lining the Apalachicola River. She had much to read and decided to glance at part of it before she faced the final leg of the drive to St. Augustine.

Lucinda found a bench along the river and began reading. The articles absorbed her attention and, admittedly, enhanced her loneliness without Macduff. She bore some physical scars from those days, but thought more about the good times.

Sometime around noon, a woman bearing the weight of considerable years sat down next to her. After Lucinda finished an article and was placing it in a pile of those she had read, the woman took advantage of the pause and spoke.

"I watched you from the next bench," she said. Lucinda had been so focused on the articles she hadn't noticed. "I saw you absorbed in your reading, but then there were occasional tears. I didn't want to bother you. . . . My name is Emma."

"You're not a bother. I'm finished with my reading for now. I have a long drive ahead. . . . There was an interesting article in today's paper about a local man named Hicks who apparently was killed and wrapped in a net of some kind."

"It was a gill net," Emma noted, and added, "He deserved what he got."

"Death is a harsh penalty. What did he do?"

"He was part of what the net ban did to our fishing families."

"Is Apalachicola a big fishing town?"

"Yes, if you include oysters. You ever heard of Apalachicola oysters?"

"I have. I had some last night at the Gibson Inn. They're delicious. I think the best I've ever eaten."

"They are the best. But they're dyin' out because Georgia wants more water. And drought. And some parasites."

"And overharvesting?" Lucinda asked.

Ignoring Lucinda's question, Emma continued. "It's really been our mullet fishermen who've been hurt, not the oyster harvesters. My sister Betty married a mullet fisherman named Joe Tanner in a little town southeast of here near Cedar Key. It's called Oyster Bay."

"I don't know the west coast of Florida. I live near St. Augustine. What's Oyster Bay like?"

For the next half hour Emma described Oyster Bay's development: a century ago supplying pencil makers with cedar, transformation to commercial fishing, and, after '94, economic collapse from the ban on gill nets, Vietnamese competition for clams, and fear of hepatitis from eating raw oysters.

"That's a sad tale, Emma."

"Oyster Bay got their revenge," Emma said, showing a different and hostile part of her personality.

"What do you mean *revenge?*"

"I mean those people who got killed and then were wrapped in gill nets."

"How many did that happen to?"

"At least four. Maybe more where the bodies were never found."

"You know who did it?" Lucinda asked. For a moment Emma looked like the cat that swallowed the canary.

"I meant whoever killed those people gave some satisfaction to that town and all of us commercial fishing folk along the whole Florida coast."

"Does your sister in Oyster Bay feel that way?"

"Not only does she feel good about it, her. . . ." Emma decided she had said enough.

"I hope there's no more violence. Retribution won't end the matter," Lucinda responded, her head shaking in wonder that an old woman could be prone to using murder as retaliation.

Lucinda filled her gas tank, left Apalachicola, and drove without a stop to St. Augustine. When she reached Macduff's driveway, she stopped and sat next to his gate, wondering whether to go in. She had a key for the cottage, on the same ring as the key she used to enter his cabin on Mill Creek. She was certain he was not at the cottage, and she knew that Jen Jennings would let her stay. She opened the gate, locked it behind her, and parked next to the cottage stairs.

As she had done so many times in the past, she walked up and entered the living room. This time she was startled. The cottage was dreary; all the signs of their living together were gone. Not because Macduff had cleaned out Lucinda's belongings, but because *she* had asked Jen to collect them and send them to Manhattan. What she especially missed were the many photos of the two taken over their years together.

As she had done less than a week before at Macduff's Montana cabin, she went into the bedroom, undressed, placed the framed photo she had brought from Montana on the bedside table, and crawled under the covers on the bed. On *Macduff's* side.

She was sound asleep in five minutes.

61

Plaintiff challenged the constitutional validity of three rules adopted by the defendant to carry out the Constitutional gill net ban. The First District Court of Appeal approved lower court summary judgment ending the case. Plaintiff appealed to the Supreme Court which rejected plaintiff's argument, thus continuing the gill net ban.

A paraphrase from Wakulla Commercial Fishermen's Association, Inc. v. Florida Fish and Wildlife Conservation Commission (2007).

THE FOLLOWING DAY

IN THE MORNING, wrapped in a towel, Lucinda washed the few clothes she had brought with her. She made a list of what to buy for the coming intensity of a Florida summer. Mostly sandals, shorts, and sleeveless tops. In the bedroom closet she hung the fleece shawl she had worn when she left chilly Montana. Some of Macduff's clothes were in the closet, and she placed her shawl over one of his long-sleeved shirts.

One light-weight long-sleeved jacket hung off to one side in the closet. She pulled it out and laid it on the bed. The right shoulder of the jacket had a dark stain. Inside was more pronounced staining. There was a single frayed-edged bullet hole. The jacket must have been worn by Macduff when he was shot. Her hands quivering, she put the jacket back in a dark corner.

Walking into the bathroom, she opened the medicine cabinet, looking for aspirin. There were none among the few shaving and dental care items. But there was a bottle of Chanel No. 5. Obviously, it was not Macduff's. Her immediate reaction was that Macduff had been *unfaithful*, but quickly realized he had his own life now, and he was a man who would attract women. She realized that her abrupt departure at St. Louis seven months ago had widened the gap between them and allowed someone new to step in and become a part of Macduff's life.

While Lucinda was feeling sorry for herself, she heard a car, looked out the door, and saw a county deputy's car coming to a halt—an array of colors flashing. She stepped out on the porch at the same time a uniformed officer stepped out of the car. He looked at her, then reached inside the vehicle and turned off the lights.

Lucinda stood in amazement looking at the figure stare at her, lift his gun a couple of inches, but not clear the holster, push it back in, and start up the stairs, no longer even acknowledging her presence.

"Where's Brooks?" he asked angrily, every half minute tugging up his belt that was lined with his Glock, Taser, and several unidentifiable gadgets.

"I said, 'Where's Brooks?'" he repeated as he brushed by Lucinda, pushed open the door, and walked in.

"He's not here. You can't just walk in here."

"Where is he?" demanded the officer.

"Who are you?" countered Lucinda.

"Deputy Turk Jensen. Now, where's Brooks," he demanded, his hand resting on the top of his Glock.

"Montana, I guess," she said.

"Who are *you*?" demanded Jensen. "What are you doing in Brooks' house?" he demanded.

"I'm Lucinda Lang, Macduff's fiancée," she fibbed.

"Then why aren't you with him? Give me some ID," he demanded, increasingly emboldened both by the presence of only a single woman and the gun he continued to fondle.

Lucinda showed him her driver's license.

"This is a New York license," he said, as though it wasn't recognized in Florida.

"What do you want? I want *you* out of my house!"

"Your house? Lady, you're under arrest for breaking and entering."

"Call Bill Muirhead," Lucinda said, using a name she knew only from some papers left on the table. Muirhead was apparently a lawyer Macduff retained after the body was found on his boat and he was badgered by a local deputy. Could this be the same deputy?

When Jensen heard Muirhead mentioned, his attitude changed. "You know Muirhead?" he demanded.

"He's our lawyer. I'd like to call him now."

"That won't be necessary. I warn you. Tell Macduff I want to see him as soon as he gets here."

"That won't be until fall, probably October. And he'll want Muirhead present when you talk."

"Goddammit," Jensen mumbled as he walked out, down the steps, got into his car, turned on both the flashing lights and the siren, and sped out the dirt drive as fast as he could without colliding with one of the pines lining the entry road.

Lucinda was shaking, more from anger that from fear. Jensen truly was a jerk.

But Jensen wore the badge.

62

THE FOLLOWING WEEK – A LATE MAY SPRING DAY AT THE COTTAGE

LUCINDA CALLED JEN AND TOLD HER about leaving Montana abruptly. Jen admired Lucinda and would do anything for her, even at the expense of Jen's employment by Macduff. In a few days Jen had found and cleaned all the photos of Lucinda with Macduff. Weeks ago she had sent those of Lucinda alone to Manhattan. Once Lucinda had rehung the pictures of the two, the rooms returned to their former brightness. Lucinda trusted Jen and valued her intelligence. Knowing no one else in the area, Lucinda decided to ask Jen a question about the gill net deaths.

"Jen, you know more than I do about the death when Macduff's boat burned. You also may have read about the body found dead and wrapped in a gill net on a flats boat in the Gulf of Mexico."

"I did read a couple of pieces in the local paper. But nothing more."

"I need to talk to someone who's working on the Bradford death. It won't be Turk Jensen, who I had a run in with here a week ago. I don't know anyone else in this area involved in law enforcement."

"There is one person you should call. Her name is Grace Justice. She's an assistant state attorney in this area. She's honest and intelligent and has a good chance of being the next state attorney—responsible for the entire state. Macduff knows her and has talked to her about the gill net deaths. He won't talk to Jensen, who arrested him for the murder of Bradford and took him to jail."

Lucinda called Grace Justice the next day, relating her conversation with the elderly woman about the death of Hicks and about Oyster Bay. Grace was dumfounded.

"Ms. Lang, this is important. Do you know I talked to Macduff about his conversation with an Oyster Bay resident?"

"Do you know Macduff?"

"We met last Thanksgiving. He called me at his attorney's recommendation. And he took me fly fishing during the Christmas holiday. When Macduff gave me a tour of his cottage, there wasn't a sign of you."

"I think there's a sign of *you*," Lucinda said, cryptically. "A bottle of Chanel No. 5 in the bathroom. I threw it out. Sorry, if it was yours." Then Lucinda felt foolish—it could have been Elsbeth's.

"Not important. . . . Let's clear the air. I don't ever come between a couple, married or otherwise. Macduff told me he'd been engaged but that she'd ended it, including giving him back her ring. I guess that was you. I saw him as a free and eligible man. When I visited the cottage and we fished together, there wasn't any indication of your relationship."

"You're not to blame. I caused our breakup. I was upset with something he planned. It involved some consulting in D.C. But what led to the breakup was my discovering I had breast cancer. I couldn't face Macduff and leave him burdened.

I left him just before the Thanksgiving holiday when you first talked to him. I went to New York City, where I have an apartment I bought when I was working there. My surgery was done in Manhattan. It led to an infection that weakened me. I seem to be recovered.

"At the same time Macduff had gone to Khar . . . he was abroad and was shot in the shoulder in an incident. It became infected and took him a long while to recuperate. I knew nothing about it until he was back in the U.S. in Walter Reed in D.C."

"This is all quite incredible. Lucinda, I don't know whether to shoot you or shoot myself. I won't be a part of your split. I've spent my last days with Macduff, conditioned on your getting back together. Lucinda, I know who is admitted to Walter Reed; my dad was an Army surgeon for three years there. Macduff's 'incident' is not something I want to know about. . . . But you were about to say Khartoum. I've read about the unidentified sniper who killed the putative heir to leading the worst al-Qaeda terrorists group. That shooting happened in Khartoum. . . . I won't ask another question."

Lucinda sat back on the sofa, trembling. Speaking softly into her cell phone, she said, "Grace, I don't know what to say. How can we help Macduff?"

"I don't know, but with a few regrets, I'm on your side."

63

I grew up fooling with these [gill nets] when I was a teenager. They would catch a lot of stuff, not only Spanish [mackerel]. Even though I have fond memories, they need to get them all. And yes, I used to shrimp trawl too, and they just kill everything that can't get out of the way. The first time I dumped a net I couldn't believe it, but you grow immune to it after a while, and it becomes 'normal' to kill all the croakers, crabs, flounder, tonguefish, trout, everything in there.

Troy Jens, citing Berry in *Gill Net Ban Introduced in Alabama* (2007). www.wmi.org/bassfish/bassboard/other_topics/message

THREE DAYS LATER AT THE COTTAGE

GRACE INTENDED TO FOLLOW UP on the Oyster Bay information. Lucinda wasn't sure what to do—but first she had to meet Elsbeth at the Jacksonville airport. She was coming for a brief three days and then flying to Montana to stay with Macduff and work for the summer at the Chico Hot Springs resort. Lucinda wondered why Elsbeth would spend even three days with her at the cottage, since she was now sure who Elsbeth blamed for the split. It *wasn't* her dad.

Elsbeth looked pallid when she met Lucinda at the airport, only partly due to being away from any sun for the past five months. Maine is not where people flock to during the winter months.

"You look pale. Are you OK?" Lucinda asked.

"Long winter. I don't know why it seemed that way; I've been through seventeen years of them in Maine. It's not where you go to work on your tan."

"Elsbeth, how much do you know about Macduff and me over the past few months?"

"Not much. Want to tell me?"

Lucinda filled her in on the breast surgery, complications, recovery, flight to Montana, and fleeing the next day to Florida without seeing Macduff.

"Why didn't you wait to see him?"

"Scared of being rejected. I pushed him pretty far."

"Then fly to Montana with me."

"I'm not ready for that."

On the drive to the cottage, Lucinda also told Elsbeth about her stopover in Apalachicola and the mystery of Oyster Bay. Perhaps it wasn't a good idea to bring a teen into another mess, but Lucinda needed someone to talk to. Then the conversation turned to Macduff and Grace Justice.

"Is Ms. Justice competition? Is she after Dad? It sounds as though he's serious about her."

"I don't know. But I like Grace. I don't think she'll see Macduff socially again, but they do have to work together to find out who killed Bradford on Macduff's boat."

"Ms. Justice seems more inclined to want to know you as a friend than to be with Dad."

"I read her that way. I think she's sincere. I'd like Grace as a friend when I'm here. Her relationship with Macduff now depends more on him than it does on her."

"It sounds as though you want to stay at the cottage," Elsbeth remarked.

Parking Lucinda's SUV, they climbed the stairs and entered. Elsbeth looked around and smiled. "The cottage looks great with the photos back on the walls. And a few of *your* things around. . . . Will you come and see us in Montana?"

"I have some things to do here."

"Involving the deaths?"

"Yes."

"Lucinda, somewhere there may be a killer after Dad. You're a good target if he's not here. . . . Remember that there have been *four* deaths."

"One was in Montana," Lucinda noted.

"But the victim was from Georgia more than Montana. And he'd talked to Dad about the gill net ban and the water issues with the Apalachicola."

"I may be able to help Macduff, with Grace's help."

"What do you plan?"

"First, I'm going to visit Oyster Bay. . . . After I drop you at the airport."

"May I tell Dad?"

"That's your call."

"Oh! I forgot to tell you. I've withdrawn from Maine. So did my friend, Sue."

"Dropping out of college?"

"Dropping out of *one* college. We've both been accepted for transfer. We'll room together."

"Where?"

"That's our next decision. We'll either be in Gainesville or Bozeman."

64

THE FOLLOWING DAY – A TRIP TO OYSTER BAY

ELSBETH LEFT FOR MONTANA after her three days' visit. Lucinda saw her off in Jacksonville and thought how good it would be to have her closer than Maine. It had to be a hard decision to transfer. Elsbeth loved her adoptive parents, the late Carsons, and it wasn't easy to leave behind seventeen years of living happily in Greenville.

Lucinda drove directly to Florida's Gulf Coast from the Jacksonville airport. After a light lunch of grilled oysters in Suwannee, she continued south to Cedar Key and back north the few miles to Oyster Bay. She had one address, that of Joe Tanner and his wife Betty. She was the sister of Emma whom Lucinda met in Apalachicola. She wasn't sure how to approach Mrs. Tanner but soon found herself knocking on the Tanners' front door, not knowing where her visit would lead.

A sixtyish lady pushed open the screen door. One disadvantage of living in Oyster Bay was that it is often called the center of the world for mosquitos.

"Can I help you, young lady?" Mrs. Tanner said, in a voice that told either that she was a naturally outgoing person or lonely for company.

"My name is Lucinda Lang. I was traveling to Florida from the West recently and stopped in Apalachicola for the night. I loved the town, and before facing another long drive, I took some papers down to the docks to read. A lovely woman shared my bench. She was your sister, Emma. We talked for an hour. She made me promise to stop by here and say hello if I were in the area. I'm to join some friends for an early dinner in Cedar Key. I hope I'm not interrupting."

"Good Lord! You're not. Emma told me about you. I'm her sister Betty. Please come in, dear. I've made some tea. Will you have some?"

"Yes. . . . Your house is lovely. So many photos!"

"They start with my husband's grandfather, John Tanner. He came here from Wales to work logging cedar. That ran out, and he had a family to feed. So he turned to fishing. His two sons began working with him when they were about nine. They both became commercial fishermen. One was my husband Joe's father, Henry. Henry's brother died at Normandy. My husband was born during the war, and he also took up fishing. We were married in the early '60s, about the time Emma moved to Apalachicola. Joe and I couldn't have children.

"Fishing was a good way to make a living; much of the time we used gill nets for mullet. But then they passed the net ban in '94. The lies told by the recreational fishermen about commercial fishing were awful. My husband was devastated. He tried to become a guide but his heart wasn't in it. *He was a third generation fisherman.* He was *entitled* to fish. Joe was never the same. Oh dear, I've talked too much."

"No, you haven't. I'm sorry, Mrs. Tanner. I didn't know about the ban until I talked with your sister in Apalachicola. I'm from Montana. We don't hear much about what's going on in Florida."

274

"It's not just me that's upset about the ban. It hurt a lot of families here and all along the coast. On the East Coast, too."

"Are you able to get by, Mrs. Tanner?"

"You're kind to ask, dear. Yes. Because we had no children, and because even before the ban the number of fish was getting poor, we knew to put money away. We did right fine."

"Do many people still fish here?"

"Not many. Some are guides. Others make enough to get along using large cast nets. But those nets can't replace the gill nets. . . . I shouldn't tell you, but there are a few families that are doing fine because they *are* using gill nets. They fish at night and keep their nets hidden."

"No one's been caught?"

"They have, several times. But we got county court Judge King here, and he's on our side. His daddy was a commercial fisherman who had a heart attack the day they announced the net ban passed. Judge King always finds a way around applying the law. . . . Not one Oyster Bay fisherman has spent a day in jail or paid a dollar in fines. But now we hear the same people who pushed the gill net ban are proposing another vote to extend it and even cover all but very small cast nets. That's so recreational fishermen can still net some finger mullet for bait. . . . That's not all; these people want to *limit* judges' power—it has something to do with not letting them withhold judgment, whatever that means."

"Mrs. Tanner, what do you think will happen? Can't you do anything about it? Change the ban to allow more netting?"

"We've tried; nothing has worked. We no sooner get some legislators on our side then the recreational fishermen step in and pass around a lot of money. . . . But we haven't sat idle."

"What do you mean?"

"Did Emma tell you anything?"

"Not about what you've done, but she did say the ban was hurting you and your friends here."

"I guess she didn't tell you that over the past six to eight months four people who supported the net ban have been found dead wrapped in gill nets."

"Here in Oyster Bay?"

"No, three in Florida—one down near Sanibel, one a little south of St. Augustine, and one found floating in the Gulf west of here. Plus, one in Montana. But he was a Georgia boy. . . . Isn't Montana where you said you were from. You must have read about it?"

"Montana's a big state. Most of the papers are in small towns and don't cover much other than local news. A few Montana trout fishermen die each year, usually falling while fishing and their waders fill with water. They're dragged under and drown.

"Mrs. Tanner, I have to go. I'm meeting with my friends in Cedar Key. I've enjoyed meeting you. I'm sorry Mr. Tanner wasn't here. I would love to hear his stories about fishing."

"Oh! Ms. Lang. You won't meet Mr. Tanner. Joe died two years ago. He was out gill netting one night. The marine police, who usually aren't out after dark, tried to stop him."

"What happened?"

"He fell off his boat into his net. And drowned."

65

They will have to pry my net from my cold dead fingers. . . . We have our rights.

Troy Jens, citing G.N.E. in Gill Net Ban Introduced in Alabama (2007). www.wmi.org/bassfish/bassboard/other_topics/message

THAT EVENING IN MONTANA

I MET ELSBETH AT THE BOZEMAN AIRPORT. When we reached my vehicle in the parking lot and I set her bags in the back, she exclaimed, "Dad, you swapped your big new Jeep for a Wrangler? Downsizing?"

"Nope."

"Is this a friend's?"

"Nope."

"You don't need two cars in Montana."

"*We* do."

"What do you mean?"

"This is for you. It's used. A friend sold it to me. You need it to get back and forth to work this summer. And you might even like to drive it to Maine at the end of the summer."

"Nope," she said, mimicking me.

"Too long a drive."

"Nope," she repeated.

"Explain."

"I'm not going back to Maine."

"So you flunked out?" She punched me on the arm.

"Dad, you don't flunk out with a 3.8 average."

"Where did you mess up?"

"Economics. Remember Lucinda telling me about her one bad grade at Oberlin? From an economics professor who was a socialist in sheep's clothing?"

"I remember."

"I think I had his son for my teacher!"

"Are you going to another university in the fall?"

"Yep."

"Do I know anything about your new university?"

"Yep."

"Stop that!"

"My friend Sue and I are going to choose between UM and MSU here in Montana—most likely MSU—and another place."

"Where's the other place?"

"Gainesville."

"Gainesville, Georgia? Good, there's a military college in that area. You could use some discipline."

"No. I need to learn how to discipline *other* people. Like my father to begin with."

"You're probably right. . . . This is wonderful news. Will you miss Maine?"

"Very much. I'll go back once a year to place flowers on the Carsons' graves."

"How are you going to decide between Florida and Montana?"

"With your help. I want to know where you'll be."

"What do you mean?"

"You talked about selling both your cabin and cottage and moving to Gainesville."

"I've thought a lot more about it. I think I'm here to stay, the same for the cottage in Florida."

"But you were so concerned with losing Lucinda that you decided to sell both. Changed your mind about Lucinda?"

"No. But I can't control what she feels about me. I have to live my life."

"You know I was with her for a few days before leaving this morning for here?"

"And?"

"She's miserable."

"Why do you say that?"

"*You* should know. She flew across the country to here, spent fifteen minutes at her ranch, went to your cabin, and slept on your side of the bed. Weeks later, when she knew you were about to arrive, she couldn't face you and fled. She drove back across the country to St. Augustine and the cottage and did the same—curled up on your side of the bed. She's rehung all the photos of the two of you."

"Sounds like she wants *memories* of me. But not me."

"Dad, do you know why she left you in St. Louis?"

"Greener grass on the other side of the Mississippi?"

"*No. . . . Cancer.*"

I didn't understand. My vision of her before she left me in St. Louis was of health and vigor, energy and enthusiasm. Trembling, I pulled over to the side of the road. "I think you'd better drive."

Elsbeth took over driving and repeated to me all that Lucinda had told her—about the lump discovered in a breast, the decisions, the operation, and her difficult recovery.

"I should have been there," I said.

"You were out of the country."

"I was. I had flown to Europe. On business."

"Is your business killing people?"

"What do you mean?"

"Does Khartoum mean anything to you? A meeting of terrorists? An assassination by a sniper? An escape up the Nile? Being shot? An operation to repair your shoulder and serious infection?"

"Are you talking about. . . . Who told you about. . . ."

"It's about *you.* Lucinda told me what little she knows. Dan Wilson told me more, including about the medals."

"Does it trouble you, Elsbeth?"

"Yes, but mostly that Lucinda is so confused."

"Can you help? I want her back."

"What can we do?" she asked. Exactly what I was thinking. We sat sipping iced tea on the rear porch of the cabin, talking about many things and watching the rapid flow of Mill Creek tumble over egg-like rocks worn smooth and elliptical by the ages. On the side of the hills that led skyward to become Emigrant Mountain, new life was rising from the ground to replace the dead. The tiny pine tree seedlings were coming back.

I'm not sure I'm coming back nearly as strong.

66

THE FOLLOWING DAY IN GRACE JUSTICE'S OFFICE
IN ST. AUGUSTINE

GRACE SET A CAPPUCINO IN FRONT OF LUCIN-
DA and asked, "So you met in Oyster Bay with, who was
it, a Mrs. Tanner?"

"Yes, Mrs. Joe Tanner," responded Lucinda. "We had a
pleasant and lengthy conversation. I feel sorry for her, her family, her neighbors, and all the commercial fishermen along the
Florida coast, both east and west."

"Do you think she was telling the truth?"

"She wasn't evasive. The feelings among the fishing families, at least in Apalachicola and Oyster Bay, run strong."

"But," Grace offered, "that doesn't mean if one or more
of the four was murdered, it was by commercial fishermen."

"How do we explain Emma's statement in Apalachicola
that the people of Oyster Bay 'got their revenge'? And her sister's statements in Oyster Bay that they 'haven't sat idle'?"

"I have to work with facts, Lucinda. We can't arrest someone for oral comments like those two ladies made. If their husbands were involved, we need more specific evidence. Let me
share a report from the state attorney in Ft. Myers about the
first death—Clint Carter. It was not issued as a press release, but

as an in-house document for limited distribution. The assistant state attorney sent me a copy. It's only a matter of time before someone passes a copy on to some Ft. Myers journalist."

Lucinda took the brief two-page report and read the conclusions:

This investigation concludes that Clint Carter died either of natural causes, such as a heart attack, or by drowning. No direct evidence exists that suggests a crime was committed. The medical examiner's report, which leaves much to be desired, found no blows to Carter that couldn't have been the result of a fall in his boat. Carter is assumed either to have fallen from his boat as a result of a heart attack or to have fallen over accidentally and drowned. The gill net is presumed to have been adrift in the water, and Carter's body became wrapped in the net, which on the outgoing tide caught on a channel marker where he was discovered by two local fishermen. Gill nets are commonly found in the water, discarded by fishermen being pursued by authorities. This investigation is officially closed; the death is ruled to have been by natural causes or by accident.

"Grace," Lucinda asked, "do you concur?"

"No, too many assumptions, but I have to accept it. We try to respect and defer to other state attorneys' conclusions. If we were to conclude that Carter was murdered, we have to have a suspect to go forward. There wasn't a suspect here, at least as far as the state attorney in Ft. Myers was concerned."

"There must be *some* suspects," Lucinda said. "There were hundreds of commercial netters. To assume not one could be a killer seems farfetched. And there may be other possible suspects who haven't been considered. The Ft. Myers report is shallow and evasive."

"Lucinda, you should have gone to law school. You think like a lawyer."

"Macduff's influence," she commented, then realizing she had chosen her words unwisely.

"Macduff was law trained? I know Macduff went to UConn undergraduate school—but not its law school where I went. . . . I don't know much about his background. He's pretty careful not to talk about his past. I suspect he has some things he'd prefer to forget. . . . But you know him better than anyone around here," she ended, making it sound like a question.

"Grace, since we're together, let's concede, or at least set aside, how Carter died," commented Lucinda, ignoring Grace's question about Macduff and law training. "Can we talk about the other deaths? Especially Bradford at Macduff's cottage and Hicks off Apalachicola in the Gulf. . . . Any reason even to discuss the Montana Hendersen death?"

"I talked to Erin two days ago. Mostly about the Hendersen death. Her conclusion is the same as it was for Carter—accident or heart attack. But not for the same reasons. Ft. Myers authorities believe they made a thorough investigation and decided the death was not a murder, while Erin's office decided, partly for a lack of funds, not to address a matter that has too many out-of-state aspects. Hendersen did have a vacation home near Livingston, but he worked in Georgia and had little known contact with Montana apart from vacations."

"Bradford's death at Macduff's cottage is the easiest to deal with," Lucinda observed. "It had to be a murder. People don't wrap themselves in a net and set themselves on fire. What the medical examiner concluded is that he couldn't determine the *cause* of death because of the fire. He identified the body conclusively, and Bradford certainly has never shown up since. So who did it, Grace?"

"Macduff?"

"Not a chance," exclaimed Lucinda. "I know Macduff. Plus, he has an alibi. He hadn't been at his cottage for weeks. I know where he was."

"You've told me he was in Walter Reed. Was it when Bradford was killed?"

"No, when Bradford was killed he was in Maine visiting Elsbeth."

"OK. . . . You never told me much about *why* he was in Walter Reed later."

"He was recovering from an infected wound."

"From being shot."

"Yes. He was outside of the country."

"Lucinda, I can get the hospital records. They have to report bullet wounds."

"Not this hospital."

"What do you mean?"

"He was in a military hospital in Germany where he had the bullet removed, and he recovered in Walter Reed in D.C. I told you about Walter Reed, and you know you'll never get access to their records."

"Why on earth was he shot?" Grace looked both mystified and curious.

"I don't know the full story, and I can't say more."

"I think I understand. Then who wanted to kill Bradford?" Grace asked.

"From what you've told me, Grace, maybe half the people in St. Augustine. Has your investigation turned up anything?"

"Turk Jensen's not been helpful. He's demanded I back off the case because it's his jurisdiction. I've made a list of a dozen people who wrote borderline threatening letters to Bradford when he was editor of the *Chronicle*."

"Any of them commercial fishermen?" Lucinda asked.

"Yes. . . . Maybe. . . . Two letters were from fishermen based in St. Augustine. One's dead; the other moved to Alaska to fish. A third letter wasn't signed. It was in an envelope with no return address. But it was postmarked Oyster Bay. It was threatening in an oblique way—not directly stating he would do anything to Bradford, but that '*if he were* a commercial fisherman, he might do something'. . . . Oyster Bay keeps surfacing," Grace continued, "especially in the last death—Tim Hicks."

"You think that it was murder?"

"A dead body wrapped in a gill net is found dozens of miles off the coast, roughly south of Apalachicola and roughly west of Oyster Bay. No marks on the body. The boat had run out of fuel. What's unexplainable is that the body was wrapped in a gill net. . . . *Tim Hicks did not do that to himself.*"

"Suspects?" inquired Lucinda.

"Apparently none in Apalachicola; I've talked with authorities there. And that talk keeps taking me back to Oyster Bay. And to both the Tanner woman, Betty, and her sister, Emma, from Apalachicola. Lucinda, it's a dead end. I don't want to close the Bradford case. And I don't want to see the Hicks case closed. But we're headed that way. It's damned frustrating."

"Grace, there's one further thing to talk about. I'll call you."

"Don't you want to tell me?"

"I don't want to *involve* you."

67

The state wildlife agency is investigating an alleged illegal netting of nearly 20,000 pounds of Spanish mackerel in the Shark River/northwest Florida Bay vicinity.
The fishermen were using gill nets . . . A mesh that traps fish by their gills, such nets are blamed for killing fish both indiscriminately and with ruthless efficiency, whether or not they are the target species.

May 6, 2009. Keysnews.com

THE NEXT DAY – OYSTER BAY REDUX

THE FOLLOWING MORNING, after breakfast alone on the rebuilt cottage dock, sitting in the bolted-down solitary chair Macduff had installed when the dock was repaired—a sign of his intentions that troubled Lucinda who missed the two seat swing—she put her small bag in her SUV and drove across the state to Oyster Bay. Lucinda had thus far talked with Betty Tanner in Oyster Bay, wife of a commercial netter, Joe, and with Betty's sister, Emma, in Apalachicola, also the wife of a commercial netter. What she hadn't done was talk to any actual commercial netters. That would be her focus on this visit to Oyster Bay.

Lucinda did not drive around the circular bay where generations of commercial fishermen's homes were mixed with an increasing number of houses owned by outsiders. Instead, she parked in front of the only place for coffee she passed in the town—a small, recently opened kiosk with three outside tables. They were all rusting except one, which was covered with a worn, faded blue-checked cloth.

The days were warming as summer approached, and she chose the outside table with the checkered cloth because it faced the channel where the bay emptied into the Gulf. On the table were sterling silver spoons, small cut-glass salt and pepper shakers with silver tops that had been polished over the years until the silver appeared worn out, and a wooden holder that held two white paper-napkins. A small glass ashtray with three places to set cigarettes was next to a "Thank You for Not Smoking" sign and was filled with an assortment of sweeteners.

It was nearly a quarter of an hour before someone came out to take her order, a woman of similar age to Mrs. Tanner and her sister. She was wearing an old, nearly ankle-length print dress that was clean and ironed, as was her white apron. She had a dignity to her that contrasted with the sadness of Mrs. Tanner.

The woman smiled and asked, "Would you like something or just sitting a bit to rest?"

"A little of both," responded Lucinda. "It's beautiful here. I love the way the marsh grasses along the channel bend in the breeze. And the breeze is certainly welcome. . . . Could I have coffee please? With a little milk."

The woman returned in five minutes with coffee in a cup resting on a saucer with a chipped edge. It looked to be part of a dinner set of blue and white Chinese Export ware. The blue on the cup was as faded as the tablecloth. Lucinda assumed it had been brought from the woman's home.

"Do you need anything else?"

"Perhaps a glass of water after the coffee. . . . This looks fine."

"It's *Paul Newman* coffee. . . . He's a good man and gives away most of his money. He hasn't been in a movie recently."

She spoke of Newman as though he were living; perhaps her memory was fading, and she forgot he died several years ago. He *was* a good man.

When the woman came out ten minutes later with the water, she wiped her hands on her apron, and said, "You aren't one of the folks who have a house and stay here on weekends, are you?"

"I'm not. I live near the other coast. The ocean's been rough the past week because of a northeaster. The surf's noisy. I wanted to be near the water where it's calm and quiet. . . . The coffee is perfect. Just what I wanted. Is this your shop?"

"Thank you. It is mine. My husband Oliver was a commercial fisherman. He's now a broken man. Wasting away in a wheelchair."

"Was he in an accident?" Lucinda asked.

"Not that kind of broken. His spirit was broke ever since the gill net ban got passed. You know about that?"

"A little. Didn't have as much impact on the Atlantic side."

"Terrible thing. He's a God fearin' man but God let him down. I think my man was weak. The bible says 'an eye for an eye and a tooth for a tooth.' He could've done something."

"But he couldn't change the law once it was passed."

"No, but maybe something else. . . . You heard of them persons who died wrapped in gill nets?"

"I have read of one on the other coast near where I live. A man who burned to death on a boat. There wasn't much left of him, but there were remnants of a net wrapped around him."

"We got one more recent this side of the state. Right off here. Boat from Apalachicola found drifting with a dead body wrapped in a net."

"Were these murders?"

"They weren't no accidents."

"Who do you suppose did it?"

"Some good Christians."

"Can good Christians commit murder?"

"Bible says 'yes.'"

Lucinda didn't want to ask what part of the bible the woman was referring to. It would only lead to a debate over the meaning of one of the many biblical phrases that people differ over.

"It sounds like there are a good number of families here who still haven't accepted the net ban."

"That's the truth. And they never will. . . . We got ourselves a group of residents who meets in the church basement here and talks about what should be done."

"What do they want to do?"

"Oh! Lord, I wouldn't repeat what I've heard goes on there."

Lucinda didn't feel it appropriate to ask if murder was one of the subjects of those discussions. She thought she had asked enough.

A phone rang inside. The woman said, "I better answer that. The coffee's a dollar. . . . By the way I'm Jessie Lowry. Nice to talk with you." She turned and went inside.

Lucinda rose, left two dollars under the edge of her cup, walked to her car, and left with more uncertainty about the gill net deaths than before. Maybe she could sort out some of the confusion as she thought more about Mrs. Lowry's comments. For the rest of the day Lucinda learned nothing further that might help.

On the drive back to the cottage, she recalled that Lowry was one of the families that controlled Oyster Bay.

68

A FEW DAYS LATER AT THE COTTAGE

FOR SEVERAL DAYS Lucinda went over and over the details of the deaths. Grace Justice called the following week and asked if they could get together for dinner, but Lucinda begged off. Erin Giffin called from Montana several times and wanted only to discuss Lucinda's relationship with Macduff. Each time Lucinda found a way of quickly ending their conversation.

Lucinda called newspaper reporters in Ft. Myers, St. Augustine, Apalachicola, and even Livingston, Montana, to fill in gaps with facts about the deaths and hopefully obtain new information. The one consistency was that there was no new information, at least partly because the authorities in each area were stumped. And partly because they didn't want to admit as much.

She broadened her research by calling several fly fishermen who were members of the Florida Council of the Fly Fishers of America, a half dozen former or current commercial fishermen in each area where bodies were found, and the few sheriffs' departments where deputies were willing to speak. Some of the deputies later called her at the cottage and talked only after Lucinda promised to protect their secrecy and not ask for their names.

Did it help? Yes, but it provided Lucinda no clear and logical answers about who killed any of the four persons. Once the deaths were ruled accidents or the result of natural causes, investigations ended and files went into storage boxes. But her persistence did produce one interesting recommendation. A sheriff's deputy in Cedar Key told Lucinda to call Freddie Towers, the longtime mayor of Cedar Key.

She found Towers difficult to locate, leaving message after message, and finally gave up. The next day her cell phone rang.

"Miss Lang?"

"This is Lucinda Lang."

"I'm Freddie Towers. You called me several times. I weren't goin' to answer, but a deputy friend in Cedar Key called me and left a message that said I should talk to you. . . . Who the hell are you, anyway?"

"I live in Montana with a longtime companion. We also share a small cottage south of St. Augustine. Last fall while I was working in New York, my companion arrived at the cottage to find his flats boats burning."

"I remember that. The body was identified as that bastard newsman Bradford. The goddam newspaper editor who wrote so much favorin' the net ban back in '94. Most of it was lies."

"Bradford's death has made it difficult for my companion. He's in Montana and hesitant about coming back here. He had a run-in with a local sheriffs' deputy. His name is . . ."

"Turk Jensen," Towers interrupted. "He's worse'n Bradford. We know about him even on this side of the state. You sure pick some winners to irritate."

"Mr. Towers, I need some help. I think one or more commercial fishermen in Oyster Bay were involved in the gill net deaths. I want to help clear my companion's name."

"I've never been close to anyone in Oyster Bay," added Towers. "I don't much care for the way they don't cooperate with other towns along this coast. There ain't no love lost between us Cedar Key folk and those in Oyster Bay."

"Is there anyone in Oyster Bay who might talk?"

"There's one known for being a blabbermouth. He is, or he was, a commercial gill netter. We don't like him. Never have. He'd cut the floats off our nets. And he'd steal fish, which ain't *ever* done among decent fishermen."

"Who is he?"

"His name's Oliver Lowry. If you can git him to talk, you'll learn more 'n speakin' to the rest of that town all together."

"Does he live in Oyster Bay?"

"Far as I know. His wife runs a little coffee and sandwich place on the channel between the bay and the Gulf."

"I know that coffee shop. That's very helpful."

"Don't use my name. And don't call me again."

Towers hung up.

Lucinda put the phone down. It was only 4:30 on a gloomy afternoon in St. Augustine. She searched the cupboards, found Macduff's bottle of Gentleman Jack, poured a drink, and took the glass down to the dock. She sat on the edge of the dock where Macduff moored his flats boat, but Jen's husband Jimmy had stored the boat for the time Macduff planned to be in Montana. She wondered how long that would be. She longed to go fly fishing in the channels that meandered through the marshes.

Her next task was to convince Oliver Lowry to talk to her. She thought of calling his wife Jessie but decided she should approach Oliver directly. It wasn't hard to find a number for Lowry. Few of the commercial fishermen and their families used cell phones; the Lowrys had a single land line with a number Lucinda was provided by the phone company.

She called the next morning, hoping he might be home alone when Jessie was at the coffee shop. Lucinda was about to give up after the phone had rung far longer than she thought necessary, when a voice came on breathing heavily.

"This is Oliver Lowry. I was on our back porch. I have some trouble gettin' around. I'm a good bit slower than I used to be. Who are you?"

"My name is Lucinda Lang. I met your wife Jessie a few days ago at her coffee shop. We had a nice conversation. I live across the state in St. Augustine. I'm curious about some matters about the gill net ban that Jessie and I talked about. I live in Montana during the summer—this is an unusual year for me, and I can't be there this month. We had a strange death on one of the Montana creeks last fall. I have a friend in the county sheriff's department in Montana who's working on the case."

"I read about that," Lowry said. "You know we had some deaths in Florida. The police haven't a clue; they think they were all accidents."

"That's what the Montana authorities believe happened, that the man was fishing and fell into the water and drowned, then floated downstream and got tangled in a net some poachers had left across the creek."

"We don't much care in Oyster Bay about what happens in Montana. . . . What do you want from me?"

"I was told you know more about gill net fishing than anyone along the coast."

294

"That's probably right, but some others who knew more ain't here anymore. Remember, '94 is almost twenty years ago."

"Would you spend time with me if I drove over? I'll buy you lunch in Cedar Key."

"That sounds good; the restaurants here in Oyster Bay don't serve lunch no more, and more often than not are open only on the weekends. I got nothin' planned tomorrow. Can you come that soon?"

"I can," Lucinda agreed. "The death near Ft. Myers and the one here have been ruled accidents. I'd like to see that conclusion for the others so we can end it."

"I don't know about the Montana death, but the three here ain't no accidents. But come to think of it, maybe it's best for the police to think they were. . . . You sound like a smart lady. We'll talk about it all tomorrow. Meet me at the Bo'suns Chair on the dock . . . at 11:45, prompt."

"I'll be there, Mr. Lowry."

Lucinda turned off her phone and looked out at the marsh, wondering why Lowry was emphatic in saying the three Florida deaths weren't accidents. She hoped she'd soon find out.

She had not yet talked to any person directly involved in commercial fishing along the coast between Apalachicola and Sanibel. She had talked to Emma in Apalachicola and to both Betty and Jessie in Oyster Bay. Now she would talk to a commercial fisherman—Jessie's husband Oliver. After talking to him, perhaps she could either eliminate the Oyster Bay fishermen from her list of those responsible or provide enough information to the authorities that charges could be brought.

Leaving St. Augustine the next morning at seven, she wanted time to spare. She had come to like Cedar Key for its simplicity. None of the tacky T-shirt and tourist junk shops that lined streets in St. Augustine. The few old buildings in Cedar Key, especially the Island Hotel, were preserved and revered. At the rate old buildings were torn down in St. Augustine, often to expand Flagler College, soon little would remain but artists' renditions of an earlier time.

Lucinda thought the long approach to Cedar Key refreshing, beginning with scrub oak and planted pine woods lining the roads and occasionally giving view to wetlands beyond. The road drainage ditches attracted grasses, swamp lilies, salt bush, glasswort, and sea lavender. Then, suddenly, the salt marshes appeared, hosting countless small and mostly inaccessible islands, scattered randomly by nature's design across the water.

Pines and palms predominate along the access road; the town's signature cedars are a part of history. Slowly, the access road becomes a causeway, buildings appear, boats are moored, and the one-street downtown is entered.

Having parked by the small beach on the southwest side of town, Lucinda walked slowly along the edge of habitation, staring west across the shallows at Atsena Otie Key that once had residents and a role in the community, but now lies largely abandoned and resuming its former natural state.

The Bo'suns Chair sat precipitously on multiple pilings over the Gulf waters, which every few decades generate a hurricane-driven fury that clears the road of buildings. But they are rebuilt, as has been the case of the Bo'suns Chair—three times in the past half-century.

The more favored tables are on the second floor overlooking the usually placid Gulf waters. Lucinda climbed the stairs slowly, enjoying the black and white framed photos of boats

and fishermen that cover the walls and carry inscriptions showing dates back to the '40s.

Entering the upper dining room, which has large glass
window panes on three sides, Lucinda discovered that Oliver
Lowry was already seated at a table by the windows. When he
saw her come in, he waved and smiled, and when she reached
the table, he extended his hand across to shake hers. She hadn't
expected that, and she liked it.

Lowry looked more than the years Lucinda believed he
had accumulated; she was slow to realize he had spent a life-
time on the water. The Gulf's sun is painfully damaging to the
complexion, and Lucinda doubted Lowry was ever addicted to
sunscreen. His face was wrinkled and bore scars, but his tan
had faded with the years. She assumed he hadn't spent much
time on the water since the net ban was imposed.

"Mr. Lowry, I'm Lucinda Lang," she said, seating herself.
"But I guess you know that. Please call me Lucinda."

"I'm Oliver Lowry. Friends call me Ollie. I hope you will,
too. . . . I know the menu well. May I make recommendations?"

"Please. . . . I prefer shellfish to fish."

"Then we both will have the shellfish platter."

The two talked at first about family and background and
everything except the gill net deaths. Lucinda thought Ollie
quite charming, with a gentle manner. Quite at contrast to the
description given her by Freddie Towers. Nearly every person
who entered the room for dinner came by the table and shook
Ollie's hand. He, in turn, introduced each of them to Lucinda
as his friend.

"You've helped me understand the fishing history of this
area," Lucinda commented, opening her last oyster.

"Now that we've finished a most pleasant meal," Ollie
said, touching both corners of his mouth with his napkin, "I

hope I may be helpful in discussing the tragic deaths you and I have avoided talking about."

"Thank you, Ollie. I don't want to impose."

"First, let me put one death aside. The man who died in Montana was in no way connected to the deaths in Florida."

"Do you agree with the Montana authorities that he accidentally drowned?"

"I don't have any opinion. But I assure you, Lucinda, he wasn't part of the deaths here."

"You seem to be saying that the Florida deaths were somehow linked."

"They were."

"How?"

"We have a group here in Oyster Bay. There are six in all. *They did the Florida killings.* With help from a person who lives in Apalachicola."

"The Ft. Myers death was a murder?"

"Yes. Clint Carter had spoken frequently about increasing the net ban and limiting judges' authority."

"How was he killed?"

"He was fishing in one of the hidden mangrove islands in Palm Island Sound. A large shallow-draft net boat entered. Six were on board. They overwhelmed Carter and drowned him. Not a single blow was needed; together they held him under until he was dead. Then they wrapped him in a gill net, took him upriver on the Caloosahatchee, and dumped him. Floating downriver, he became hung up on a channel marker. That wasn't planned."

"What about Bradford, on the east coast?"

"Bradford was the worst of the group. He used his position as editor of a newspaper to write scurrilous editorials about gill net fishing. The Oyster Bay group followed him from the bait shop on the Intracoastal Waterway where he launched his skiff to go fishing. He powered back into the marshes where the six caught and drowned him the same way as they did Carter—held underwater by the six until he no longer struggled.

"Then they saw a dock and flats boat and dumped the body in the boat after wrapping it in a gill net. They siphoned all the fuel into the bottom of the boat, shoved off, and tossed in a lighted stick. They watched the boat burn on their way out with the tide."

"The last was Hicks in Apalachicola. Why another?"

"My sister-in-law Emma lives in Apalachicola. Her husband was a commercial fisherman. He was arrested for violating the net ban. He spent four months in jail before a local judge ruled his net wasn't illegal. But it was too late. He had never received proper medication in prison for a heart condition. He died the day he got home. . . . Emma wanted revenge. We agreed to help."

"How did you get Hicks?"

"A friend of Emma's hired him to guide fishing in the channel west of Fort George Island. When they got there, our boat was waiting. Our six took Emma's friend on board. She feigned illness, and they offered to take her home. Hicks was overwhelmed and drowned. His body was wrapped in a gill net and then the steering wheel was tied so the boat would head south and it was set on course. The six and Emma's friend came directly here to Oyster Bay."

"Why are you telling me all this?"

"Did I get up when you came in and hold your chair?"

"No."

"Do you see something in the corner behind me?"

"A wheelchair."

"That's mine. I got here even earlier than you so I could be moved into this chair and my wheelchair set in the corner."

"I'm sorry. I should have realized. Your wife told me about the wheelchair."

"There's no blame cast. . . . Lucinda, I'm an old man. I don't have long to live. My final wish is letting the public know they can't enact laws that kill commercial fishing without expecting retaliation."

"But there were five other residents in your group. They'll be charged with murder."

"That's very unlikely."

I couldn't speak I was so overwhelmed by the depth of their hatred and the audacity of their actions. And their spouses have to live with the murders.

"How will your wife Jessie deal with this when you're gone?" Lucinda asked.

"She'll feel compensated and live out her life, along with the others, knowing their families had the last say. They plan to meet in the basement of the old church every month and drink a toast."

"Ollie, I don't know what to say. It raises questions why the various local investigators didn't do more than dismiss the deaths as accidents."

"Lucinda, if you make this public *after* I'm dead, which won't be long, the authorities may have no one to prosecute."

Lucinda drove home slowly that evening, worried that being distracted by what Ollie Lowry had said would precipitate an accident. Should she call Grace immediately and tell her what transpired? She didn't approve of waiting until Ollie died. Perhaps that would make her guilty of a crime.

That night at the cottage, finding the Gentleman Jack bottle empty from the night before, Lucinda opened a bottle of South Australian *Pinot Noir* and drank successive glasses on the dock, the end of the pier, the top step of the stairs, and the porch swing.

Until the bottle was empty.

69

Commercial net fishers have other legal options to catch mullet. Many use hand-thrown cast nets in conjunction with seine nets. The seine nets with two-inch or less mesh corral the fish, which are then caught by the cast nets. Cast nets are also used during fall migrations in rivers and bays when mullet are aggregated in large schools. Landings data [confirm] the viability of using cast nets and other legal nets. In the four-county area of Wakulla, Franklin, Jefferson and Dixie County commercial fishermen landed 493,614 pounds of mullet in 2011 and 579,027 pounds in 2010. Statewide more than 12.5 million pounds of mullet were landed in 2011.

Fly Fishing in Salt Water, October 11, 2012.

THE FOLLOWING DAY IN ST. AUGUSTINE

IN THE MORNING Lucinda turned on Jacksonville public radio. After stories about another budget battle in Greece, a double murder in Savannah, and the indictment of a county commissioner in Duval County, the announcer briefly noted that an Oyster Bay commercial fisherman, Oliver Lowry, confined to a wheelchair during the final stages of a terminal illness, had taken his own life. He used a shotgun, bought in 1994, on the day after the net ban was passed, but to this date had never been fired.

Lucinda's eyes clouded as she fought back tears. Tears for Ollie and for Jessie. Now Lucinda could tell the story that Ollie told her. She called Grace Justice.

"Grace, it's Lucinda. I spent yesterday at Cedar Key, having lunch with a man named Oliver Lowry. He apparently committed suicide the night after I left. It was on the radio this morning. He was a well-known and respected commercial netter in Oyster Bay."

"Why did he commit suicide?"

"He was wheelchair bound from weakness caused by a broken heart. . . . We had lunch. He was charming. I think there's another reason he killed himself."

"Why?"

"What he told me at lunch. About the three gill net deaths here in Florida."

"Are you comfortable talking about it on the phone?"

"No. Can we meet?"

"It's Saturday. I'm at home at Camachee Cove. Can you come here?"

"Yes, about noon."

Lucinda knew Grace had a condo at Camachee Cove, where she believed that Macduff had spent at least one night. She wasn't thrilled with the idea of going there. But she wanted to talk to her.

Grace answered Lucinda's knock. She had been swimming in the condo association pool and was drying her hair with a towel. She was taller than Lucinda, with a manner of moving and posing that would attract men.

They sat on the condo's small porch overlooking the yacht basin. Grace brought out snacks and a bottle of wine. After the previous night, the wine didn't look enticing to Lucinda.

"Now, tell me about yesterday," Grace said to start their conversation. Lucinda tried to relate every detail of her lunch with Oliver Lowry, down to his final comments about the three deaths.

"Grace, does all this have to be made public?"

"If you sign a statement that includes everything you've just told me, one way or another the statement will appear in the papers—at least papers in the three Florida cities. It's certain you'll be mentioned by name."

"What will that serve?" asked Lucinda. "Oliver Lowry is dead. Oyster Bay has had enough problems with the net ban prohibiting gill netting. I think the town will come back. . . . This news won't help the town; it may do nothing more than satisfy curiosity about murders for some readers. What if I *don't* give a statement and deny anything you say I said. No one will corroborate your statement."

"I know. If you don't provide a signed statement, I won't go any further. We'll close the Bradford case for lack of evidence of murder. Ft. Myers authorities have already made Carter little more than a note in a dead file—a cold case. Apalachicola will soon follow with Hicks. What happens in Montana is their business, but I know after talking to Erin Giffin that nothing more is planned. Again, a lack of evidence."

"So, it's over?" Lucinda asked.

"It's over if you say so," Grace assured.

"I do. . . . Grace, what would you do in my shoes?"

She rose and hugged Lucinda warmly, stepped back and said, "I'd do exactly what you're planning. I wouldn't sign *anything*. . . . Please don't repeat that."

"I should go," Lucinda said in nearly a whisper. "I've caused you enough trouble."

"There is one more thing. Not related to the murders."

"What's that?" asked Lucinda.

"Macduff."

"That may also be a cold case."

"Only *you* can reopen that case, Lucinda. But I'd like to help."

70

The net ban is probably the most contentious fisheries management measure implemented in Florida. ... The short-term negative impacts of the net ban have been absorbed primarily by small-scale commercial finfish businesses, many of which are owned and operated by independent families. ... Benefits resulting from the net ban will continue to be realized as the stocks of finfish continue to improve.

Univ. of Florida IFAS extension publication #FE123 (2013).

THE FOLLOWING DAY

MUCH OF SATURDAY AFTERNOON AND SUNDAY MORNING, not to mention hours when she couldn't sleep Saturday night, Grace spent thinking about Lucinda. Partly about her conversation with the deceased Oliver Lowry, but mostly about her fractured relationship with Macduff. Plus, Grace had come to believe that Lucinda was jeopardizing the relationship between Elsbeth and her father.

Grace knew Lucinda had not talked to Elsbeth since she flew west in June to begin her summer job. By now Elsbeth must have made her decision about where to transfer. Most universities began the fall term in mid-August. Grace knew how much Lucinda wanted to be a part of Elsbeth's life—the daughter Lucinda could never have.

Never one to turn down a challenge, Grace began a plan. Her first call was to Lucinda.

"Thanks for coming yesterday. I think it's best you're through with the cases. But there are a few details I should discuss with you. Like how to handle inquiring reporters who want to dig up the case in the future. Or dealing with Turk Jensen if he causes further trouble. Let me come to your place. I'll be busy most of this week. Could we get together on Monday a week from tomorrow?"

"Yes, what time?"

"Nine a.m. all right?"

"I'm writing it in my date book as we speak. See you."

Grace next called the sheriff's office in Livingston. Erin answered, "Deputy Erin Giffin. Who am I speaking to?"

"It's Grace Justice at the State Attorney's office in St. Augustine. We've talked before."

"You're not going to ask me again what's new with the Hendersen death, are you?"

"No. That was an accident as far as we're concerned. But it's your jurisdiction."

"That helps. Thanks. What's on your mind, Grace?"

"I'd like you to come here and help with *our* three cases. I've been asked by the State Attorney in Tallahassee to oversee an investigation comparing all three deaths. I think you could help. It would be good to have another person whose judgment I trust look at what we have. We'll pay for your flight."

"I don't know how I can help. But I can come, name the date."

"Next Sunday. We'll meet Monday. . . . While we're on the line, one other matter. How's Macduff?"

"He's a mess, trying to do the best he can with Elsbeth. She leaves soon for college, and I don't think she'll be unhappy to go. She hasn't said where."

"Are she and Macduff not getting along?"

"Elsbeth has been coercing him to talk to Lucinda. He says it's over, that Lucinda has gone back to her old life."

"Well, she hasn't," said Grace. "I've seen her a few times in the past two weeks. I hope we're becoming friends. At least we respect each other."

"Competitors?"

"No. As far as I'm concerned, we never were. And I'll see to it that we won't be."

"How is Lucinda?"

"Lonely," Grace answered. "Being in the cottage with all the photos of better days doesn't help. She's living in the past—like a widow. Do you know if Macduff's coming here for the winter?"

"No reason to think not," replied Erin. "He hates the winter weather here. But he hasn't talked about it."

"Does he ask about Lucinda?"

"No. He can't seem to talk about it . . . or doesn't want to. He spends a lot of time alone."

"Women? Any new flames?"

"If there are, Elsbeth has snuffed them out."

"Will you stay with me, Erin, please? And bring Elsbeth with you. Lucinda doesn't know I planned to call you."

"Fine. I've known Macduff and Lucinda for years. I've never seen the cottage. I haven't ever been to Florida!"

"I've never been to Montana. . . . You'll love Florida. You'll want to stay, at least for the winter."

"You wouldn't say that if you'd been to Montana. Even with our crummy winters, I love it here. Maybe you'll visit."

Grace felt good about having Erin come east. Erin and Lucinda had been close for years. The past year they'd drifted apart. Grace thought she might rectify that. . . . She was embarrassed by the one night she spent with Macduff.

She'd had too much to drink.

71

AT THE MILL CREEK CABIN

I KEPT BUSY AROUND THE CABIN AND PROPERTY doing jobs I left unattended for the past couple of years. It had never been difficult to convince Lucinda to put off some maintenance and head up Mill Creek to fly fish. That is, until our last trip when we discovered the body under the Passage Falls Trail bridge. I don't think she's been fishing since.

For the biggest change to my cabin, I sought help. I added a wing off one side that includes a bedroom with a comfortable seating area, a desk in the corner, a generous bathroom, a walk-in closet, and a porch overlooking the creek.

The wing is for Elsbeth. But I haven't told her that. I told her I need more guest space, not wanting her to think I'm trying to influence her decision to choose a university. If she goes to MSU, fine. There will be room for her to bring a friend. But she has to make the decision herself.

Elsbeth has asked with increasing frequency about when Lucinda will be returning. I finally told her I didn't know and to please not raise it again. That didn't help our relationship. She hasn't spent much time with me at the cabin; a week after she started working at Chico Hot Springs, she was given a promotion and her own lodging.

She hasn't asked me for advice on universities. Time is short; enrollment will start in a few weeks. She frequently talks with Sue on the phone; Sue has a summer job at Little Palm Island in the Florida Keys. Elsbeth tells me they've all but decided where to enroll, but she's not saying more.

I'm planning on leaving for Florida in late October. Mid-September to mid-October has become my favorite time to be in Montana. The leaves turn; tourists depart; school starts.

The fishing is never better, and it takes my mind off the couplet spoken as the curtain fell:

Never was a story of more woe
Than this of Juliet and her Romeo.

72

The court is not saying that preserving our marine life is absurd. Instead the absurdity is created in the law and how it is being applied. It is abundantly unfair for the courts to continue to attempt enforcement of laws that contradict each other ... An absolute mess has been created. [Circuit Court Judge Jackie Fulford ruling at the peak of the mullet spawning season when mullet are filled with eggs, both that the net ban was unfair and ordering the Florida FWC not to enact any further rules dealing with gill nets. October 22, 2013. Gill netters immediately flowed in from as far as North Carolina.]

Wakulla Commercial Fishermen's Association, Inc. v. Florida Fish and Wildlife Conservation Commission (October 22, 2013) [same parties as in 2007].

THE MIDDLE OF AUGUST AT MILL CREEK

ELSBETH'S SUMMER JOB WAS OVER. She returned to the cabin but kept to herself. Her questions and comments were few and far between.

"Dad, when are you going to Florida?" she asked abruptly one morning.

"Mid- to late-October. I promised John Kirby I'd fish with him in early October. A Jackson Hole church auctioned our donated guide services for two floats on the 10th. Two guys from Texas with summer palaces in Jackson paid $3,000 for

John's guide trip. A wealthy, forty-year-old former Miss Wyoming paid $9,500 for mine!"

"What is she buying other than a day on your wooden *Osprey* and a few lessons about fly casting?"

"I guess I'll find out."

"What *are* your intentions? I know how you still feel about Lucinda. When you're back in St. Augustine, I assume you'll be spending time with Grace. Lucinda has to realize you won't pine away forever."

"I guess my intentions about Miss Wyoming are clear. She gets a day on the boat and some lessons. Hands-on contact."

"Dad!"

"Miss Wyoming is spectacular. I can't wait to get her alone in my boat."

"I don't believe you!"

"Elsbeth, she's blind. One of the most respected philanthropists in the valley. I've taken her fishing on the Snake each of the last three years."

"I'm sorry."

"As for Grace, the truth is we spent one night in her condo. Believe me, *nothing* happened."

It was an hour before we said another word to each other. I spoke first.

"When are you leaving for college? It can't be long. Do I get to know where?"

"Sue and I decided last week. We're taking more time off. I'm going to join her on the Keys next week. We both have jobs at Little Palm Island."

"Putting off your choice for a year?"

"No. I plan to start in January for the winter term. . . . But not until *you* get your life in order. I can't focus on academics not knowing where you'll be or who you'll be living with."

"Is that fair? Did I drive Lucinda away? Or did she go because of her own needs?"

"Did you kill Isfahani? Was that part of your needs?" Elsbeth asked, cryptically.

"I wish you wouldn't raise that. But yes, I did shoot him."

"I saw the bullet scar on your shoulder when you were working on your dock. I don't want to see any more scars."

"You won't. The rifle I used in Guatemala and Khartoum is gone."

"Rifles can be replaced. Fathers can't be."

"I've told Dan Wilson it's over. He understands."

"Then you're not concerned about Juan Pablo Herzog?"

"That's different. But he's busy getting ready to run again for president of Guatemala."

"Would you assassinate him if Dan Wilson asked?"

"Yes."

"Why? This can't go on."

"I need closure."

"Meaning?"

"If Herzog is dead, no one's after me."

"And then what?"

"Who knows?"

"You could be Professor Maxwell Hunt again."

"Yes and no."

"What do you mean? Why not?"

"I'm a decade older than I was my last year as a law professor."

"And?"

"I don't want to teach again. The last decade of teaching wasn't good. I missed your mother."

"Then what would you accomplish be killing Herzog?"

"Be free from worrying."

"Do you worry a lot?"

"Constantly."

"About being killed?"

"No."

"About what?"

"Lucinda."

"What about her?"

"Will you please not repeat this?"

"Promise."

"Two hopes. First, to spend the rest of my life with her. Second, to marry her."

"But you have to kill Herzog to do that?"

"I don't have to kill him. He just has to be dead for me to believe Lucinda's out of danger."

"Can't Dan Wilson arrange that?"

"Five years ago, yes. Now Herzog's a loyal friend of our government."

"Friend?"

"Yes, he keeps Guatemala safe for U.S. investment."

"At the expense of the Guatemalan people?"

"Mostly."

"Are you talking to Dan now about Herzog?"

"No, because of our government's position. It's clear that Herzog must to be allowed to live."

"Do you think you're safe from him because the U.S. is protecting him?"

"Not for long. Only as long as he wants to be president. He's an evil man. He's determined ultimately to find me and kill me. And anybody around me."

"Meaning Lucinda."

"Yes. You understand it clearly."

"What can I do?"

"Help me get Lucinda back."

"Even though you might be willing to kill Herzog in the future?"

"It's not like Isfahani. He wanted to kill every American he could. Herzog is different. He wants only me. I would not kill him unless I were sure he was still after me."

"So you think Lucinda and you could be together under such threat?"

"That's for her to decide."

Was this Elsbeth asking these questions? Is she mature enough to understand what's going on?

"Dad, do you love me?"

"Beyond my ability to define love."

"Aren't I at risk from Herzog?"

"That's even more reason for him to die. . . . But you're not leaving me."

"Because I'm your daughter?"

"Exactly."

"And Lucinda is not related to us."

"Yes. And she's already left me."

"So the gap between you is that you're not married."

"I guess."

"Do you regret not marrying her when you could?"

"Every moment."

"You could tell her this."

"No."

"No?"

"She might refuse."

"What if I told you she wouldn't?"

"I might not believe you."

"But I'm your daughter. You know I don't lie to you."

"Yes."

"I'm going to Florida, Dad. First to St. Augustine, then on to the Keys to work."

"Good."

"I'm going to meet with Lucinda."

"Good."

"Grace Justice will be there. . . . And Erin Giffin."

"Why?"

"To set aside the gill net deaths once and for all."

"Can you all do that?"

"I think so. We're four pretty strong women."

"Four of the best. . . . I've been looking into the deaths for the past year. Possibly I could help."

"Then come," she pleaded.

"Will you be with me?"

"Every step, every word."

"I'll go."

73

In 2002, Circuit Court Judge N. Sanders Sauls deemed unlawful a rule enacted by the FWC [Florida Fish and Wildlife Conservation Commission] that defined any net with a stretched mesh size greater than 2 inches a 'gill net' and thereby prohibited under the amendment, which was overwhelmingly approved by the voters in 1994. But Saul's ruling was overturned a year later by the 1st District Court of Appeal. Two other lawsuits also ultimately ended in favor of FWC, with the mesh-size limit being upheld.

Tallahassee Democrat, October 23, 2013.

THE FOLLOWING WEEK AT THE ST. AUGUSTINE COTTAGE

A MOCKINGBIRD WAS BALANCING ON A POST set near the bottom of the cottage stairs solely to attract winged musical soloists. The bird was warbling as only a mockingbird knows how, changing melody and pitch with the vocal range and timbre more associated with Kiri Te Kanawa or Luciano Pavarotti.

Two cars ghosted along the drive from the gate to the cottage through a dense Maine-like fog that had settled on the Pellicer Creek marshes. The cars parked in the yard, and two people exited each vehicle. One by one three of them quietly climbed the stairs and entered the door that was ajar. The fourth person walked down to the dock and sat on the solitary seat.

The main living room of the cottage had been miraculously transformed by Lucinda from the starkness she discovered when she arrived to a room of warmth and comfort with the return of dozens of framed photographs. Between two windows hung three new black and white photo portraits, intriguing renditions of three women in their seventies, reminiscent of the elegant work of Lord Snowdon depicting royals and aristocrats and the realism of Margaret Bourke-White depicting migrant workers in the depression.

First to enter the cottage was Grace Justice wearing pleated shorts and a long sleeve white linen shirt with upturned cuffs. Behind her was the diminutive Erin Giffin; the deputy sheriff's uniform she so often wore had been left in Montana. She was in jeans and a light cotton sweater that extended nearly to her knees. Erin had arrived the day before and stayed at Grace's condo. Lucinda was overcome with surprise and joy at seeing her best friend and held her close and long.

"Erin!" Lucinda exclaimed, standing back and looking incredulously at her. "Why are you here?"

"Grace asked me to come. Besides, you've never invited me. I was beginning to think the cottage didn't exist. . . . It's beautiful; I can see why Macduff loves this place."

Behind the two stood Elsbeth, who Lucinda had not seen at first while greeting Grace and seeing Erin.

"Elsbeth!" Lucinda cried, bending her arms up at the elbows with palms open in greeting. Elsbeth moved quickly to bury her head against Lucinda's shoulder and block her own tears. Elsbeth wore shorts and a charcoal T-shirt with large blue letters edged with orange spelling "Florida."

Any one of the women would have drawn stares; the four together were sure to stop any male in his tracks. But this was not a beauty pageant. These were serious women who had gathered for a serious purpose.

"Grab some coffee from the kitchen counter," Lucinda told her company, "and there's some very fattening French pastry from a new bakery in town. I haven't dared to sample a piece—yet."

The next hour passed quickly with conversation that covered nearly everything but two subjects: the gill net deaths and Macduff. But everyone in the room knew the reason they had gathered was to discuss both. Finally Grace began.

"Lucinda and I have been talking about the gill net deaths for weeks. We have some information you might think should be reported to the local authorities. I'm one of those authorities, and I'll express my views.

"There's a small town on the west coast of Florida, about the same latitude as here. It's called Oyster Bay. I'll give Erin and Elsbeth some background about the town that Macduff, Lucinda, and I collected on separate visits."

For the next twenty minutes Grace presented a capsule history of Oyster Bay, concentrating on the disappearance of the cedar trees, commercial fishing, the gill net ban impact, and views about the net ban held over the past two decades by residents of the town. Then she turned to specifics.

"Macduff stumbled upon Oyster Bay. Two days into this new year, he went to the west coast of Florida, hoping to discuss with residents their views on the net ban. He had been to

Cedar Key many times, but never the few miles north to Oyster Bay. He was sitting on a bench looking at the water when a local resident, who had been drinking, sat down next to him. It was clear this person was a disaffected Oyster Bay resident, speaking in strong words about the disastrous impact the net ban had on the town.

"Comments were made about the two deaths in Florida and the one in Montana. Of course, when Macduff was there, the death off Apalachicola hadn't yet occurred. It was clear to the resident that finding blame had to focus on recreational fisherman, both for the passage of the ban and the deaths. The ban had largely been ignored in Oyster Bay. After the ban, gill nets were used frequently and surreptitiously by locals. Once the ban was in place, the local police wanted nothing to do with implementing it. The Florida Fish and Wildlife patrols were spread so thinly along the coast that they rarely visited the area. When they did patrol, word quickly spread, and the gill netters hid their nets.

"What troubled Macduff," continued Grace, "were both the attitude of the resident and some of the resident's specific comments. Macduff asked if anything could be done, and the resident said something to the effect that it *already* had been done and that the locals took care of their own problems. But, remember that the person had been drinking."

"That doesn't sound like very much to go on," suggested Erin.

"It isn't," replied Grace. "But there's more. Macduff called me when he got back to St. Augustine. We talked about his conversation. I didn't see Macduff for weeks afterwards. I called a few times but there was no answer."

"Grace," Erin interrupted. "Ken and I talked to Macduff on the phone from Montana. He said he'd been away. He told us a little about his conversation in Oyster Bay."

"Right after that," Grace continued, "the death off Apalachicola occurred. When Macduff left here for Montana soon thereafter, he went by way of Oyster Bay. He had his hair cut by a long-time Oyster Bay barber, who proved to have extensive knowledge of the net ban and strong opinions against recreational fishermen, legislators, and what he insisted was a misinformed voting public.

"He told Macduff the names of six residents who controlled the town for years. Easy to remember because the first letters of their last names spelled 'Mullet.' They were Murphy, Unser, Lowry, Lumpkin, Edwards, and Tanner. The barber said that the townsfolk had 'rights' to the mullet and that the six families retaliated against anyone who challenged those rights. He didn't say the six killed anyone, but I didn't rule it out."

Erin added, "That's still not enough to take to the authorities. Those conversations alone aren't much evidence."

"Then it got interesting," said Grace, not commenting on Erin's observation. "Macduff continued on to Montana. When he got there, he didn't know Lucinda had been in his cabin. Like one of the three bears, she'd been sleeping in his bed. But as soon as she knew he was in the area, heading for the cabin, she fled, driving east and leaving Montana for what she thought would be the last time. The fourth and final night of her drive, she stopped in Apalachicola, where the Hicks death had occurred two months earlier. Lucinda, you can tell this better than I."

"Grace is right about me leaving Montana and heading back here," Lucinda began. "I did stop in Apalachicola. The evening I arrived was balmy and star-filled. In the morning I took the local paper down to the docks. The paper had a piece about Hicks' death. It was critical about those who supported the net ban, including Hicks.

"While I was reading the article, a woman noticed me, and I suspect she saw what I was reading. She sat down and introduced herself as Emma. She didn't give her last name, but she did mention her sister Betty lived in Oyster Bay and was married to a commercial fisherman named Joe Tanner. She went on to condemn Hicks and say he 'deserved what he got.' She said her sister's family and the other commercial netters 'got their revenge.'

"She seemed to imply that the people in Oyster Bay were involved in the three Florida deaths. When I asked her who did the killings, she said she meant only that the deaths provided satisfaction to Oyster Bay and 'all of us commercial folk.'

"I wanted to visit Oyster Bay after talking to Emma in Apalachicola. Macduff had been there; I thought a different face might start someone else talking. I especially wanted to talk to Joe Tanner, Emma's brother-in-law. I got his address and drove to Oyster Bay. When I knocked on the Tanner's door, Mrs. Tanner answered. She was very pleasant and invited me inside for tea. We talked about several women's issues and eventually got to the net ban, after I told her I had met her sister in Apalachicola. She talked about how the men in Oyster Bay fished at night and avoided being arrested, but it was psychologically stressful for them. Then, when I asked her what was being done, she said they hadn't 'sat idle.'

"I asked what she meant, and she asked me what Emma had told me. I told her as best I remembered. When I asked her if I could meet her husband, she informed me that Joe died a couple of years ago, falling off his boat trying to get away from the fish and wildlife authorities. He had a huge haul of mullet. He fell into his gill net, became entangled, and drowned.

"I revisited Oyster Bay a short time ago," Lucinda continued. "I didn't go to the bay where the homes are, but to a small coffee shop on the channel that leads to the Gulf from the bay. A fifty- or sixtyish woman brought me coffee and stopped and talked. I asked if it were her coffee shop. She said that it was, that she needed to work after her husband became a broken man because of the net ban. She thought her husband had been too passive in dealing with the net ban. When we talked about the deaths, she said they weren't accidents, but were done by some 'good Christians.'

"She then spoke about a group of residents who met in the basement of the church to talk about what to do. When I asked her what they wanted to do, she said she didn't dare repeat what she'd heard. When I paid the bill, she said her name was Jessie Lowry. Lowry is one of the six families."

Erin broke in and said, "There's a lot that points to the murders being the work of one or more of these six men. But it still seems lacking in something."

"There's one more meeting about Oyster Bay that's important," Lucinda said. "I thought about the killings when I got back here. Finally, I was asked to call a sheriff's deputy in Levy County who, in turn, told me to call Freddie Towers, long time mayor of Cedar Key. The deputy said Towers was an honest but gruff man who had tried to bring the commercial and recreational fishermen together to talk.

"When I called Towers, he said to call Oliver Lowry in Oyster Bay. I did. Lowry agreed to meet, and I offered to buy him lunch. We met at a nearly empty Cedar Key restaurant. Lowry was a charming man about mid-sixties. We had a wonderful meal overlooking the Gulf, talked about his wife's coffee shop, and then began to discuss the gill net deaths. He was adamant that the Montana death had nothing to do with those in Florida. He then shocked me by saying—and I will remember it to my last day—that 'We have a group here. Six in all. They did the murders.' I remembered that the barber had mentioned that six families controlled Oyster Bay. Over the following hour, Lowry explained how that happened and described how each murder was committed."

"Did he name names?" asked Grace. "Specifically saying which of the six did the murders?"

"No."

"Do you think he did it?"

"No. I know he did not."

"Why are you so sure?"

"He was in a wheelchair, weak from illnesses that would likely take his life within a year."

"What about the other five," asked Grace.

"I told Lowry they would be charged with murder."

"He said 'no, they would not be charged,' without explaining why."

"The police would at least charge Lowry," said Grace.

"Possibly, but I learned the next morning that he had committed suicide shortly after I left. I'm not sure why but I shed some tears."

"So it's over," said Erin. "Those responsible are all dead."

"Yes," responded Lucinda.

"Thank God," said Grace.

Lucinda nodded.

74

Decision of Judge Fulford automatically stayed. Judge Fulford was asked to overrule the automatic stay. *'There is in fact irreparable harm if I do not lift the stay,'* Fulford said. *'The status quo, I believe, has resulted in unnecessary killing and waste, and by the adoption of the FWC rules after the net ban amendment, it's resulted in an unfair application of the net ban to some and not to others.'*

Wakulla Commercial Fishermen's Association, Inc. v. Florida Fish and Wildlife Conservation Commission (November 4, 2013).

THE CONVERSATION CONTINUES

A VOICE DRIFTED IN AN OPEN WINDOW from the front porch and said, "It's not over."

Lucinda was aghast; someone could have been listening for the whole conversation. The other three women merely smiled.

The door opened slowly. I entered and sat in a distant corner, avoiding eye contact with Lucinda. But I was back; it was my first glimpse of her for months.

"I've been listening," I said. "Since the men are all dead, you assume the case is closed."

"Yes," said Grace, followed by Erin's agreeing nod.

"That may not be the case," I remarked.

"But they have admitted it," Grace responded.

"No, Lucinda said that Oliver Lowry told her details about how each of the three Florida deaths occurred. There is no doubt that the murders involved, to one degree or another, Murphy, Unser, Lumpkin, Lowry, Edwards, and Tanner."

"But you don't believe they did it?" asked Grace in surprise.

"I didn't say that."

"Can you explain that?"

"Was Oliver Lowry one who carried out any one of the murders?" I asked.

Lucinda responded, speaking to the group and not directly to me. "Oliver Lowry could not have been actively involved in drowning the three. Lowry had been in a wheel chair for a year. And he was much weakened from his illnesses."

"But he might have been part of the conspiracy. Anyway, there are five others who did the murders, assuming Lowry wasn't able to participate," added Grace.

"What conspiracy?" I asked.

"The meeting in the church that Oliver's wife Jessie talked about," replied Grace.

"Have you ever been in that church?" I inquired, assuming the answer would be no.

"All four shook their heads."

"I visited that church early one weekday morning. The six met in a basement room that has one entrance. It has a very narrow staircase with no railing on the side open to the room."

"Meaning that for at least the last year Oliver Lowry couldn't get down to the basement with his wheelchair," offered Grace.

"Not a chance," I said, "unless he was carried."

"But there were five more residents," Erin stated.

"Yes. We know there were six residents at the church meetings. And recall what Tanner's wife said. Her husband Joe fell off his boat and died, *before* the first gill net death."

"Macduff," Lucinda asked, hearing her use my name for the first time in almost a year. "Are you playing 'and then there were none' with us?"

"We'll see," I answered, rising and moving from my corner stool to sit next to Lucinda on the couch. She looked tired, was uncertain in her movements, and had lost weight.

"We have four fishermen left from the group of six," I said. "When Glen Unser is eliminated, we're down to three."

"What's wrong with Unser?" asked Erin.

"Unser was working on a boat that had a drum used to pull in and roll up the nets. Three years ago he was standing on the edge of the frame of that drum. He fell; the drum crushed his leg. He's been receiving federal disability payments ever since. He hasn't been on the water since the accident. Unser gained weight; he must weigh 350 pounds. He uses a walker and never leaves his house."

"There are three more, including Lumpkin," Lucinda noted, turning directly to me for the first time.

I turned my head to meet her glance and wanted to touch her. I could smell her and see her clear, penetrating green eyes. But the Cheshire cat grin was absent.

"Ben Lumpkin is like Charlie Babbitt in Dustin Hoffman's portrayal of an autistic savant," I said. "Ben can recite the names of every species of fish inside and off the coast of Florida, what the fishing limits are on each, and the world records for each using any weight of line. But he can't be touched by anyone else. His sister has cared for him by herself since his brother—his only other friend— was killed in a car wreck. He was in his old Ford 150 pickup and collided with one of the weekenders of Oyster Bay driving his Cadillac Escalade SUV. The Escalade survived; the pickup did not. The outsider was drunk. Ben has been worse since his brother died."

Lucinda turned to me again, setting her hand on top of mine and giving it a squeeze. She asked, "We're down to two. Do they also have depressing stories?"

I was so startled by her touch I had to ask her to repeat the question. She did, and smiling, also repeated the squeeze.

"Eddie Edwards was a strapping man," I began, "the youngest of the group by fifteen years. He was in the National Guard. Each week he drove to Gainesville for meetings and training. His unit was called up. He served most of a tour on patrols. He was shot four different times. He thought he was invincible. After he saw a Humvee driven by his best Army buddy hit by an IED and be blown through the air, ending upside down, Edwards ran to save his buddy. He got to the Humvee, extracted the severely injured buddy, threw him over his shoulder and ran to cover. He made it one step short of safety. A bullet hit him in the back of the head, and he died instantly. His buddy lived. Edwards was given a Silver Star posthumously to go with his four Purple Hearts. He's buried in the small cemetery behind the church where you all assumed, incorrectly, that he conspired to kill the three persons."

Grace spoke in a trembling voice. She has a cousin currently serving in Afghanistan. "Do we even need to talk about the sixth fisherman, Murphy?" she asked, visibly exhausted from hearing the stories of these unfortunate fishermen.

"I can do that quickly," I answered. "Pete Murphy died peacefully in his sleep from a stroke the day Clint Carter was killed. He had been taking heavy dosages of medicines for four years."

Grace quickly regained her composure. Looking at me as though she wanted to ask me a question but didn't dare, she set down the empty coffee cup she had been holding throughout the discussion. "Macduff, I . . . no, forget it . . ."

"Take your time," I suggested.

"We're nowhere! Somebody killed the three."

"That's right. Six people did it."

"You know who?"

"I think so."

"Share it?"

"Of course. There *was* a conspiracy to kill an undecided number of recreational fishermen who had spoken out in favor of the original net ban and were promoting new and more severe rules and punishments."

"Was Oyster Bay in any way involved?" asked Erin.

"It was the very center of the conspiracy. . . . The conspiracy took place in the basement of the church. Six people were there. Their names were Murphy, Unser, Lowry, Lumpkin, Edwards, and Tanner."

"But they were dead . . . or disabled." Erin said, not sure she was asking a question or making a comment.

Elsbeth had been sitting quietly. She knew some of what had happened. But she had never talked to any of the six Oyster Bay residents or visited that town. She now spoke. "Actually, weren't there seven involved."

"Seven?" said Grace. "Who are you talking about?"

"Emma, the sister of Joe Tanner."

"But she's from Apalachicola."

"Exactly," Elsbeth nodded. "She must have helped arrange the Hicks murder."

"By herself?" inquired Lucinda, wondering if Elsbeth would embarrass herself.

"Not by herself."

"With a group of fishermen from Oyster Bay?" Lucinda asked.

"No," Elsbeth said quietly.

"Then with who?"

"A group of six fishermen's *wives*—sister in the case of Lumpkin—in Oyster Bay."

There was silence in the room. The other three began to nod their heads. I sat staring at my daughter Elsbeth with a pride I could never explain.

"Could women have done these killings?" asked Grace.

"You shouldn't have to ask that, Grace," I interjected. "Are you referring to their age?"

"Not only that," she responded. "Women don't do these things!"

"Tell Lizzie Borden that," I said. "Or better, tell Elizabeth Bathory, the Blood Countess in Slovakia centuries ago. She was said to have bathed in the blood of her alleged 650 victims in order to keep younger. . . . Do you doubt that the four of you could overpower me and drown me in the marsh?"

"There have been times when I've thought of that," said Lucinda, beginning to show hints of her humor I have so missed.

"I've been listening," said Elsbeth. "You're all so focused on the men as murderers, you've overlooked the women. And these seven women are all *alive*. Also, they're all able bodied. They can all be indicted, tried, convicted, and even executed."

"They won't be," said Grace quietly. "The Ft. Myers authorities ruled Clint Carter's death an accident. The Apalachicola police determined the same about Tim Hicks. Turk Jensen in St. Augustine is so incompetent he won't get anywhere without my help in solving Bradford's murder. And he won't get it."

"Is this a women's thing?" I asked. "Women protecting women?"

"No," Grace responded. "What will be gained by reporting what only we five know?"

"We'd be reporting three murders," I answered.

"According to a dead man's statement. Not one of the women has admitted anything," Grace countered.

"Three people were murdered. Their lives are over. Plus there may be families," I added.

"No," Grace exclaimed. "I've investigated that. Carter was a known loner. Parents deceased. No siblings. No spouse. Not even a significant other."

"Tim Hicks?"

"One conviction for rape in Georgia. Suspected of two others. Disowned by his parents and siblings. I don't know why his wife stayed with him. He beat her. He was scum."

"What about Bradford from St. Augustine?"

"Engaged in a messy third divorce. My office has been involved because of child abuse. One thing we've found is he had a lot of money in Cayman Island accounts. His three wives will share it. . . . Macduff, I don't know how I'd feel if they had left dependent families. But I think the world's better off without them."

"Murder is murder," I muttered.

"You're right!" Grace said. "But I'm certain these seven women will never go to prison. First, the evidence is very circumstantial. And who's going to testify? Second, what jury in Cedar Key or Apalachicola will convict these women after what they've been through caring for or losing husbands and a brother? . . . I hate the way they responded by killing. . . . I wonder how any one of us would have reacted in the same place? . . . One more comment. There's been closure to the Ft.

Myers death—ruled accidental. The Apalachicola authorities are close to a similar conclusion. Bradford, on my turf, will be ruled accidental if they don't come up with new evidence. They're not getting any from me."

Erin interrupted, "Macduff, I'm not sure Hendersen's death was an accident or killing. We simply don't know. I hope it was an accident. His wife died more than a year ago. No kids. He was a good husband as far as we know. . . . I don't like to say this, but most murders go unsolved. That includes some of the worst offenders. Murderers we wouldn't hesitate for a moment to send to trial. . . . It's a very imperfect system."

"What's to prevent more of these killings, especially if the ban is extended?" I asked.

"We can't regulate unlawful future conduct." Grace replied. "The seven women range in age from 55 to 70. Each one of the six from Oyster Bay was devoted to her man. Is there anyone who can take care of autistic Ben Lumpkin like his sister has over the past years?"

"Are we like vigilantes?" I asked no one in particular.

Erin answered. "No. Vigilantes take the law into their own hands. They do the acts. We haven't done that. We're refusing to talk. Macduff, if you learned someone raped Lucinda and I saw it happen and later killed the man, would you report me?"

"Not in a thousand years," I said. I felt Lucinda's hand squeeze more tightly.

"Case closed," said Grace. . . . I'm hungry."

75

'What we're doing is just trying to feed our families, really,' fisherman Robbie Bell said. 'We're not trying to harm the environment. Yes, we are catching fish, but it's not what it's made out to be. . . . We want to make sure there are fish for our grandchildren to catch. It's a lot of propaganda. We don't want to upset anybody. We are not trying to disrespect anybody or do any of that, just catch some fish.'

November 5, 2013. News4Jax.com

LUNCH AT THE COTTAGE

LUNCH WAS NOT A CELEBRATION. Nor was it a wake. Erin and Grace cornered me while Lucinda and Elsbeth were talking, a discussion mixed with hugs and happy faces.

"Macduff," Erin said. "Grace and I know a lot more about human nature than you do. Police work makes you become a realist. We're not closing in on a perfect world. We're just hanging on."

"Erin's told me something interesting which relates to this, Macduff," said Grace. "She also filled me in on some of your past, but only going back to your move to Montana. Your first incident involved the killing of a friend by a shot meant for you. The killer tried again, while in your boat. He wounded you and Lucinda and Wuff. But he was killed. No trial needed.

"Then the following year three of your shuttle service women were murdered. One by a Mexican woman who fled to Mexico and could never be tried. Another by a PARA member and a Montana law professor. By the time it was clear they were responsible, they were dead from a vehicle accident. Last year, actually over a fifteen-month period, there were five wicker man and mistletoe murders. All those killed were good people. It was clear who committed the murders, but the two have never been caught. Justice isn't perfect, Macduff. But Grace and I keep trying."

Grace and Erin edged me toward the door and out onto the porch. Grace spoke first. "Erin is staying with me. She's going back in two days. I promised her a day seeing St. Augustine. Tomorrow evening I'm having a dinner at my condo. Sit down, candlesticks, linen, and my best china and silverware. We'll expect you to bring Elsbeth and Lucinda."

"Have you talked to Lucinda?"

"Yes. She's got something to do tonight with Elsbeth. They'll be back here tomorrow afternoon, in time to change for dinner. For you, Macduff, no jeans. And no Stetson."

Grace and Erin went back inside, gave warm goodbyes to Lucinda and Elsbeth, came back out, and without another word drove off. I didn't know what Lucinda and Elsbeth were discussing, but I didn't want to interfere and sat in one of the rocking chairs on the porch. Fifteen minutes later they came out, each carrying a small overnight bag.

Elsbeth kissed me and said, "Dad, we'll be back tomorrow afternoon. Don't ask questions. Lucinda brushed my cheek with her lips and they left."

I was alone, again.

I poured a Gentleman Jack and put a few roasted pecans in a tiny sterling silver dish. The dish had been passed on to me by my mother, who had been given it by her ninety-year-old grandmother, who received it as a wedding present. She was married May 24th, in 1819, the day Queen Victoria was born. Family is everything, I thought. I haven't remembered that very well over the past half dozen years. Somehow I have to make up for that. I walked down to the dock with the silver dish and my drink. When the sun set three hours later, I was still on the dock. The glass and dish were long empty. I had an idea of what I would do. Or at least try.

The day had been long, and I was tired. Before I went to bed I searched my drawers for something I had misplaced. The bed was inviting. Lucinda had slept there the night before. I drifted off wishing she were here now.

76

By order of the Court: The appellant's [Florida Fish and Wildlife Conserva-tion Commission] motion for reinstatement of automatic stay ... is hereby reinstated. Enforcement of the law is once again allowed.
[Florida First District Court of Appeal re-imposing the stay of Judge Ful-ford's decision setting aside enforcement of the Constitutional Amendment banning gill nets.]

Just hours after the Recreational Fishing Alliance (RFDA) blasted Leon County Circuit judge Jackie Fulford for overturning the voter-approved, constitutionally protected Florida net ban, the Florida Fish and Wildlife Conservation Commission (FWC) sent official notification to all law en-forcement personnel that enforcement of the net ban would officially re-sume.
The latest ruling in the District Court of Appeal, First District in Tallahas-see, a motion for reinstatement of an automatic stay . . . was reinstated putting the net ban back in place.

RFA website, November 7, 2013, discussing Wakulla Commercial Fish-ermen's Association, Inc. v. Florida Fish and Wildlife Conservation Com-mission.

THE FOLLOWING EVENING

I DIDN'T WAKE UNTIL TEN. The house was silent. I missed the vibrancy the four had given to the cottage yester-day. I don't know what to expect from the dinner.

Grace had said no jeans and no Stetson. One suit hung in the very back of my closet, left over from my days of teaching. I wore it when I went to Washington on business. Behind the suit was my even less used black tux, which I had last worn almost two decades ago to a formal dinner with El. Along with it was a white Brooks Brothers dress shirt with a wing-collar, half-inch pleats, and holes for studs and cufflinks. I found both in a drawer, small gold circles with burgundy inlays. A black bow tie was next to them. I wondered if I remembered how to tie a bow tie. A shoe box was on the floor beneath the suits. The dusty black, plain tip shoes needed polishing and there was a can of Kiwi Black Gloss tucked in one shoe, a pair of folded black socks in the other.

Grace did say *formal.* I laid the tux across the bed and polished the shoes I hadn't worn in years. Elsbeth called and said she and Lucinda would meet me at Grace's.

On the way to dinner, I stopped at a wine and cheese shop on the outskirts of St. Augustine. Passing on the month's special *Pecorino Sardo* cheese, I bought *foie gras* for five and three bottles of an old Spottswoode 1987 Napa *Cabernet*, which the *New York Times* food section last week had said was a "worthy splurge" at $195—*per bottle.* It may have been a typo—really meaning "wealthy splurge." That amount would normally provide me wine for six months. "Oh, well!" I thought. It was "Buy America"; I wasn't sending the money abroad for a French wine. And the store did wrap each bottle quite elegantly.

I arrived at Grace's at 7:30. From the scene in the living room, the others had gathered one drink sooner. There were hugs all around. When I got to Lucinda, I buried my face in her hair and whispered, "Last night I crawled into the bed you'd slept in the night before. There was a touch of the fragrance I'm smelling now. I've missed it."

The women were elegant, a mix of subtle complementary colors. Elsbeth was wearing a dress I was certain I had once seen on Lucinda. Lucinda was wearing the same clothes she had the first Thanksgiving night we met at her ranch and dined together alone. Smart jeans and a pleated, collarless cranberry tunic that dropped a foot below her waist. A single strand neckless of tiny hollow metal egg-shaped beads repeated as earrings with smaller beads.

I noticed on Grace's living room wall the same three photo-to portraits of elderly women as Lucinda had placed on the cottage walls. Looking closer, at the bottom left corners were titles: Portrait of a Woman #1, Portrait of a Woman #2, and Portrait of a Woman #3. At the bottom right corners was simply "LLL." I knew who took the three transcendent photos. And I was certain I knew the names of the three women, although I had never met any of them.

Grace had set out name cards at each place at her table, which was beneath a crystal chandelier that cast sparking streaks of light through the Waterford stemware on the champagne colored tablecloth. The china was elegant Wedgwood that had belonged to her mother.

When I found my place card, I glanced left and right. Elsbeth was to my left, Lucinda to my right. Grace and Erin were directly across.

After a Gentleman Jack to catch up, I did the wine honors. In the shimmering crystal goblets, the wine added twisted cabernet-red shadows to the tablecloth every time someone lifted a glass to take a sip.

Not a word was spoken at dinner about gill nets, drift boats, fly fishing, or murders. Nor were the names Abdul Khaliq Isfahani or Juan Pablo Herzog uttered. The conversation, shifting throughout the meal from changing groups of two or three, was about good times. I had forgotten how many such times there had been in the past eight years. Erin, Elsbeth, and Lucinda knew my whole background, and I felt comfortable bringing Grace into this inner circle. She now knows why I am Macduff Brooks and work at trying to be a decent fly fishing guide. Grace understands the potential consequences of my life's history becoming more widely known.

When dinner was over, ending with an exquisite mango and key lime pie, and the last inches of the third bottle of wine, all four women set down their forks, wiped their lips, and turned toward me.

I was surrounded by both the prearranged seating assignments and the stares of this beautiful foursome.

77

It ain't over 'til it's over.

Yogi Berra, N.Y. Yankees' baseball catcher.

THE END OF THE MEAL

WHILE I WAS THINKING ABOUT HOW BEST TO PROCEED, Elsbeth raised a finger to gain our attention. When we all nodded to her, she began in a soft voice that demanded our attention.

"Dad, before it's your turn, I need only a few minutes to let you know about my plans. You may have sensed something from the T-shirt I wore at the cottage with FLORIDA across the front. What you may not have noticed was the Gator logo on one sleeve. Sue and I will start classes in January at UF. The dorm rooms were awful, and we didn't like the party scene at the apartments we visited. We're both serious about studying. Sue ultimately wants medical school. I want to go to the UF law school. I may not practice, but I want the education in thinking, self-expression, and writing that's missing from most baccalaureate programs.

"You won't guess where we'll be staying together in Gainesville. We looked at some small houses and found a couple we liked. And we looked in Golf View. Dad, your old house was empty. We called the agent, and they said the house had been donated to the University. But they haven't completed the gift because the University can't accept a house donation when there's a mortgage. The mortgage on the property has about eight years remaining. The monthly payments are less than what we would pay for a small house in the student ghetto north of the university. We've signed an agreement to stay in *your* house, maintain it except for major repairs, and pay directly to the bank the monthly amount that's due on the mortgage. It's awesome! Sue and I are so excited."

"You were conceived in that house," I said. "Your mother carried you for eight months living there before the accident on the Snake. It's been almost a decade since I lived there alone for ten years after El died. Those were lonely years. . . ."

"There are three bedrooms. You'll have one made-up for you—and Lucinda—all the time. Don't let Dan Wilson ever know you've come to Gainesville to visit us."

"I'll be there. Maybe you'll buy me lunch," I told her.

"That's *your* job. . . . And, you can't sell your cottage. . . . It looks much better right now than when you were here alone," she added, nodding at Lucinda.

"OK, you two. It's my turn," said Erin. I couldn't think of issues I had outstanding with Erin. But it did defer reaching the real reason for this dinner—what's to become of Lucinda and me?

"Macduff, you're impossible when it comes to hanging on to who and what you love most. You, and the same is true of Lucinda, don't communicate. When the two of you parted in St. Louis, Lucinda hadn't been fair to you by not telling you about her concern about the lump in her breast. You weren't fair not telling her your real reasons for wanting to kill Isfahani. It wasn't because you're a good shot and a patriot. You can't forget what Isfahani would have done to Lucinda if he had flown his plane into the Chrysler Building. There's no doubt about how dangerous he was. Whoever replaces him will likely be just as bad. But whoever that is doesn't have a personal vendetta against you. Am I right so far?"

Lucinda and I answered with the smallest nods that could be considered assent.

"What else is there?" Erin asked rhetorically, continuing to answer herself. "Macduff, you've put Lucinda in harm's way too many times to count. But nobody ever forced *you* to be there," she added, looking at Lucinda. "Whenever you and I have talked, it's mostly been about some new adventure you've shared with Macduff. You thrive on the kind of difficulties he attracts. Look at what's just happened. You went to Oyster Bay three times until you got an admission from Oliver Lowry that the residents killed the three in Florida. Can you deny that since you two met your lives have been anything but dull?"

Turning toward me, Erin continued, "You're not Harrison Ford, Macduff. Life is not a movie. You may be a great shot with your rifle, but you're a danger to anyone around you—including Wuff—when you use a pistol." Erin sat back.

"My turn," said Grace. "Look what's happened the past year since you two split. Lucinda had to go through a serious operation alone in New York. She's told me not one Manhattan acquaintance visited her in the hospital. Macduff would have been there every day. Is your memory so bad, Lucinda, that you forget Macduff was with you constantly when you were in a coma after you were shot on the Snake River and again when you had amnesia?"

Lucinda's hand was now on my knee under the table. She was trembling.

"You two fished together and succeeded in making it across the Great Plains states twice a year," Erin reminded the two. Turning more serious, she went on. "I think one thing troubles Lucinda that Macduff appears to be taking for granted. Macduff has said he will kill Juan Pablo Herzog. Half the problems you two have faced together involved Herzog. Macduff shot and killed his niece. Someone protecting both of you shot and killed his nephew. Herzog's determined to respond. But right now he's in a dilemma. He wants U.S. government support to unseat the new leftist Guatemalan president who beat him in the recent election. He's far more determined to be president than to be your assassin," she ended, frowning at Macduff.

"At least for now," Lucinda murmured.

I was convinced we'd been foolish to stay apart. I wasn't sure Lucinda agreed, but I had to try something.

"Lucinda," I asked, turning toward her and holding both her hands. "Are we still engaged?"

"I don't think so. I sent the ring back to you."

"It's right here," I said, pulling the battered black velvet box from my tux jacket pocket, opening the box, and placing the ring between us, and asked, "Will we be engaged if I put this on your finger?"

Elsbeth's lips were moving; I could read them enough to know what she was quietly chanting: "Marry her, marry her, marry her."

"We'll be engaged," Lucinda advised, "on condition we set a date to marry before I'm old and you cast me out onto the streets. And I mean set it *now*, before these witnesses. Erin and

Grace are lawyers; Elsbeth will be one sooner or later. If you back out, we'll sue the hell out of you. Or we'll hire some fishermen's wives in Oyster Bay to take you out on their boat."

"*Take the ring, Lucinda,*" cried out Grace. "*Put it on.* Macduff's so spaced out when he sees you wearing it in the morning he'll forget you ever gave it back."

Lucinda took the ring, slipped it on her finger, and looked at me with that full Cheshire cat grim, her elbows resting on the table and her chin resting on her hands. I took full advantage of her lips being no more than six inches away.

"Macduff, you're pretty quiet," Erin said. "Nothing to add?"

"You've all done fine. Oh! There is one thing." I turned to Lucinda and took both her hands in mine. She was grinning. "Will you marry me and set a date, Doctor Lang?"

"Yes, Professor Brooks," she said.

"I do need to know one thing," I added. "When do we get to consummate our engagement."

"We did it the *first* time," Lucinda said, "but then; remember the famous musician who was asked 'How do you get to Carnegie Hall?'"

The four women answered in unison: "Practice, practice, practice."

And we did.

EPILOGUE

Elsbeth's Diary

I have read every word of Dad's fourth manuscript. And then read it again. For years I've wondered why Lucinda and he separated. I remain mystified by that time in their lives. Dad loved Lucinda as he had loved my birth mother El. But for years he never really believed that he deserved a second chance at the kind of happiness he had with El. He will take that to his grave. I'm uncertain to this day why he didn't fight more for Lucinda when she left him that day in St. Louis and went off to Manhattan alone.

It was difficult for Dad to understand how much Lucinda loved him and was hurt by his avoidance of discussing marriage. But after the gill net deaths and especially knowing that Lucinda had cancer and he had not been there by her side, he knew that marriage was what both he and Lucinda needed and wanted.

Grace Justice and Erin Giffin have both crossed the bar and joined Lucinda in death. That too has been hard on Dad. I am the only surviving member of the four women who knew who killed the three persons in Florida who were wrapped in gill nets, and now only I, and of course Dad, retain the knowledge of who was responsible for the killings. Of course, all the six women in Oyster Bay, and Emma in Apalachicola, have long since passed away.

I count my blessings every day.

AUTHOR'S NOTE

I enjoy hearing from readers. You may reach me at: **mac-brooks.mwgordon@gmail.com**

Please visit my website: **www.mwgordonnovels.com**
I am also on facebook at **www.facebook.com/ m.w.gordon**

I will answer e-mail within the week received, unless I am on a book signing tour or towing *Osprey* to fish somewhere. Because of viruses, I do not download attachments sent with your e-mails. And please do not add my e-mail address to any lists suggesting for whom I should vote, to whom I should give money, what I should buy, what I should read, or especially what I should write next about Macduff Brooks.

My website lists coming appearances for readings, talk programs, and signings.

CPSIA information can be obtained at www.ICGtesting.com
Printed in the USA
LVOW07s2141290714

396659LV00001B/120/P

9 780984 872343